I saw Gilley pushing his way through the crowd over to me, his face flush with excitement. "Cat!" he began.

"What's happened?"

"Yelena's dead!"

I gripped the top of my chair to steady myself from the shock of that announcement. "Dead? What do you mean, she's dead?"

"She's been murdered!"

"How is that possible?"

"She was stabbed backstage during intermission!" Gilley exclaimed. "Someone murdered her, then fled the scene . . ."

Books by Victoria Laurie

COACHED TO DEATH

TO COACH A KILLER

COACHED IN THE ACT

COACHED RED-HANDED

Published by Kensington Publishing Corp.

Coached in the Act

VICTORIA LAURIE

Kensington Publishing Corp.
www.kensingtonbooks.com

KENSINGTON BOOKS are published by

Kensington Publishing Corp.
119 West 40th Street
New York, NY 10018

All Kensington titles, imprints, and distributed lines are available at special quantity discounts for bulk purchases for sales promotion, premiums, fund-raising, educational, or institutional use.

Special book excerpts or customized printings can also be created to fit specific needs. For details, write or phone the office of the Kensington Sales Manager: Attn.: Sales Department. Kensington Publishing Corp., 119 West 40th Street, New York, NY 10018. Phone: 1-800-221-2647.

The K and Teapot logo is a trademark of Kensington Publishing Corp.

First Kensington Hardcover Edition: September 2021

ISBN: 978-1-4967-3441-9
First Paperback Edition: June 2022

ISBN: 978-1-4967-3442-6 (ebook)

10 9 8 7 6 5 4 3 2 1

Printed in the United States of America

Chapter 1

I found Gilley in the kitchen, tearfully sniffing as he stared at his laptop screen. "Gil?" I asked, surprised to find my permanent guesthouse resident and dear friend so upset. "What's happened?"

Gilley jumped at the sound of my voice. He obviously hadn't heard me come downstairs. Once he recovered himself, he swiveled the laptop around so that I could see. There, on the screen was a video clip of M.J. Whitefeather, Gilley's best friend and former business partner, sitting in a rocking chair, with two babies cuddled against her and a towel draped over her chest. She was obviously nursing the twins.

Entering the screen to the right was a toddler, stumbling a little as she walked, obviously still half asleep. Suddenly, the voice of Heath, M.J.'s husband, could be heard. "Such a good mama, feeding the babies at five a.m.," he cooed.

M.J. glanced up at the camera, revealing dark circles and half-lidded eyes. She looked so tired, the poor love. I could sympathize. I'd had twins when I was about her age. It's not for the weak.

"Is she getting *any* sleep?" I asked Gilley.

He wiped at his cheeks with a tissue. "Not a lot," he said. "According to Heath, Skylar seems to be nocturnal, and Chase has trouble with gas or something that makes him fussy. Margot just entered her terrible twos, so the whole thing's a disaster, if you ask me."

I chuckled and came around the side of the island where Gilley was sitting to hug him around the shoulders. "You really miss them, don't you?"

"Is it that obvious?" he asked in a choked whisper. "But I especially miss M.J. We were inseparable for almost thirty years, and now the only time I get to see her is when she has the energy to call or Zoom with me, or when Heath sends me a clip, like this one."

I sat down next to Gil and took up his hand. "It's going to be really hard for her until the twins are in kindergarten," I said. "Then things will settle down, and she'll be in touch more."

"They're three months old, Cat. You're telling me I have to wait five years to connect regularly with my best friend again?"

I squeezed his hand. I understood that, deep down, Gilley was actually happy that M.J. had found her soul mate and was building a family with him, but I also knew that the adjustment of giving her up to Heath, Skylar, Chase, and Margot was exceptionally difficult.

"You could always fly out to see her," I suggested. The Whitefeathers lived in New Mexico.

Gilley scowled. "I don't do babies. The dirty diapers *alone* would have me running for the hills."

I cocked my head at him. He'd been living in my guesthouse for nearly two years now, and I was still learning new and interesting things about him. "You and Michel have never considered having a baby together?" I asked, referring to Gilley's husband.

"Nope," he said, a note of tension in his voice. Michel had spent much of the pandemic locked down in the UK, and it'd put a definite strain on their marriage. And ever since the vaccine had been widely distributed, Michel still continued to take assignments as an in-demand fashion photographer, out of the country.

"Although," Gilley continued, "I *have* been contemplating adopting a puppy."

My brow arched in surprise. "Really?"

"As long as it's okay with my landlord, of course," he said.

I waved my hand. "Of course, it's all right, Gilley."

In fact, it was more than all right. Poor Gil had been a bit lonely of late, ever since my boys went back to boarding school and I had more time to spend with my current love interest, Detective Steve Shepherd.

I realized as I stared at my dear friend that since the boys left two weeks earlier, I'd hardly spent any of my free time with Gilley. Oh, sure, we saw each other at work—he was my personal assistant—and we typically shared lunch together, but we hadn't really spent any quality time together, and I suddenly found myself feeling guilty over that.

"Gilley," I said, trying to pump a little enthusiasm into my voice. "Why don't you and I go out on the town tonight?"

Gilley slid his gaze toward me, his lids weighed down by skepticism. "Don't you have a date with Shepherd?"

"We have nothing planned," I lied, knowing I'd have to cancel our plans for dinner the moment I was out of earshot. "Come on, Gil, it's supposed to be a beautiful night, and we can go out to eat, do a little shopping, and . . . Ooh! I've got it! We could take in that hot new show at John Drew Street Theater!"

I'd wanted to catch the show everyone in town was talking about ever since I learned it was opening in late August. The show was a take on a famous classic, but with a clever twist. "You and I have both said we'd love to see *Twelve Angry Men*. Why not go tonight?"

Gilley frowned. "You're kidding, right? Tickets are impossible to get, Cat. It's totally sold out for the next three months."

Clearly, Gilley had been doing a little research into this very subject, which made my smile all the wider. "I can get us tickets," I said.

"You know a scalper?"

"Better. I know Yelena Galanis's best friend." Yelena Galanis was the star of the one-woman show, aptly titled *Twelve Angry Men*, in which she told the story of the twelve rich and powerful East Hamptonites she'd used and abused over the years. Word on the street suggested it was a scintillating hoot.

"You do?" Gilley said. "Who?"

"Sunny D'Angelo," I said, with a bounce to my brow. "She and Yelena go way back. I think they were college roommates or in the same sorority. And Sunny has already mentioned that she can score us tickets anytime we want."

Still, Gilley looked doubtful. With a sigh, he said, "I don't know that I'm in the mood for it, Cat."

I rubbed his arm. "Oh, come on, Gil. It's been forever since the two of us were out on the town together. Besides, what else are you going to do? Sit home and watch VH1?"

Gilley frowned, and I knew that was exactly what he'd planned on doing. "Ru's doing a special on the best of the drag racers," he said.

"Record it and watch it later," I suggested.

He made a face, but I could tell his resolve was cracking. "Where would we go to dinner?" he asked.

"Well, the Beacon is still open for another two weeks, and we haven't been there in forever. What do you say to that?"

"Hmm, I do *love* to be seen at the Beacon," Gilley said of the yacht-club bistro.

I grinned. I knew I had him. "What'll we wear?"

Gilley couldn't resist planning his outfits ahead of time. "You should wear that red, off-the-shoulder number," he said, referring to the new Versace deep red dress with flared sleeves and skirt that I'd purchased only a week earlier. I'd been saving it for a special occasion out with Shepherd, but I could certainly wear it out tonight for Gilley.

"Done," I said. "And you, sir? What will you wear?"

A smile began to form on Gilley's lips. "I think," he said, tapping his lips, "that I've been looking for an opportunity to wear my new Ted Baker suit."

"The light gray plaid?"

Gilley nodded. "I've got a gorgeous black silk shirt to wear with it. The contrasts are delicious."

"Then you *must* wear it," I said, watching as Gilley began to show some enthusiasm.

"Okay," he said after taking another moment to think on it. "It's a date, Cat."

"Excellent!" I said, moving in to hug him around the shoulders. "I have a few errands to run before my client today at one, but I can call Sunny from the car and see if she can't scrounge up a pair of tickets for us."

"Cool," he said, hopping off the chair at the island. Pointing to the counter near the sink, he added, "There's a quiche that I took out of the oven a bit ago. It should be cool enough to eat by now. Let me know if we're a go for tonight so I can pull out the suit and steam out the wrinkles."

"Did you want to come with me to run the errands?" I asked.

He shook his head. "Can't. I've got a massage with Reese at ten."

My brow arched. "Again?" I asked carefully. Reese was an absolutely breathtaking man, who reminded me very much of the late Christopher Reeve at the height of his Superman career. Reese was also someone I knew Gilley had a monstrous crush on.

"Yes, *again*," Gilley said moodily.

"You've been seeing a lot of him lately," I said, undaunted, because I needed to understand Gilley's thinking here. Even though I knew he and Michel were struggling in their relationship, I felt strongly that if Gilley strayed, he'd regret it.

My dear friend sighed. "There's nothing going on, Cat."

"Okay, but *could* there be at some point, Gilley?"

Reese's sexual exploits into the beds of many of the Hamptons elite were an open secret. He was rumored to be a very . . . shall we say, *talented* lover, and he had no preference as to which team he'd pitch for on any given day. He was as sought after by women as he was by men.

Gilley glared at me. I held his eyes and didn't look away. At last, he threw up his arms and said, "I don't know. Maybe?"

"If you don't know, Gilley, then it might be best to resist the urge until you deal with your relationship with Michel. And I say that as a friend to both you and him, okay?"

Gilley nodded. "It's just nice to get some attention, you know?"

I bit my lip, the guilt of a few minutes ago returning. "I do," I said. "And I'm sorry that I haven't been paying nearly as much attention to our friendship as I should have."

The edges of Gilley's mouth quirked up in a smile. "You're forgiven."

"Good. Now, come with me to run those errands."

To my surprise, Gilley shook his head no again. "I'm going to keep my appointment with Reese." When I again arched my brow, he added, "I may be married, but I'm not dead. I'm allowed to flirt."

I held back the protest I badly wanted to make and settled for a simple nod. It was Gilley's life and relationship to work out, not mine. "I'll text you if I hear back from Sunny before I meet you at the office."

"I'll get there a little early and throw on some tea for you and your one o'clock."

"Thank you, lovey. You're a doll." With that, I leaned in to kiss him on the cheek, before I headed out the door.

As soon as I pulled out of the driveway, I called Sunny.

"Hi, Cat," she said, sounding weary.

"Sunny?" I said. I hadn't seen much of Sunny over the summer, which, I'll admit, was odd, given that she was Shepherd's twin sister. And I definitely hadn't seen much of her while the pandemic was on. As the mother of a baby—and now toddler—she'd been especially careful to protect little Finley.

"Yes, I'm here," she said, probably thinking that I hadn't heard her the first time.

"Are you okay?" I asked. Shepherd had told me that his sister had been struggling recently, and by the sound of her voice, I wondered if she might be ill.

"Yeah," she said on a sigh. "I'm fine. Just a bout of insomnia, and Finley started becoming a real handful just after his second birthday."

"Ah, the terrible twos," I said. My boys had gotten up to all sorts of mischief when they were Finley's age.

"He'll be the death of me," she said, but added a tired smile.

I could tell she was trying to appear like her old self. Sunny had been very aptly named.

I grinned when I heard the old playful enthusiasm back in her voice. "Do you remember when you said that you had an in with Yelena Galanis?"

Sunny chuckled. "You want tickets, don't you?"

"Only if it won't cause you any trouble."

"It won't," she assured me. "I've been meaning to take Finley over to see her for ages. This'll give me an excuse, and Yelena always has extra seats on hand for just such an occasion."

"Have you caught her act yet?"

"Not yet. I'm waiting for Darius to come home from L.A., and then we'll go."

"Is he away again?" Darius worked in the music business, and he spent more time on the West Coast than he did at his home here in East Hampton.

It secretly upset me because it left Sunny to care for Finley for long stretches at a time without any help from the boy's father.

"Yes, but he's on his way back," she said. "He'll be here late tonight, in fact."

I let out a relieved sigh. "Well, that's good. And you promise it's no trouble to ask Yelena for a couple of tickets?"

"I promise, Cat. I'll call you in a bit to let you know, though, okay?"

I said my goodbyes to Sunny and called her brother.

"Hey there," he said, his voice warm and throaty. I shimmied a little in my seat. Shepherd could light the home fires with just a greeting, and it was a delicious thing to be the object of his affections.

"Hey there," I repeated. "Got a second?"

"For you? Always."

This was a lie, as I knew from experience. Whenever Shepherd was knee-deep into working a case, my phone calls went straight to voice mail. But I was hardly going to remind him of that at the moment. "Listen," I began. "About tonight . . ."

"Something's come up," he said, beating me to the punch.

"Yes."

"What?"

"Gilley."

Shepherd chuckled. "Ah," he said. "Our third wheel."

"Hey, he's not a third wheel, Shep, okay?" I'd adopted the nickname Shep for Shepherd after I recently discovered that was what most of the other men in blue from the East Hampton PD called him.

"Okay, okay," Shepherd said, and I could almost see him holding up his hands in surrender. "He's feeling neglected, though, right?"

"Yes," I said. "So, I've decided to take a rain check with you and focus on Gilley for tonight."

"That's fine, Cat," he said, using the nickname common to most of my friends and family, instead of the more formal Catherine, which he'd insisted on using for the first few months of our relationship.

"I'm free most of this week," he continued. "Just let me know when your schedule clears up, okay?"

"I will," I promised. "And if you want to come over late tonight, I won't say no."

Shepherd made a growling sound. "You're a temptress, you know that?"

"I do," I said, smiling wickedly. "I'll tell Sebastian to let you in if you feel like spending the night. Gilley and I should be home around eleven, I think." Sebastian was my AI butler. Much like Google Nest, but much more sophisticated.

"See you then," he promised.

A bit later, after I had run all my errands, I was headed back to the house to drop off a few packages before driving across town to my office when Sunny called me.

"Hey, where are you?" she asked the moment I picked up the call.

"Um, I'm driving back to my house. Why? Do you need something?"

"I got the tickets," Sunny said. In the background I could hear Finley fussing, and there was that exhausted tone in Sunny's voice again. "Can you swing by to pick them up? Finley and I both need a nap."

"Of course," I said. "I'm rounding the corner onto your street as we speak."

"Oh, I see your car," Sunny said, and up ahead I saw her Range Rover pull into her driveway.

I parked and was out of the car first, and then I trotted over to hold Sunny's car door open so that the windy day didn't bang her door against her as she reached in to get Finley out of his car seat. The poor tyke was red faced and crying, and as Sunny backed up with him cradled in her arms, I was taken aback by the dark circles under her eyes and the sag to her shoulders.

"Thanks," she said. "The tickets are in my purse. Come on in and I'll fish them out for you."

I held my arms out toward Finley, who was kicking and fussing in his mother's embrace, and made a "gimme" motion with my hands. I'd been that overwhelmed and exhausted mother once. I knew when it was time to volunteer to take charge.

Sunny's expression was a bit apprehensive but also relieved. "He's super fussy, Cat," she said.

"Yes, which is why you should give him to me so that I can help you, instead of standing around waiting for you to be supermom and super friend all at the same time."

Sunny hesitated one more second, but then she lifted Finley away from her and pivoted him around to me. I took the tyke and held him close, relishing the feeling of holding a small toddler again. It made me miss my sons even more than usual, but it was also the right thing to do.

"Shhh, shhh, shhh," I said to Finley, bouncing him gently in my arms.

He pulled his head back, probably startled to be in someone else's arms, and that was all the opening I needed. I made a goofy face, and his expression turned from sour to unsure and then to nearly a grin.

"Who's a boogley boo?" I asked him, still bouncing him up and down playfully, while Sunny retrieved a bag of groceries from the car.

"We can go in through the garage," she said, clicking a switch on her key fob. The garage door creaked open a few feet then stopped. "Oh, come on," Sunny grumbled. "Not today!"

"What's wrong?" I asked as Sunny clicked the button on her key fob again and the door came down.

"It's the stupid garage door. It keeps sticking. Sometimes I can't get it to come down. Sometimes I can't get it to go up."

She clicked the fob a third time and the door slowly rose and this time it went all the way to the top. "Whew," she said.

I smiled, bouncing Finley in my arms as he played with my hair.

"This way," Sunny said, leading us into the garage. "Watch your step," she added as she pointed down to a pile of supplies made up of a big carton of disposable water bottles, paper towels, laundry detergent, and various other household cleaning supplies. "I went to Costco yesterday," she explained as I waited for her to unlock the door.

"I love Costco," I said, following her through the now unlocked door into the kitchen. "Gilley and I go once a month, so if you ever need anything from there, just ask, Sunny, and we can pick it up for you."

She glanced over her shoulder as she moved to set down her groceries. "You two are my angels," she said. Then she pointed to a high chair at the table. "You can set Finley down in the high chair."

I shook my head because I wasn't about to put the child down. He was mocking my facial expressions and giggling along with me, and it was a glorious exchange that was also allowing Sunny to get herself organized.

"Oh, where did I set my purse?" she said, spinning around and looking at the counter and nearby breakfast table.

"I didn't see you bring it in," I told her.

Sunny sighed heavily. "It's still out in the car," she moaned.

"Hey," I said to her to get her attention. "When was the last time you had a proper meal?"

Sunny pushed at a stray strand of her long blond hair that had pulled free of her ponytail. The way her hair was pulled back today showed how thin she'd become since the last time I saw her. It worried me.

"I eat when he eats," she said.

"Uh-huh," I said. "And I bet it's about the same size meal too."

Sunny ignored my concern. "I'll eat as soon as I get him down."

"Or you could fix yourself a little nosh right now, my friend, and let me put him down for a nap." Not waiting for an okay from her, I edged toward the hallway leading to the stairs. "The nursery is the first door on the right past the stairs, correct?"

Again, Sunny's shoulders sagged with relief. Finley had fallen against my shoulder, the novelty of making funny faces at me having lost out to exhaustion.

"Yes," she said. "But, really, Cat, you don't have to—"

"I want to," I told her. "Now, get yourself a sandwich or something. I'll be down as soon as he's asleep."

I took Finley up the stairs slowly and carefully so as not to jostle him. I'd picked up a pacifier off the kitchen drying rack as I'd passed it on the way to the stairs, and the little tot was sucking on it with heavy-lidded eyes as I crested the landing.

"Here we go," I said, walking down the hallway and heading into the nursery.

I'd last been here when Finley was a newborn, just as the pandemic was starting to exact its terrible toll on the world. I smiled as I entered, remembering the photos lining the wall that Sunny had been in the middle of putting up.

A series on the far left wall was the most inviting—it began with a breathtaking shot of Sunny, radiant in the early evening light, her hands placed protectively over her belly, as she leaned against the porch railing of the D'Angelos' old home in L.A. The twinkling lights of downtown could be seen at the bottom of the image. I knew from Sunny that Darius had taken the photo in the moments after Sunny had revealed her pregnancy to him. She'd said he'd been so excited to capture the moment that he'd insisted on the photo and every one after it, taken one a month for nine in total. The last one included a tiny baby, laid against the bare chest of his mother.

What always took me by surprise was the look of un-conditional love on Sunny's face as she smiled at her husband while he chronicled her pregnancy. I didn't really understand their marriage—Darius was gone far too often for my taste—but the adoration in Sunny's expression was so obvious that it was unmistakable. They loved each other, and their marriage worked for them, so who was I to judge?

I laid Finley down in his bed, then gently eased off his shoes and socks to expose his little feet and button toes. I placed my hand around one of his feet and smiled at the feel of baby skin against my palm. My mind's eye filled with images of my sons, Matthew and Michael, at Finley's age, and I teared up a bit as I laid a blanket over the toddler, who was already asleep, his mouth still working the pacifier.

Pulling up the guard rail on his toddler bed, I moved over to the photos of Sunny through her pregnancy. Darius had quite the artist's eye for photography. The backdrop for each photo was nearly as eye catching as the central figure.

The second photo in the series, taken when Sunny was about two months along, featured Sunny perched atop the railing, staring out at the early evening view of downtown L.A., where a few twinkles of light could already be seen. It gave the viewer the impression of Sunny as the Greek goddess Aphrodite looking down from Olympus to Athens below.

A few images to the right was one of a playful Sunny clad in a tiny bikini, which even five or six months along in her pregnancy she could still pull off beautifully. She was laughing in the spray of an outdoor shower, and there was such joy on her face. I stood in front of the image and mentally noted how different Sunny looked back then compared to today.

As if on cue, I heard the sound of something behind me and turned to see her there, a weary smile on her face, watching me standing in front of the photos. "Did he go down okay?" she whispered, glancing toward the bed.

I nodded.

Sunny came over to stand next to me as I looked back to the photos. "Where was this one taken?" I asked softly.

"Here," she said, smiling at the memory. "That was the day that Darius closed on the house in L.A. and we played in the surf most of the afternoon to celebrate. That shower is so cold," Sunny chuckled. "Darius loves it but I don't think I've used it since."

"You look like you're having fun," I said, grinning too.

"Oh, he probably said something hilarious. I just remember I was so relieved to have Darius back here, and be rid of the fake, money-fame-success-focused crowd. I'd already moved back to this house, which we bought, oh, about ten years ago. It was our vacation pad, if you can believe it, but as soon as I found out I was pregnant, I packed up and moved. No *way* was I about to raise my kid in La-La Land."

"What's wrong with L.A.?" I asked. I'd been there only a few times, but I'd found it okay.

Sunny made a face. "It's full of fake people with far too much money and privilege. I didn't want our son to grow up a spoiled brat, surrounded by other spoiled brats, so I told Darius that I was headed home to New York, and I expected him to split his time between here and there. He agreed, and we sold the house, because it was a total drain on our finances. Anyway, that photo was taken the day Darius officially made his residence here in the Hamptons."

"Where does he stay when he's out there?" I asked.

"He bought a condo, and he rents out the spare bedrooms to two of his old college buddies. They're very sweet men, actually. Noah and Jason used to be lovers, but now they're just friends, and they watch over the place when he's back here with me. I like the arrangement because it keeps Darius honest. If he's living with those two, no way would they let him get into any mischief."

Sunny laughed softly, but I asked, "Mischief?"

She shrugged. "He works in the music industry, Cat. Women, desperate to sign a contract with a successful music producer, throw themselves at him all the time."

My eyes widened. "How are you okay with that?"

Sunny's lids drooped heavily, and she yawned. "I trust my husband, and so far in our fifteen years together, he's never given me a reason not to."

I placed a hand on her shoulder, knowing it was far past my time to take my leave. "I think I should let you get some sleep."

She nodded. "Thanks. I took half of a sleep-aid tablet, and it's hitting me hard all of a sudden."

"A sleep aid?" I said with concern. "Did you want me to stay in case Finley wakes up?"

Sunny yawned again. "No, it'll be okay. I took only half a dose, because I'm so exhausted by this bout of insomnia that I need something to help me get a little rest. And I called Tiffany, and she's coming over now to hang out and tend to Finley when he wakes up while I get some z's."

"Ah, the famous Tiffany," I said. Sunny raved about Tiffany. I'd never met her, but I'd heard a great deal about her over the summer, when the young woman had been touring Europe as a graduation gift from her parents.

"Yes," Sunny said, her eyes droopy. "She's finally back from across the pond, and I'm so relieved. I don't know that I could've held on one more day without her."

"I'm so glad you've got someone you can rely on to take up some of the slack."

Sunny nodded, stifling a yawn. "You know what's a funny coincidence?"

"What?"

"It was Yelena who recommended her to me. She's friends with the Blums—Tiffany's parents. She's known Tiff since the girl was a tiny tyke, so I felt good about trying her out with Finley. I never realized how well the two of them would get on together. It's like they speak the same language."

"How long was she away in Europe again?" I asked.

"Six long, impossible weeks," Sunny said, with a tired smile. "But she's finally back, and she'll be here in ten minutes or so." Sunny again put a hand up to cover another yawn. "Sorry," she said.

"Please don't be," I told her. "You look exhausted, and I should leave you to your rest."

I was turning to go when Sunny reached out to grab my hand, and holding it, she said, "I almost forgot. The tickets are on the island counter. When I told Yelena that two of my dearest friends were hoping to attend tonight, she gave me her best two reserved seats and said that tonight was a perfect night for you guys to come, because she just might name names before the night is through."

"Ooh," I said, with an eager smile. "Sounds juicy."

Sunny giggled. "With Yelena, it wouldn't be anything but."

After leaving Sunny in the nursery, I made my way

downstairs and found the tickets in an envelope marked VIP. Taking a peek inside, I discovered that Yelena had generously offered us front-row-center seats, and I made a promise to myself to come up with a way to thank both her and Sunny for the generous gift.

Looking back, I wish more than anything that I'd known then that I'd never be able to make good on my promise.

Chapter 2

After a quick pit stop home, I arrived at my office building in the heart of East Hampton's downtown. I'd purchased the building nearly two years earlier, even before my house—Chez Cat—had been built.

Charmed by the office building's historic roots and architecture, I'd invested a great deal of time and money to bring the neglected old relic to its current glorious state. And I was proud to say that every suite in the building was currently leased and bringing in a tidy income.

My office occupied the largest suite on the first floor, with an entrance onto Main Street. The building itself took up a corner lot, so its main entrance was on Pondview.

And because my suite was hemmed in by two walls of floor-to-ceiling windows, I had to ensure that it stood as the showpiece for the entire building, which was why I'd taken such care to decorate it in the most neutral but still stylish tones of stone, white, and sand. The combo gave the feeling of a fresh start, which was an important subliminal message to send to my clients, not to mention the subliminal message I was also sending to myself.

After twenty years spent building a marketing firm, which I'd sold for a tidy profit a few years back, I was now a professional life coach, and I was proud of the fact that almost all the people who'd come seeking a little wisdom were in better positions now to tackle whatever life threw at them. Slowly but surely, my client base was building, and I now had at least two to three clients on the books at any given time.

That afternoon I was meeting a brand-new client, and I was excited to see what life issues we could tackle together.

"Gilley," I said after pacing a little around the office.

"Hmm?"

"Did you confirm the time with Mr. Nassau?" Aaron Nassau, my new client.

"I sent him an email yesterday."

"Did he reply?"

"No."

I glanced at my watch. It was seven minutes past one, and I had to take a deep breath to push back the hint of irritation bubbling up from my insides. I'm a stickler for punctuality, and it drives me crazy when people show up late to their first session. I always wonder what they could be thinking, as it's their first opportunity to make a good impression on me.

Still, I realize not everyone places a high value on punctuality. But they should. They really, really should.

I crossed my arms and tapped the sleeve of my blouse

impatiently while glancing out the large front windows for any sign of Aaron.

I didn't know what he looked like, but I expected at any moment to see someone hurrying toward the door, perhaps a bit disheveled and certainly out of breath.

Instead, the sidewalk was sparse of pedestrians, and those walking past hardly seemed to be in a rush.

So, with a sigh, I moved to my wing chair, took a seat, and sat back to wait. Meanwhile, Gilley was busy at his computer, going through what looked like rescue sites, in search of his new pup.

"Any of them stand out to you?" I asked into the silence.

Gilley's shoulders jumped slightly at the sound of my voice. "What?" he asked, peering over his shoulder.

"The dogs. Any of the dogs stand out to you?"

"All of them," he said wistfully. "I wish I could adopt every single one."

I made a sympathetic mewing sound. "I really get it, Gilley, but please don't."

He chuckled. "Not to worry, Cat. I'll keep it to one pup."

I headed over to stand behind him so that I could better see the screen. It was now a quarter past one, and I'd decided that Aaron had simply changed his mind and would be marked off in my book as a no-show. Bending down to have a look at the screen, I jerked when the door suddenly opened and in stepped an elegant man, whom I'd put somewhere in his midfifties, dressed in Versace loafers, silk khaki slacks, and a blue blazer with gold buttons mostly covering a crisp white shirt.

"Hello," he said, a bit flustered. "I have an appointment."

"Aaron?" I asked, taking a mental note at the hint of a European accent coming from him.

He nodded enthusiastically and stuck out his hand. "Catherine?"

"Yes," I said, reaching my own hand forward. His palm was dry to the touch, and his handshake had the perfect amount of pressure. Still, Aaron's gaze darted around the office a bit nervously.

To put him at ease, I decided not to mention the fact that he was nearly twenty minutes late and instead smiled pleasantly and motioned toward the seating area. "Won't you please come in and make yourself comfortable?"

He gave a nod to Gilley, who was eyeing him curiously, and followed me to the plush love seat and wing chair that made up my seating area. I motioned again to the love seat, and Aaron sat down with a whoosh of air escaping his lips.

I sat down, too, and leaned toward him slightly, hoping that my body language indicated that I was focused on him and intent on listening. "Can I get you something to drink?" I asked. The man had a bit of a sheen about his forehead.

"Water would be wonderful," he said. "Sparkling, if you have it."

"We do," I said and nodded to Gilley, who got up and hurried to the beverage counter.

I waited until Gilley had removed a small bottle of Pellegrino from the minifridge and brought it with a frosted glass over to Aaron before I got down to brass tacks. Taking up the yellow notepad I kept on the side table next to my chair, I said, "So, Aaron, what brings you to my little coaching corner?"

Aaron blanched as he unscrewed the cap of the Pellegrino. "I could really use some help."

"Of course," I said gently. "But about what, specifically?"

He sighed and took a sip of water. "To be honest, Catherine, I'm having some difficulty moving on after a breakup."

"Oh?" I said. "Were you married?"

"Yes, but that's not the woman I'm having trouble getting over, which is sad, given that my ex-wife and I were married for twenty years before we split. And I've dated a smattering of women, some of them seriously, since then too, so it isn't that I'm a fool for love. But recently, I split from a woman I was absolutely mad for, and I'm having a hard time getting over her."

"How long were you two together?"

"Six months."

My brow rose in surprise. "Only six months?"

"I know it seems like too short a time to develop any real feelings for a person, but I did develop feelings. Deep feelings. I'd planned to propose, and I wanted to spend the rest of my life with her."

"So, what happened between the two of you to cause the breakup?"

"I have no idea," Aaron said, with a sigh and a shake of his head. "One day we were mad for each other, and the next she wouldn't answer my calls or texts or the door when I went to check on her. It was bizarre."

"She ghosted you," I said.

Aaron's brow knit in confusion. "No, she's still alive."

I held back a grin and explained, "'Ghosting someone' means 'to cut off all contact, as if they never existed.' It's a cruel way to end a relationship, but it's becoming more and more common, I'm afraid."

"Oh," he said, his shoulders drooping. "Well then, yes, she ghosted me."

"Could there have been someone else?" I asked carefully.

"Not that I was aware of when we were together. Frankly, I don't know how the woman could've had time for another lover. We were always together, inseparable, in fact. We acted as one unit for most of our relationship."

"Ah," I said. "So, her abrupt departure from your life is part of the problem."

"What do you mean?"

"Well," I began, trying to choose my words delicately. "If you two were always together, your life as an individual morphed into your life as part of a couple. And I understand that you were very happy in your relationship with her, but when it ended so abruptly without closure or even an explanation, I can see how it would've left you feeling set adrift, without benefit of a life preserver or any way back to her."

Aaron pursed his lips, and to my surprise, his eyes watered, then leaked a tear or two. He wiped them away self-consciously. "I'm shattered," he whispered.

I inched forward to the edge of my seat in order to reach out and squeeze his hand. Behind Aaron, I heard a loud sniffle, and my gaze momentarily darted to Gilley, who was dabbing at his own eyes. He caught the look of disapproval on my face—he wasn't supposed to listen in on these private conversations with my clients—and he quickly grabbed his headphones and shoved them on to let me know he understood my look of disapproval.

Focusing back on Aaron, who thankfully seemed not to have noticed Gilley's eavesdropping, I said, "Aaron, I understand how heartbreaking this must be for you, and what I think you need is some time to ease back into your old identity as a single man with a lot to offer the world."

Aaron nodded, but his eyes were still welling up. I had to fight against my own emotions, because it was difficult to watch such an elegant, regal man be brought to tears over the insensitive, cruel, and abrupt dismissal from a woman he'd clearly loved.

"Listen," I said softly. "I know exactly what you're going through. Three years ago, my own heart was broken when I discovered the affair my husband was having with another woman. I was devastated, but after a time . . . I got through it and realized that I could have a wonderfully happy life without him. Right now, you're in the worst part, the swamp—the place where every step forward feels a little like you're also sinking into the muck—but you've also already taken the bravest and hardest step. You've come to me for help. I'm so proud of you for that, Aaron, and I promise, you won't have to move forward alone. I will help you take every step forward through the muck until you're on safe and solid ground again."

Aaron lifted his gaze then to meet mine, and the smallest hint of relief played across his expression. "Thank you, Catherine."

A bit later, Gilley came over to stand next to me as I watched Aaron cross the street after he'd left my office. "He's sweet," he said.

"He really is, the poor man. It's hard to see such a nice person get his heart stomped on by someone so callous."

"There are always two sides to every story, Cat," Gilley reminded me. "Right now, we know only his."

I pointed to Aaron's retreating form. "Agreed, but no one deserves to be simply cut off like that, Gilley. Without any explanation or even a formal goodbye. What she did was cruel, and even in the small amount of time I've spent with Aaron, I can tell you he likely didn't deserve to be treated like that."

Gilley sighed. "True," he said.

At that point Aaron had reached the side of a silver Bentley, and after unlocking it, he got in.

"Wow," Gil said next. "Aaron comes from money."

"And did you catch that accent?" I asked.

"It sounded Danish to me," Gilley said.

Gilley had traveled extensively across Europe, so I trusted that he was probably right.

He then moved back over to his laptop, lifted the lid, and began typing.

Aaron had pulled away by now, and I turned my attention to Gil. "Whatcha working on?"

"A little sleuthing."

My brow furrowed with curiosity. "Oh? What are we sleuthing?"

"I'm curious about him," he said.

"Aaron?"

"Yes," Gilley said, squinting at the screen. His eyes then widened, and he looked at me in surprise.

"What?" I asked.

"He's a count."

"A what?"

Gil swiveled the screen toward me. "I was right. Aaron is from Denmark, and he's a count from the royal house of Rosenborg."

"But his last name is Nassau."

"I know, but he's still a member of the Danish royal family, currently sixteenth in line for the throne."

"Whoa," I said. I'd never met a royal before, much less sat with one for an intimate conversation.

Gilley then looked up at me with a perplexed expression. "*Who* would dump a count?"

I shrugged. "Maybe she didn't know."

Gilley scoffed. "She knew," he said. "You're the only person left on earth that doesn't immediately Google a prospective romantic partner."

I rolled my eyes. "It's rude to snoop into someone's personal life before actually getting to know them."

"It's rude only if you get caught," Gil replied.

I sighed. On that note we'd have to disagree, and I changed the subject. "What's a Danish count doing in the Hamptons?"

Gilley shrugged, but then he said, "There's money here, so he'd be among his own kind, and a certain anonymity. I'd imagine that the members of the royal family are well known among their countrymen. Especially if they're eligible bachelors."

I tapped my lip thoughtfully. "Which, to your point, makes it odd that this ex of Aaron's would dump him without so much as an 'It's not you, it's me' speech. If you knew your boyfriend was connected to royalty and all kinds of influence, would you really want to cut ties so succinctly?"

"What do we know about the girlfriend?" Gilley asked. "I mean, it's hard to imagine someone not caring about those kinds of connections, unless she herself was even better positioned."

It was my turn to shrug. "We know nothing about her," I admitted. "I didn't think to ask."

Gilley closed the lid to his laptop and stood up. "It's probably not relevant to helping, anyway, so maybe we're better off not knowing."

I nodded. "Agreed." Changing the subject, I asked, "What's next on my schedule?"

Gilley offered me a slow blink. "You've already hit the highlight of your workday, sugar."

"Nothing?" I asked. "No calls? No emails to return?"

"Zippo," he replied.

I sighed. Launching a life-coaching business had proven to be a much more arduously slow endeavor than I'd ever expected, and while I now typically had a few clients on the books, it still wasn't enough to fill a full workday.

What was truly frustrating was that I knew that there were so many people out there in need of a little reassurance and life advice, but it was hard to get any of them to reach out to me for help. Thus, my client list was still relatively small and far less needy than I'd hoped.

"What shall we do with the rest of the workday?" I asked with a hint of exasperation.

Gilley scooted his chair in. "Let's go look at puppies," he said.

I laughed, thinking he was joking. Then I realized he was serious. "Where are we going to look at puppies, exactly?"

"The Southampton Animal Shelter, duh," he said.

I thought about telling Gilley to temper his enthusiasm until he'd had a chance to talk to his husband about bringing a dog into their lives, but then I decided there was no harm in looking. "Okay," I said.

Gilley clapped his hands happily and came around the desk to offer me his arm. I took it, and out the door we went.

Several hours later, as I was slipping into my dress, I heard the front door open and Gilley call out for me. "Yoo-hoo! Cat? Where you at?"

"Up here!" I called back.

Quick footsteps up the stairs suggested that Gilley hadn't lost any of the enthusiasm he'd arrived home with.

I pulled my dress up over my shoulders and settled it around me before he came through the doorway.

"Hey!" he said, slightly out of breath.

"Hey, yourself," I replied. Then I turned my back to him and said, "Would you help me with the zipper?"

Gilley obliged, and I could feel his hot breath on the back of my neck. I doubted the run up the stairs was totally to blame. "You seem excited," I said.

"I just finished the paperwork," Gilley said. I turned around and saw his face flush with happiness.

I reached out and grabbed his hands. "Congratulations, Papa. When does the little tyke come home?"

"Hopefully soon! Like, maybe tomorrow or the day after, which, I suppose, is okay, because it'll give me time to buy everything I need to welcome him home."

Gilley's face was aglow with happiness, and I knew exactly how magical the trip to the shelter had been for him. I was still trying to wrap my own mind around the kismet moment when, after walking up and down the aisle of adoptable dogs, Gilley had come to a pen where a small dark silver Staffordshire terrier with gorgeous blue eyes sat. The dog had immediately started wagging his tail and gazing up at Gilley while wearing—swear to

God—a huge smile. Gil had stopped in his tracks and squatted down to the dog's level. There was something that passed between them in that moment, some sort of knowing, which caused goose bumps all up and down my arms. It was a sort of acknowledgment, like Gilley and the pup were destined for each other, and now that they were face-to-face, the pup actually seemed to recognize Gilley as his new human.

"This one," Gilley whispered, and that was when the pup walked forward to lick at Gilley's hands through the steel-mesh door of the pen.

The woman who'd been escorting us through the area came a little closer to gaze at Gilley and the pup. With a chuckle, she said, "You won't find a more lovable dog than Spooks."

Gilley and I turned to look at the woman, with mouths agape.

"What'd you say his name was?" I asked.

The woman—Peg, according to her name tag—pointed to the pup and said, "That's Spooks. His name when he came to the shelter was Ghost, but we changed it to Spooks because we thought it'd be cuter and make him more adoptable. Oh, but don't worry. You can change it again to whatever name you'd like. He won't mind."

Gilley and I then exchanged a look of our own, and I shook my head in wonder. Gilley had spent more than a decade as a ghostbuster, and he and his partner M.J. had come to call the ghosts they hunted "spooks," so finding such a perfect mascot seemed to be an incredibly magical thing.

"His name is perfect," Gilley said as he got to his feet. Then he added, "And I definitely want to adopt him."

We came home with a whole packet full of information, and a link to the online adoption forms. Peg had promised that as soon as Gilley filled out all the forms and submitted them, she'd make sure to process his application and check all his references quickly, in order to get Spooks to his new, "furever" home.

"It'll be exciting to have a bundle of love around here," I remarked as I reached for my wrap and clutch. "And I know you'll feel less lonely while Michel is off on his photo shoots."

Gilley bounced on his feet. "True, true," he said, but then his expression changed, and I saw a hint of worry in the creases around his eyes.

"Gil?" I asked.

"Yeah?"

"You mentioned Spooks to Michel, didn't you?"

"Not yet, but I will."

My eyes widened. "You mean you haven't even called or texted him?"

Gilley glanced down at his suit coat and pretended to pick a piece of lint off the lapel. "I need to figure out a gentle way of telling him."

"A gentle way to tell him? Why? Does he not like dogs or something?"

Gilley cleared his throat uncomfortably. "Something like that."

My jaw dropped. Michel was the gentlest of souls. If I could peg anyone for a dog lover, it would be Michel. "He doesn't?" I asked.

Gilley shrugged. "He likes little dogs, but when he was ten, a Rottweiler bit him on the leg and cheek, and he had to have surgery. He still has the scars."

I thought of Michel's handsome face and recalled the very small divot to his left cheek.

"Yikes," I said. Spooks was on the small side of medium for a dog, but his head was large. And while he certainly wasn't Rottweiler size, as he weighed only about forty-five pounds or so, I could see how he could be a little intimidating to someone who'd had a terrifying experience as a child.

"What if Michel says no?" I said, hating that I had to ask Gilley the question I knew he was dreading Michel's answer to.

"Spooks is my dog," Gilley said firmly, and it wasn't lost on me that he was already claiming ownership. And then his voice turned bitter. "Besides, he's never here, so he doesn't get a lot of say about it."

I bit my lip. I'd been married for almost twenty years before my ex-husband began an affair that led to our divorce. In those two decades I'd learned that marriage sometimes meant depriving yourself of the things you needed to live your fullest, happiest life. It was a trade-off, really. On the one hand, you received love and support. On the other hand, you sometimes had to give up something that your heart really wanted, all to keep the delicate balance of the partnership intact.

So, I understood Gilley's position, but I worried what that hard stance would do to a relationship that was already showing significant signs of strain.

I moved over to lay a hand on Gilley's arm. "Listen," I began. "I know you've already fallen hard for Spooks, and I will support wholeheartedly your efforts to claim him—even if it means adopting Spooks for you—but, Gilley, before you talk to Michel, just try to see it from his point of view. It might take him a minute or two to adjust to the idea, so give him that time before you dig in your heels, okay?"

Gilley sighed and nodded almost reluctantly. "The instant I saw him, Cat, I *knew* he was my dog. So, yeah, I'm a skosh concerned that Michel is going to give me a hard time about it."

"Then say that to Michel," I suggested. "Tell him about that immediate connection, and hopefully, he'll understand."

Gilley pushed a weak smile to his lips. "We should go," he said.

"We should," I agreed, feeling a bubble of excitement. "I'm so glad we're doing this. I've been dying to see this show!"

Little did I know in that moment that someone else was about to die for the show too. . . .

Chapter 3

We arrived at Guild Hall, home to the John Drew Theater, after a simply scrumptious meal and lively conversation. Gilley's mood had been practically giddy by the time we arrived for dinner, and the maître d' had complimented him on his choice of suit. The walk to our table had also turned a few heads, which Gilley had eaten up like free beer at a monster-truck rally. Our dinners had both been absolutely delicious, which had only added to the magic of the evening.

I had held off telling Gilley how good our seats were and delighted in his expression when the usher led us to the front-row-center seats at the foot of the stage. I felt so relieved and happy that Gilley was having such a wonderful day. He deserved it, and the change in him since that morning was readily apparent.

"I'm so excited to see the gorgeous Yelena Galanis

giving it to the fat cats here in East Hampton," he gushed. "Practically everywhere I go, people are talking about who they think the twelve are."

"I wonder who we'll recognize," I said.

Neither Gilley nor I ran in any of the same social circles that many of my socialite peers did. I didn't exactly care for the "high-society" crowd, often finding them excruciatingly dull, materialistic, and shallow.

I did have a few friends in the area, of course, including Sunny and Shepherd, but most of my friends kept to the outskirts of the Hamptons' "in" crowd.

"Supposedly, Tucker McAllen was her first lover," Gilley said, which I'd also heard. "And Reese told me today that there's a rumor going around that Joel Goldberg was Lover Number Four."

Tucker McAllen was a big deal around town. The New York real estate developer owned several high-rises in the Big Apple and was always in the society papers. Gilley and I had actually had a brief encounter with him at a local eatery when McAllen had been exceptionally cruel to a female server that had dared to put the wrong dressing on his salad, berating her loudly and insulting her intelligence and her looks. McAllen had sent the young woman to the kitchen in tears, and the scene had been such an appalling display that I'd excused myself from Gilley's company, suggesting that I had to visit the powder room, and on the way there I'd stopped by McAllen's table to offer him a withering look and a very soft "Shame on you." He glowered at Gilley and me for the rest of our meal.

In an added display of solidarity with the female server, after I paid our bill and we were about to leave, I managed to intercept the young woman—who was still obviously shaken from her encounter with him—and I offered her a folded hundred-dollar bill in plain view of McAllen. Glaring hard at the insufferable ass, I told her in a loud and commanding voice, "Consider this hazard pay, my friend. And please know that my companion and I think you're doing an absolutely *marvelous* job!"

Next to me, Gilley grinned broadly, then turned to stick out his tongue at the boorish tycoon as we practically flounced out of the restaurant with our noses in the air. It was deliciously satisfying.

And, if I was honest, part of the reason I was looking forward to Yelena's show was that I wanted to take some delight in the dressing-down of Tucker McAllen.

Neither Gilley nor I had ever encountered Joel Goldberg, but we knew of him, and he was an equally big deal around town. Joel came from old money, mostly gold and diamonds. His family were some of the first and finest jewelers in the City, and they'd spent generations catering to the wealthiest citizens there and in the Hamptons. Goldberg had a fine jewelry store in every major town on Long Island, with several boutiques in Manhattan.

In the society papers, he was known to throw the most lavish parties. I had been invited to one a few weeks earlier but had sent my regrets because Shepherd had a low opinion of the man. Shep had told me in confidence that Goldberg had recently had a DWI charge thrown out, even though there was substantial evidence at the hearing that he had been quite intoxicated on the night in question. The incident had happened in East Hampton's jurisdiction, so Shepherd had been well aware of it, and he'd even done a little digging into the presiding judge's background and discovered that the Honorable Judge Waterson was a regular attendee of Goldberg's parties, where the judge's wife had been photographed wearing a new diamond pendant.

"There's a part of me that both loves the idea of this play and is also slightly repulsed by it," I confessed to Gilley.

"Oh, pish," Gilley said with a wave of his hand. "It's perfectly normal to delight in someone else's public shaming as long as that someone is a total turd."

I laughed. "Well, when you put it like that . . ."

At that moment the lights dimmed and the buzz of conversation in the packed theater came to an abrupt halt. For several seconds nothing happened, causing a palpable expectant and excited vibe to flitter across the audience. Finally, a single spotlight appeared, shining bright but empty on the center of the stage, and the excited tension in the audience ratcheted up a notch.

More seconds ticked by, and Gilley and I exchanged a look of confusion, and Gil even lifted his wrist to mimic looking at his watch. Where was the star?

Just when a low murmur began to hum out from the audience, the unmistakable sound of heels clicking against a wood floor reverberated across the stage.

I looked toward the source of the sound, but the bright spotlight made the background all the darker, and it was impossible to see anyone approaching.

And then the sound of clicking heels stopped, and more expectant seconds ticked by, until finally, the spotlight moved quickly—almost violently—several feet to land squarely on a statuesquely shapely woman in a dramatic pose, with her chin lifted and one arm raised high overhead while the other rested demurely on a hip jutted out just so.

Gilley gasped, as did many members of the audience. The sight of her standing under the spotlight was like watching the birth of a goddess.

Yelena's floor-length, sequined blush-pink dress was scintillatingly revealing, allowing her ample décolletage to bulge from the deep V at the neckline. A slit up the side from floor to hip allowed for one gorgeous leg to peek out from all that sparkling fabric. And while she stood still as a statue in that dramatic pose, her dress shimmered under the light, making it appear like a living thing adoringly wrapping itself around a celestial being.

"Oh, my goddess . . . ," Gilley whispered breathlessly.

"Indeed," I whispered back.

I'd had no idea that Yelena Galanis was such a vision, and just looking at her, I could understand why so many men reportedly fell at her feet.

I was about to say as much to Gilley when Yelena's extended arm floated down to her side, and her chin dropped, along with her gaze. It settled on us, her audience, and I felt myself subconsciously sitting a little straighter in my seat.

Gilley also shifted. Glancing at him sideways, I saw he was bug eyed, staring up at Yelena, totally entranced. In that moment, I'm rather ashamed to admit, I felt a small needle of jealousy thread its way into the pit of my stomach.

It wasn't that I had any romantic designs on Gil. . . . It was more. . . . Well, he usually wore that particular look for *me*. Not all the time, but sometimes when I'd dolled myself up extra special, he would swoon appreciatively, and it always filled me with such a lovely little ego boost.

And a further look back to Yelena told me she seemed

to sense Gilley's adoration, because I swear she looked directly at him, the corners of her lips lifting in a knowing smile.

My eyes narrowed involuntarily, but I quickly pushed the expression back to neutral, just in case Gilley took his eyes off Yelena for two seconds to glance my way. I didn't want him to see the hurt and envy etched onto my face.

I needn't have worried. Gilley seemed to sense his connection with Yelena, and he leaned forward toward her and nodded. She blinked slowly, demurely, then took a step closer toward the audience.

"Lover Number One," she said, her voice low and smoky à la Kathleen Turner, "was from the mean streets of Lower Manhattan."

The audience chuckled appreciatively. Gilley giggled loudly and squirmed in his seat. Yelena came closer still, and I could see her very clearly now under the glare of the spotlight. Her long black hair shimmered in the brightness, and her delicate nose wrinkled a little distastefully when she spoke of Lover Number One, who we all knew was Tucker McAllen.

"His trust fund was built by the timber industry," she continued drolly, holding a microphone up toward her lips, and then she turned her palm over, as if to inspect her nails. "His lovemaking . . . was not." Yelena let the microphone fall forward limply, and the audience roared, with Gilley laughing loudest of those around us as he also clapped his hands in glee.

And yes, even I chuckled. Still something about it felt a tiny bit shameful.

"We met at an art show," Yelena went on, swinging the microphone back to her hand while continuing to study her nails. "He liked my dress. I liked his car. He told me he called his mother twice a week, and I told him, 'What an odd name to call your mother. . . .'"

Again, the audience erupted in laughter. I giggled again, this time a little easier.

"Lover Number One was also quite the connoisseur. In particular, he loved all things French . . . *du vin, la bouffe, l'art, la culture, l'architecture, les French fries, le milkshake, l'hamburger, les McDonald's* . . ."

Yelena winked at the audience, and her hand then made a curving motion out away from her trim stomach to indicate that Lover Number One had had a belly.

Gilley squealed and slapped his knee. He was eating Yelena's act up. It was, I thought, deliciously gossipy, but I didn't know. . . . There was something a bit too wicked about laughing at McAllen so publicly. Even though he'd been absolutely wretched to that server, laughing at his expense like this didn't feel as satisfying as I had thought it would. Instead, it almost felt like we were stooping to his level.

Yelena carried on, telling us all the naughty things she'd learned about Lover Number One, winding her way through their three-month relationship and sparing him no expense. Her humor was deft. She could deliver a punch line with such casual ease that if your mind drifted for a moment, you'd be out on the joke.

Ten minutes later she'd thoroughly emasculated Lover Number One, and I had stopped giggling. I found her act more cruel than humorous, but all around me there were peals of laughter. As I glanced around at the audience, I could see people here and there mouthing, "Tucker McAllen," to each other and nodding agreeably. It was obviously no secret whom they were laughing at, and it was a bit disturbing, actually.

"Lover Number Two," Yelena announced, "had a thing for fast cars, loud music, loose women, and big money, honey."

A murmur of anticipation spread through the crowd. Yelena road out a pregnant pause, gleaming at the audience as she continued to cast her spell. "He spent his days at the house on the hill," she said, giving us another juicy clue. "Looking down his nose at all the fools that bought his act. He wasn't born into money, but he worked the phone and always came away with a generous donation or two all the same."

"A congressman," Gilley said, leaning over to whisper in my ear.

I nodded. "That'd be my guess too."

"He spent his nights cheating at cards and commitments, working his way through the wives of close friends," Yelena went on.

Gilley joined the audience's chorus of "Ooh."

"And I . . . ," Yelena said, adding another lengthy pause, "worked him out of a new Lexus and a pair of diamond earrings."

For emphasis, she offered the audience a little hip bounce and flicked her hair with a wave of her hand, exposing the bling in question.

Again, I shifted uncomfortably. I didn't like the fact that she felt so entitled to cheat men out of things. Even if those men were cads. It just didn't sit well with me.

Still, I seemed to be the only one who didn't find it amusing. The audience appeared to hang on her every word as Yelena wound her way through the sordid details of their fling.

She then moved on to Lover Number Three. "Lover

Number Three thinks this show is about him, don't you? Don't you? Don't you, Lover Number Three?"

Yelena giggled as she moved over to put her mic in the stand and fluff her long black hair for effect. Blinking her eyes demurely at us, she continued. "Speaking of love, Number Three never met a camera he didn't love. Or a mirror. Or his image in any reflective surface he passed by. He spent more time preening than I do. And, honeys, let me tell you, I spend a *lot* of time preening!"

There were murmurs in the audience; clearly, everyone around us thought it was someone different. And, for his part, Gilley was pitched forward, his brow knit in concentration, as if he could tweeze out the identity of Number Three from just a few clues.

"Now, Lover Number Three is a man of traditional values, and by that I mean he enjoys a neat house, a good meal, and a boisterous romp in the hay, but only if the woman does all the work. Which is odd for a man that likes to throw his weight around so much." Yelena pretended to have an extended belly again, and she swiveled her hips back and forth, stumbling a little, as if her belly was so heavy, it was creating momentum and causing her to nearly trip.

Gilley kicked his feet as he squealed with laughter. I forced a smile, but inside I was wincing.

Yelena giggled again, clearly enjoying herself. "Ahhh, and if he were here, my dear, sweet, gossip-loving friends, he'd probably lead his introduction with a 'Do you know who I am?'"

She'd lowered her voice to quote the man and added more of the stumbling belly act, and people were laughing and laughing at her antics. Gilley looked over at me, eager to share the boisterous time he was having. I forced a laugh and nodded, intent on not spoiling his fun.

She carried on this way for another grueling half hour or so, winding her way through Lovers Four and Five and Six. Each sordid affair seemed to be worse than the last, and I stopped laughing long before Yelena waved to us, announced the intermission, and walked offstage to the beat of some loud, sassy music, which continued to play even as the lights flickered on and Gilley and I got up with the rest of the audience to move out into the lobby for the fifteen-minute break.

"Isn't she a hoot?" Gilley asked when we had cleared the doors into the lobby and were away from the loud music, which made it easier to speak to each other.

"She's something," I muttered, rubbing my temples. I'd developed a headache during Lover Number Four, and that last wave of music ushering us out into the lobby to purchase a drink or a snack hadn't helped.

"You don't look happy. What's wrong, Cat?"

I sighed. "She's mean."

Gilley's chin pulled back in surprise. "Duh. It's what makes it all so delicious."

I shrugged. "It's just not my cup of tea."

Gil seemed to study me for a long moment. "You're probably thinking about your first days here, when you were the topic of gossip around here, am I right?"

I shrugged again. "I suppose much of it might be that, but overall, I just find her to be a narcissistic, gold-digging, self-involved bully."

"Gee, Cat, don't hold back. Tell me how you really feel."

I smiled, and my hand went to my temple again. "I'm

sorry, lovey. I've been pushing back against a terrible headache for the past half hour."

"Do you have anything for it?"

"Not with me. There's a pharmacy down the street, next to the coffee shop, though."

Gilley eyed his watch, and I knew he was nervous about missing any part of Yelena's second act. "If we hustle, we can probably make it back in time."

I shook my head. "No, Gilley. I'll go. You get yourself a little wine before you head back to your seat."

"But, Cat, if you come back after the second act starts up again, they won't let you in."

"I know," I said, eyeing him intently.

It took Gilley a moment, but he suddenly understood. "You don't want to watch the second half."

"Not particularly."

Gil frowned. "Well then, I'll definitely come with you."

I put my hands on his shoulders to block him. "No, my friend. You're loving the show. I've just got too much of a headache to put off taking something for it any longer. If I don't make it back here in time, I'll wait for you in the coffee shop next to the pharmacy, okay?"

Gilley arched a brow. "Really? You think I'd actually be selfish enough to let you wait in a coffee shop with a splitting headache while I'm back here enjoying the show?"

I grinned, genuinely amused. "In point of fact, I do."

Gilley chuckled. "You know me too well." But then he sobered and let out a sigh. "I'd feel too guilty, Cat. Let me come with you."

I took his chin in my hand and kissed his cheek. "My

sweet Gilley, we're out on the town tonight for you, and just because I've got a blistering headache doesn't mean I should ruin your good time. No, you go back and catch the second act. If this is intermission, then it's only going to be another hour and fifteen minutes. I'll be fine just down the street."

"You're sure?" Gilley pressed.

"Positive," I assured him. Then, after squeezing his chin one last time, I turned and headed toward the exit.

In short order I made my way to the pharmacy, bought some pain-relief tablets and a *Town & Country* magazine, and headed outside. I looked first toward the theater and took note of the time on my phone. I still had about three minutes left to get inside and to my seat, and I knew that it'd be close but that I could make it, and still, I just couldn't muster up the will.

So instead, I walked the ten feet to the coffee shop— cutely named Thanks a Latte. Entering the shop, I was immediately charmed by the smell of baked goods and an eclectic decor.

Only one table appeared to be occupied, by a couple in their late teens, huddled in the corner booth by the window. They were sitting side by side, displaying lots of PDA, with eyes only for each other.

I squashed an amused smile and looked away. *Young love is adorable.*

After I ordered a signature latte, a bottled water, and a raspberry scone, I settled down at one of the many open tables in the middle of the shop, close to the door so that Gilley would spot me immediately when he came to find me. After popping two of the headache-relief tablets, I eased back in the chair, opened up the magazine, and took a sip of the latte, prepared for a luxurious hour spent quietly perusing the pretty pictures and stately homes of *Town & Country*.

No sooner was I feeling an easing to the set of my shoulders than the door opened abruptly, startling me, and in came a man of short stature, with white, wispy hair and a wild-eyed expression, nearly completely enveloped by a raincoat that was several sizes too large.

After the door behind him shut, he shuffled toward me a few paces before glancing over his shoulder back at the door, and that was when his foot seemed to catch the hem of his raincoat, and he stumbled forward, then reached out to brace himself against the table where I sat.

The movement seemed to startle both of us, and as our eyes met, I asked, "Are you all right?"

"Fine," he squeaked, standing again, but he looked pale and shaky. He wiped his brow, which was beaded with sweat, and belatedly, I saw that his hand was smeared with blood.

"Oh, my," I said. "Did you cut yourself?"

He stared at me with those big bug eyes and furrowed brow, so I pointed to his hand.

The man looked down and quickly covered his injured appendage with his other hand. "It's fine!"

I bit my lip, concerned for him, but also fearful of making him even more agitated. "All right," I said gently. "Would you like me to get you a coffee or a bottled water?"

The elder gentleman was quivering and pale, and I was fearful he was having some sort of episode.

"No," he said, again glancing back toward the door. "I just need to get to the men's room."

It was my turn to look over my shoulder, where a sign above a dark hallway said RESTROOMS.

Pointing to the sign, I said, "I believe it's that way."

He gave a sort of half-hearted nod, glanced back behind him one last time, then headed toward the men's room.

I hoped he'd be okay and vowed to ask him to sit a spell with me so I could assess if he needed some kind of medical assistance. He'd been awfully pale, and I'd noted that his whole body had seemed to be trembling. I worried that he could be having either a heart attack or a stroke.

After getting up from my seat, I approached the counter to get another bottle of water which I intended to offer to the gentleman when he came out of the men's room, but the store's barista was nowhere to be found. Leaning over the counter, I could hear some rustling behind a curtain leading to what was likely the stockroom. At last, the curtain parted, and out came the young man who'd waited on me, carrying an armload of coffee cups in all three sizes.

"Did you need something?" he asked when he paused to set down the cups on the counter.

"A bottled water when you get a moment," I said, fishing out a five-dollar bill from my purse.

The barista got the water, took my five, and gave me change. I went back to the table and waited for the stranger to come out, but minutes ticked by, and he didn't appear.

I bit my lip again, anxious to know if he was all right, and after another five minutes had passed, I approached the counter again and got the barista's attention.

"Excuse me," I said. The young man turned around from where he was wiping down the espresso machine to raise a brow in question. "A gentleman came into the shop about fifteen minutes ago and headed to the men's room. He hasn't come out yet, and when he went in, he looked unwell. Would you mind checking on him to see if he's all right?"

The barista blanched, and I could tell that, after hearing an older gentleman had been in the men's room for fifteen minutes, that was likely the last thing he wanted to do. "Aw, man," he said. "I hope he didn't get sick in there. I just cleaned it."

I nodded, even though it irritated me to hear the young man complain when I'd just expressed concern over a patron in the restroom. Still, he moved from behind the counter and headed toward the hallway leading to the restrooms.

I went back to my seat but turned so I could see one or both of them come out.

The barista appeared again and approached me. "There's no one in there," he said.

I blinked in surprise. "There isn't?"

"No, it's empty."

"You're sure?"

"Yes, ma'am. No one's in there."

"All right. Thank you for checking," I said.

Once the barista was back behind the counter and busy with his side work again, I slipped from the seat and quietly made my way to the hallway leading to the restrooms. It wasn't well lit, but I easily found the men's room door, first on the left. After pushing it open, I peeked inside. A vacant row of urinals and two empty stalls with the doors open showed me clearly that the barista was right. And there was no window through which the stranger could've climbed out of, either—not that he would've, but still the thought did cross my mind.

After backing out of the men's room, I made my way a bit farther down the hall to the ladies' room and pushed that door open as well.

Four empty stalls and two vacant sinks were all that were in there. While backing out of the ladies' room, I glanced a bit farther down the hallway, and there I saw a door marked with a faded EXIT sign.

I walked to the door, checked it for any OPEN ONLY IN AN EMERGENCY signs—there were none—and pushed it open, revealing a darkened alley.

A shudder went through me as I looked up and down the alleyway. It was creepy back here, but there was no sign of anyone either coming or going.

Logically, I knew that the elderly man had either by-passed the men's room and exited out the back or had used the facilities and exited out the back without my seeing him go. My back had been to the hallway leading to this exit, so it wasn't surprising that I hadn't seen him leave.

Still, something really bothered me about the entire in-teraction. He'd seemed to be in such a heightened state of anxiety, and when I'd looked into his eyes, there'd been the unmistakable note of fear there.

With a shudder, I closed the door and decided there was nothing more I could do for the poor man. I had no idea who he was or where he'd gone, so worrying over him was an effort in futility.

Yet, as I made my way back toward my seat, I couldn't help but worry over him. It was an unsettling encounter all around.

When I came out from the hallway, I was surprised to see a bustle of energy toward the front door. Patrons were streaming in and buzzing loudly with conversation. All were well dressed—clearly the theater crowd—but one glance at my phone to check the time told me that Yelena was only about thirty minutes into her second act.

"What the devil . . . ?" I muttered after I reached my chair. Just then I saw someone waving out of the corner of my eye.

I glanced toward the motion and saw Gilley pushing his way through the crowd over to me, his face flush with excitement. "Cat!" he began.

"What's happened?"

"Yelena's dead!"

I gripped the top of my chair to steady myself from the shock of that announcement. "Dead? What do you mean, she's dead?"

"She's been murdered!" Gil shouted above the din of the crowd.

"Murdered?" I repeated. "How is that possible?"

"She was stabbed backstage during intermission!" Gilley exclaimed, still clearly excited by this turn of events. "Someone murdered her, then fled the scene!"

I stared at him with big wide eyes before looking over my shoulder toward the hallway leading to the exit. "Oh, my God," I said, focusing on Gilley again. "I think I just met the murderer!"

Chapter 4

"*What?*" Gilley shrieked. Several people nearby glanced our way.

I grabbed up my belongings from the table and took Gilley by the hand, and then we weaved our way through the crowd to the exit and outside. I walked with him a little way down the street until we were sufficiently out of earshot.

"Tell me everything you know," I instructed him.

"Hold on," he said, his hands finding his hips in a defiant posture. "Tell me what you meant by 'I think I just met the murderer!'"

I clenched my teeth, impatient to hear the details of what'd happened at the theater. "I will, but you tell me what you know first."

Gilley scowled at me, but he complied. "Right after the audience was seated for the second act, there was some kind of commotion that we could hear coming from backstage. After another lengthy pause, a guy showed up onstage and told us to sit tight because there'd been an incident and the police were on their way.

"One or two people got up and tried to leave the theater, but they were stopped by the ushers. It was all really unnerving until your main squeeze appeared onstage and told us that the star of the show had been violently attacked and that the police would need to get everyone's name and phone number before they'd be allowed to leave."

"He said she'd been *attacked*? How do you know she was actually murdered?"

"Shepherd spotted me, front row, center, and called me up onstage. He gave me the skinny, or as much as he knew, and then he asked where you were, and told me to come find you and take you home—*immediately*, as he put it."

"Why the rush to get me home?" I asked.

Gilley shifted on his feet. "Um, mind you, these are his sentiments and not mine, but he said that he wanted me to take you home immediately because right now there's a killer on the loose, and when trouble comes to town, you're usually at the center."

I scowled. "That's not true."

Gilley gave me a doubtful look. "This coming from the woman who just said to me that she thought she met the murderer."

I growled. "Fine. I just hate it when he's right."

"Me too," Gilley said, but I could tell he was still mocking me a little. "Now, come on, fess up. What makes you believe you've already met the killer?"

I explained my strange encounter with the gentleman

at the coffee shop, and Gilley's eyes bugged wide. "Wow. He actually had blood on his hands?"

"Hand. Just the one, but truly, Gilley, the more I think about it, the more it could've been quite innocent. I mean, he was fairly short and somewhat frail to be a killer, now that I think about it. Maybe he cut himself and didn't realize it until I pointed it out to him."

"How much blood was there?"

I bit my lip. His hand and nail beds had been smeared with it. "Quite a bit, actually."

"Whoa," Gilley said. "And you say that he kept looking back over his shoulder? Like he was nervous about being caught for the crime?"

"Well, I didn't say *that*, but yes, he did seem preoccupied with who might be coming through the door at any moment. And he *did* slip out the back door into an empty alley, which probably was so that he wouldn't be seen or further questioned by me."

"Cat, I think you have to tell Shepherd about this."

"But what if I'm wrong, Gilley? What if this man was just having some sort of medical episode and is innocent of any crime?"

"What if he wasn't, though?" Gilley replied. "I mean that truthfully, Cat. What if he really *is* the killer?"

I sighed heavily, feeling the weight of the responsibility to report what I'd seen to Shepherd, but concerned that I might spark unwarranted suspicion of an innocent man.

"Listen," Gilley said, obviously sensing my indecision. "If this guy with blood on his hand who was acting all suspicious had nothing to do with Yelena's murder, then Shepherd can clear him quickly and move on to another possible suspect."

I weighed the argument out in my head one more time, then said, "Okay, Gil. Let's go find Shep."

Gilley glanced across the street, where the crowd was still snaking its way out of the theater's exits. "Good luck getting through that," he said.

After taking out my phone, I placed the call to Shepherd. It rang twice and went to voice mail. "He's not picking up," I said while the outgoing voice-mail message played.

"He's probably really busy working the case. Text him that you need to talk and it's urgent."

I hung up the call and texted Shepherd, then set the phone in my open palm so that Gilley and I could watch the screen for any telltale bubbles with his response. We waited at least two minutes in silence, and nothing but a "delivered" notification indicated that my text had gotten to Shepherd.

"Jeez, what's taking so long?" Gilley whined.

"He's probably ignoring his phone."

Gilley again looked across the street. "The crowd's starting to thin out. Should we head over and try to find him?"

"Yes," I said and took up Gilley's hand again to cross the street, now determined to tell Shepherd what I'd seen.

Gilley and I checked for traffic before trotting across the street to the theater, which was now blocked off by yellow crime-scene tape and at least half a dozen EHPD officers, who were keeping onlookers at bay.

I led us straight to a female officer, smiling as I neared her. "Officer Labretta," I said, recognizing her from the station.

"Catherine Cooper," she replied coolly. "What're you doing here?"

I pointed to the theater. "Gilley and I caught the first act, and I may have seen something suspicious at the coffee shop down the street during intermission that Shepherd would want to know. Can you ask him to come out here and meet us? Just for a minute?"

"You saw something?" she asked. "You mean, related to the homicide?"

"Maybe," I said. "Either way, it was pretty suspicious."

Labretta nodded and raised her radio, then turned slightly away to speak into it. I tried to make out what was said, but a lot of it was in police code and somewhat garbled.

Turning back to me, she put away her radio and said, "He'll be right out."

Sure enough, Shepherd appeared a few minutes later. He looked stressed and not exactly pleased to see me. "I'm working," he said quietly when he got to us. "So, if this some sort of a social visit . . ."

Gilley sucked in a breath, and I raised my brow and scoffed at Shepherd. "You're kidding me, right?" I snapped. "Do you *really* think I'd interrupt a homicide investigation simply to say, 'Howdy-high-ho!' to my boyfriend?"

Shepherd winced. "Sorry," he said. "That crime scene has me on edge. I didn't mean to take it out on you."

But I was still a little miffed. I'd come over here with the sincerest of intentions, and it hurt my feelings that Shepherd would think me so self-involved. "Whatever," I said moodily.

Shepherd rubbed his face with his hand. It seemed like he was frustrated that I was still miffed. With a sigh, he said, "How about you tell me why you called me out here?"

"I saw something that looked very suspicious," I said curtly.

"Suspicious?"

"Yes."

"Suspicious how?"

I pointed to the coffee shop a block down the street. "I was sitting at Thanks a Latte, waiting for Gilley to finish up watching the second act of Yelena's show, when a disheveled man, who appeared to be upset, came into the shop, stumbled at my table, then dashed into the men's room before heading out the back door before I could question him further."

Shepherd blinked at me, then rubbed his face with his hand. "That's it?" he said. "Cat, are you kidding me with this?"

Again, I was taken aback by his tone, and my defenses went up. Crossing my arms, I adopted a clipped and curt tone. "Yeah, Detective, that's *exactly* what I'm doing. Kidding you. A woman was brutally murdered this evening, and I couldn't *wait* to prank you about it!"

"Cat?" Gilley said next to me.

"What?" I growled. I was in *no* mood for Gilley to take Shepherd's side.

Gilley cleared his throat. "Um . . . you forgot to mention the man had blood on his hand."

Shepherd had been wearing a scowl since I snapped at him, but his brow lifted the minute Gilley offered up that additional clue.

"Wait a second, Cat, you saw *blood* on his hands? How much blood?"

"His left hand was smeared with it. When I initially noticed it, I thought he'd injured himself."

"Was it dried blood?"

"No," I said, making a face. "It seemed to be . . . fresh."

"And he went into the restroom?" he said, glancing down the street toward Thanks a Latte, which now had a line out the door.

I turned to look too. "Yes," I said, gulping a little.

"Damn," he swore through gritted teeth before looking to his left at Officer Labretta. Shepherd whistled loudly to get her attention, and she hurried over. Pointing to the coffee shop, he barked, "That's a possible crime scene. Take Winnacker, get those people out of there, and secure that entire area."

"Yes, sir," she said and ran to get another officer just down from where she'd been standing.

Shepherd again rubbed his face, and I could see the strain of such an unruly crime scene, one spreading out to two separate locations, with literally hundreds of possible suspects, was beginning to take a toll on him.

Still, he flipped out a little notebook he carried and a pen and asked, "Give me a description of this guy, in as much detail as you can remember."

I spent a few moments with my eyes closed, recalling every detail of the man in my memory, and described him as well as I was able to.

"You're sure he was only about five feet six or seven?" he asked me when I'd finished.

"Yes," I said. "He was right around Gilley's height." For emphasis, I looked at Gilley, who was trying to stand as straight and tall as he could in an effort to squeeze a little more height out of himself.

"I'll have you know that I'm only an inch under the average," he said.

Shepherd ignored him and kept his focus on me. "And you used the word *frail*. Did you mean *thin*?"

"Yes," I said. "There wasn't much to him. Just a little old man in an oversized raincoat."

"Did the coat have any blood on it?"

"No," I said.

Shepherd snapped the cover of his notebook shut. "None of that fits with what I've seen of the actual crime scene, Cat."

"No?"

He shook his head. "Yelena was stabbed repeatedly and in quick succession. At least six times, by my count. Believe me when I tell you that that kind of attack takes some brute strength. It also would've left more of a mark on the killer. No way did he leave the scene without a lot of blood on his clothing."

"Could the raincoat have been covering up his clothes?" Gilley asked. We both turned to look at him. "Maybe he grabbed the raincoat from somewhere to cover up the blood on his clothing."

I thought back to the stranger stumbling into the table, and for the life of me, I couldn't remember if the raincoat had been buttoned at the chest or not. It seemed like it should be an easy thing to remember, but all I could see in my mind was the man's extremely stressful expression and the bloody hand.

Finally, I shook my head. "I don't know, guys. I'm sorry, but I don't know if his clothing underneath the raincoat was bloody."

Shepherd sighed. "Okay," he said. "I'll definitely have

my CSI guys check it out. For now, you two should go on home, and, Cat, I'll follow up with you later."

"Tonight?" I asked.

He shook his head. "I'm gonna be here for hours, so I won't be over tonight. But I'll make a point of finding you tomorrow, okay?" Shepherd reached out and gripped my hand for a moment. It was, I thought, a half-hearted attempt at an apology for snapping at me earlier.

I wanted to stroke his cheek and hug him, to let him know we were okay, but it wasn't the time or the place for any PDAs. "Sounds good," I said, squeezing his hand.

He let me go and turned to leave, and so did Gilley and I, but then I thought of something and turned back toward his departing form.

"Shep?" I called.

He glanced back at me. "Yeah?"

"Did you tell Sunny?"

The look of surprise on Shepherd's face at the mention of his sister told me he hadn't. "Damn it," he swore, closing his eyes, as if to rein in any further commentary. When he seemed more composed, he opened his lids and said, "I haven't. This is gonna kill her. She and Yelena go way back. They've been really close friends since college."

"Do you want Gilley and me to go to her place and break it to her?" I asked next. I hated the thought of Sunny being alone when she got the news, and there was no way Shepherd could leave the crime scene to go break the evening's tragic turn to his twin.

"Would you?" he asked hopefully.

"Yes," I said. "Absolutely. I'll text you to let you know how she's doing, and we'll stay with her until Darius gets home."

"He's in L.A.," Shepherd said, a look of disapproval crossing his features.

"Sunny told me earlier that he'd be home tonight."

The tension in Shepherd's shoulders eased a bit. "Good," he said. "If you could stay with her until he gets home, I'd appreciate it."

"Consider it done," I said.

Shepherd offered me a grateful smile and then turned back toward the theater. Gilley and I resumed our walk across the street, and I suddenly realized that Gilley was rather quiet, a pained look on his face.

"You okay?" I said to him.

"Hmm?" he asked. I'd obviously roused him from his troubled thoughts.

"Are you okay?" I repeated.

"I'm thinking about Sunny," he said. "And I'm wondering how we're going to find the words to tell her that her dear friend was just murdered."

I sighed heavily. When I'd volunteered to deliver the news, I don't think I'd thought it through as thoroughly as I should've. "I think that we should approach it with great care," I said.

"Duh," Gil replied.

"What I mean is, I think we should prepare her from the second she opens her door to us. We should say something like, 'Sunny, we have some difficult news to break to you. How about we all go inside and sit down?' and then you can guide her inside to the sofa and hold her hand while I offer her the news."

"I like that," Gilley said. "I mean, I don't *like* it, but I like the approach. We'll be gentle yet truthful, and we'll make sure to stay with her until the hubs gets home."

"Good," I said, feeling relieved that Gilley was along with me on this terrible errand.

By this time, we had reached the other side of the street and were passing by the alley on our way to the parking garage where we'd parked, when I stopped and looked down the length of the darkened alley.

"What?" Gilley asked.

"That's the alley the murderer slipped out the back door into," I said.

"So now he's the murderer?" Gilley said.

I rolled my eyes and, using air quotes, said, "Okay, the 'suspicious person.'"

"Should we check it out?"

"I don't know. It looks creepy."

Gilley pulled his chin back in mock surprise. "*That* looks creepy to you? Pish, gurl. You never would've made it on one of our ghost busts back in the day."

"Nor would I have wanted to. They sounded horrendous."

"You don't know the half of it," he said. "Come on, I'll hold your hand. Let's see if, in his haste to run out the door, he dropped something that could identify him."

I took Gilley's hand, and we crept into the alley.

"Which door is the coffee shop?" he asked.

"I think it's the one down there," I said, pointing a little way down the alley.

"Okay, let's go all the way to the end of this block. It'll let out on the right side of the parking garage, too, so this will end up being a convenient shortcut," Gilley said.

We walked along, and Gilley had the flashlight on his phone pointing toward the ground. Mostly there was just some random garbage, puddles of water, and the foul smell of a full dumpster. We passed the back door to Thanks a

Latte, which was clearly marked, and continued on, with only about a quarter of the way left. Neither one of us spoke, and I began to relax, because with Gilley's flashlight, the alley wasn't nearly as creepy as it had seemed at first.

Mostly I couldn't wait to get away from the dumpster smell.

We passed another door, which led to a hardware store, and opposite the door was a tall stack of pallets. Gilley raised his flashlight to flash across the pallets, and I followed the beam as it trailed up the stack of wood. As I was waiting for it to swoop back down to the street, the beam passed over something that didn't belong in the scene.

I gasped.

Gilley made a startled squeaking sound, his beam now to the right of the pallets.

Slowly, he moved it back to the stack, my free hand now gripping his arm, which had begun to tremble. That was how I knew we'd both seen what I thought we'd seen.

At last the beam landed on a hand that was dangling down and wedged against a torso, which was wedged against the side of the stacked pallets.

Gil and I took an involuntary step back, the beam shaking in a perfect reflection of our mutual fear.

"Hello?" I whispered, unable to make a noise any louder than that.

There was no reply.

"Hello?" Gilley tried to speak a tad bit louder than me. Still no reply.

My own hand trembling, I moved the arm Gilley was using to hold his phone, and the bright light moved slowly left again, until it came to rest on a blood-soaked rain-coat, where it froze, because I froze, and so did Gilley.

That is, we froze until the adrenaline kicked in and we both ran as if our lives depended on it.

It took me a bit to realize that we were also screaming bloody murder (pardon the pun). As we came out into the cross street, we nearly ran headfirst into Officer Labretta, who had probably come running when she heard the screams.

"What's going on!" she yelled, even though we were right in front of her.

Gilley and I both pointed forcefully back toward the alley. I couldn't seem to make my vocal cords work to form words, and neither, it seemed, could Gilley, which was doubly odd as we'd just been screaming at the top of our lungs.

Labretta pulled up her flashlight, blinding us for a moment, but then she swept the beam toward the entrance to the alley. "Someone in there?" she asked.

Gilley and I nodded. Vigorously.

"Are they armed?" she said next.

We both shook our heads. Equally vigorously.

"Did they try to hurt you?" she asked next, her eyes darting from the alley to us for a quick up-down scan, then back to the alley again.

"D-d-d-d-dead," Gilley managed as he once again pointed to the alley.

Labretta's eyes widened. "You saw a *body*?"

We both went back to the vigorous nodding thing, but I managed to add, "B-b-b-blood!"

Labretta unholstered her gun and pointed it, along with the flashlight, at the area behind us. "Anybody else in that alley besides you two?"

We both did the shaking head thing.

Labretta reached for the mic to her radio, which was snapped in place at her shoulder. She spoke in code into it, but I thought she was likely calling for backup. Sure enough, in short order the sound of pounding footsteps approached, and from around the corner emerged two uniformed police officers.

By now I thought I had some of my breathing under control, but I felt the need to clutch Gilley's arm with both of my hands. He wrapped his palm over them and inched closer to me. We were both still trembling, but the nearness of each other was comforting.

Labretta spoke to the two officers off to the side, then motioned to me and Gilley to move toward the brick wall of the building right in front of us. We shuffled over and waited as all three uniforms cautiously approached the alley, their guns drawn and their flashlights on.

Then they disappeared in the dark, but we could see the light of their beams emanating from the alley. We waited for what felt like a very long time, but it was only likely another two or three minutes, and then Labretta emerged, her gun holstered again, and a granite set to her jaw.

"Found him," she said.

Gilley and I squished together a little more.

"I radioed Shepherd. He's on his way over," she said. And then she leaned in toward us and added, "Best brace yourselves. He didn't sound thrilled that you two had found the body."

Neither Gilley nor I said a word in reply, but I saw out of the corner of my eye that Gilley wore an expression that likely matched my own: *Yikes!*

Still, I managed to square my shoulders a bit as Shepherd rounded the corner and stopped short in front of us. "*What* did you two *do*?"

I glared at him. "We used a shortcut on our way to the parking garage and discovered a dead body in an alley," I said sharply, to let him know that I wasn't about to put up with him giving us the third degree.

Shepherd ran his hand down the front of his face—a gesture he'd employed liberally tonight and one I knew he only made when he was particularly frustrated. He then seemed to consider us again and gave a half-hearted nod before leaving us standing there. We then watched as he moved in the direction of the entrance to the alley.

Labretta met him there, and the two disappeared into the darkness together.

"How long do we have to stand here?" Gilley asked.

The wind had picked up, and I was starting to shiver. I had only a simple pashmina to wrap around my bare shoulders.

"Who knows?" I said. There wasn't much more that we could offer the investigation at this point, and I was still somewhat anxious to get to Sunny before she heard the news. It was a little past nine, and I knew that Sunny would be up by now, getting ready to greet her husband when he returned home. I was worried that someone within her friend circle would learn the news and tell her over a phone call or text.

Shepherd reappeared after just a few minutes, wearing black gloves and holding his phone. He approached me and covered the face of the phone with one hand while looking critically at me. "I took a picture," he said. "The guy wasn't wearing any ID. Are you up for taking a look at his face?"

I gulped and braced myself. "Okay," I said.

Shepherd held the phone up to reveal the photo, and although he'd been very careful not to include anything gruesome in the shot, there was still a smudge of blood on the man's chin, and his eyes were half-lidded and staring sightlessly out into space. He was also very, very pale and very, very dead.

I swallowed hard. It was unsettling to look at the image of a dead man, especially one I'd spoken to earlier that night. "That's him," I said. "That's the man I saw in the coffee shop."

Shepherd pulled the phone back and slid it into his pocket. "Sorry you had to see that."

"It's okay," I said. "I understand."

"How're you going to figure out who he is?" Gilley asked.

Shepherd pulled out a small baggie from his other pocket. "He had his key fob on him. I'll have a uni walk around and see if he can find the car by pressing the alarm."

"I do that in the parking lot of the grocery store," Gilley said.

"It's effective," Shepherd replied. Thumbing over his shoulder, he added, "By the looks of it, we think this was a mob hit."

My eyes widened in shock, as did Gilley's. "A mob hit?" we both said.

"Yeah. His throat was cut, right through the carotid, hit-man style. And he's got some money on him."

"Why would having money on him indicate a mob hit?" I asked.

"The money is stuffed into the lining of the raincoat he's wearing. All hundred-dollar bills. Not sure how much he's packing, but it's a lot. We think it's counterfeit—otherwise the hit man would've taken the coat with him after doing the deed."

"Who knew that East Hampton would be such a den of Mafia murderers?" Gilley mused.

I shuddered, thinking how close I'd come to yet *another* Mafia hit man. Or hit woman. Hit person. Still, I couldn't help wondering something, so I asked, "What's the connection to Yelena?"

Shepherd shook his head slowly. "Hell if I know, honey. I've known Yelena for almost twenty years, and never once did her name come up in any investigations into mob activity around here."

"Still, it can't be a coincidence that she was killed within a half hour of this man, right?" I pressed.

"Not in my book, it can't. I'll dig a little into the guy's background once we ID him, to see what I can find out about any connection to her, but right now, these will be two separate investigations."

I shuddered again, feeling cold all over. "Did you need us to stay and give our statements?"

Shepherd's expression turned soft. "No. Sorry. You two should get going. I'll get a statement from you both tomorrow."

"Okay," I said, taking Gilley's hand, ready to leave this horrible scene on this horrible night.

"Hold on a sec," Shepherd said as we turned to go.

We stopped and waited for him to tell us why. Instead, he called out to Labretta, and she hurried out of the alley and over to us.

"Officer Labretta, would you please escort these two to their car and make sure they leave the area safely?"

"Absolutely, sir," she said.

"Oh, and take this with you and see if you can locate the vic's car."

Shepherd offered Labretta the baggie with the key fob, and she took it dutifully. "Yes, sir."

Shepherd then turned his attention back to me, and I offered him a grateful smile as I moved to give him a quick peck on the cheek, but his phone buzzed, and he lifted it out to read the display. "I gotta go," he said quickly. "They think they've found the murder weapon."

I didn't know which murder he was talking about, but after squeezing my arm, he ran past me to jog across the street toward the theater, and that told me it must've been the weapon used to kill Yelena.

Labretta walked us all the way to our car in the parking garage, and we took our leave and were off to break the heart of someone we knew and loved. Little did I know that other hearts would soon be broken too.

Chapter 5

Sunny lived only a few streets over from me, and as we wound our way there, I tried to rehearse the words that I'd need to say to break the terrible news to her as gently as I could.

"I think you should get to the point right away," Gilley suddenly suggested, like he'd been reading my mind. "She's gonna find it weird that we're showing up at her place this late at night, and we don't want her to think that something's happened to her brother."

I nodded. "Great point. There isn't any easy way to say it, though, is there?"

"No," Gilley said. "And Sunny's such a sensitive soul. This is going to be very hard on her."

"What would you say to her?" I asked.

"Well," Gilley replied, taking a moment to think about

it. "I suppose I'd tell her that I had news, that it wasn't about Shepherd, but that it was still difficult news to hear. Then I'd ask for us all to sit down, and I'd take her hand and I'd say, 'Sunny, I'm so, so sorry, but your brilliant, talented, gorgeous friend Yelena has left this earth, never to return.'"

My brow furrowed. I liked most of that. "'Left this earth' sounds like she's gone on a space mission."

Gilley nodded and waved his hand poetically. "Crossed the rainbow bridge . . ."

"That makes her sound like a pet."

"Yelena has gone off to meet Jesus. . . ."

I stared at him. "*Was* she Catholic?"

Gilley's brow furrowed. "Okay, how about 'Sunny, your brilliant, talented friend Yelena has been taken from us too soon'? 'She died tonight doing what she loved best, entertaining the masses and bringing laughter and light to this world.'"

"A bit melodramatic, but that's not bad," I said.

Gilley scowled. "Everyone's a critic."

I allowed myself a small smile. "We'll tell her together as gently as we can and be there for as long as she needs us."

"Agreed," Gilley said.

We pulled into Sunny's driveway a short time later and parked near the front door. I noticed an unfamiliar car in the drive.

"Who's that?" Gilley asked.

"It could be the babysitter's car."

"The babysitter?"

"Yes. Sunny was so exhausted this afternoon that she took a sleep aid and made arrangements for Finley to be looked after while she caught some z's. Darius is coming home tonight, and Sunny wanted to be fresh and alert for her husband's arrival."

"Aww," Gilley said. "That's so romantic!"

"It's sweet," I agreed. "But it's not going to be the evening that Sunny had anticipated."

Gilley's expression fell. "Yeah. Almost forgot."

As we began to climb the steps to the front porch, I couldn't help but notice that most of the downstairs lights were on, which hopefully meant that Sunny was up.

Pausing before ringing the bell, I said, "You ready?"

"No, but let's get on with it," Gilley said.

I rang the bell, which had such a happy chime for two guests who were bringing such dark news. As approaching footsteps sounded on the wood floors inside, I squared my shoulders, prepared to keep my emotions in check, but I did take a small step back when the door was then opened to reveal a pretty young woman with a heart-shaped face, deep-set eyes, and long, dark, wet hair. She looked like she had just gotten out of the shower and had dressed quickly in a baggy XL men's sweatshirt and black leggings.

"Hi?" she said, obviously startled by our appearance.

I pushed a smile to my face. "You must be Tiffany," I said.

"I am," she said, a bit surprised, I thought, that I knew her name. "Can I help you?"

"Is Sunny home?" I tried.

"No. She went out."

"She went out?" I said.

"Yeah. I don't know when she'll be back."

"Did she say where she was going?" Gilley tried.

"No."

Gilley offered her his hand. "I'm Gilley Gillespie, and this is Catherine Cooper. We're very good friends of Sunny, and we've both heard marvelous things about you."

"Hi," Tiffany said, and she seemed to relax a bit in the presence of Gilley's charm.

"Tiffany, could Sunny have gone to pick up Mr. D'Angelo?" I asked.

Tiffany shrugged. "I don't know," she said. "She didn't say anything about where she was going when she went out the door."

"She didn't?" I pressed. This was confusing. Why would Sunny not give her sitter any information about where she was going or how long she'd be out?

Tiffany shook her head, shrugged, and said, "I was in the basement playroom with Finley, and I thought I heard footsteps above us in the kitchen and then the sound of the garage door opening and closing, but when I came upstairs to see if Sunny was up and around, she wasn't anywhere in the house, and when I looked in the garage, her car was gone."

"Did you call her?" I asked. This was very strange indeed.

"Yeah, about an hour after she left, 'cause I didn't know when she'd be back, but Sunny left her phone here."

"She . . . she left her phone behind?" Gilley asked, and he was as shocked as I was. What mother of a toddler would leave behind her phone? And if Tiffany's timeline was correct, wouldn't Sunny have realized by now that she'd left it at the house, and come back for it?

In answer to Gilley's question, Tiffany said, "Mm-hmm. I followed the sound of the rings from my call upstairs to the master bedroom. I found her cell phone on the nightstand, and I left it there, but right around nine o'clock it started ringing and pinging like crazy. So many people were calling and texting Sunny that I had to put it on silent so that it didn't wake Finley."

I turned to Gilley. "No doubt word of what happened at the theater has gotten around, and people are calling and texting her."

"Could that be why she left?" Gilley asked me.

"What word's going around?" Tiffany asked innocently, but I wondered if she didn't already have some clue about what'd happened if people had been texting Sunny. Tiffany probably couldn't access Sunny's phone due to the phone's security protocol, but she could've read the first part of the incoming texts.

Instead of answering her question, I asked, "What time did Sunny leave, Tiffany?"

"It was right before I was gonna give Finley his bath and put him to bed, so I think, like, seven thirty or eight. The weird thing is that I swear I heard her come back into the house a little after nine. I was on the treadmill in the workout room." At this admission, Tiffany's face flushed. "They let me use it as long as Finley's sleeping and I have the baby monitor with me," she added quickly. My gaze traveled to her wet hair, and she added, "And they let me shower here too."

"Hold on," Gilley said, blinking as he spoke. "You thought she came back to the house but left again?"

"Yeah. I was only into my second mile when I swear I heard someone in the laundry room, which is next door to their workout room. It totally creeped me out, but when I went to check, nobody was there, and Sunny's car was still gone from the garage."

"That is creepy," I said.

"Right?" Tiffany agreed. "I mean, I could've imagined it, but I swear that when I passed the laundry room on the way to the workout room, the door was open, but when I went to check to see if Sunny had come back, it was closed. I could be wrong or it could be my imagination again, but it still freaked me out."

"Is Finley sleeping now?" I asked.

"Yeah. He went out like a light. I think he was pretty tired. Sunny said he hadn't been sleeping well, so I made sure to tucker him out in the playroom."

"Good thinking," I said. And then I sighed when I struggled to come up with a plan to track down Sunny.

"We could drive around and see if we spot her car," Gilley suggested, reading my thoughts.

I nodded and glanced at my phone, noted the time was now after ten. "We have no other choice. But where could she be at this hour?"

Gilley shrugged. He had no clue, and Tiffany shook her head as well.

"Are you okay to stay with Finley for another hour or so?" I asked her.

"Sure," she said. "I've got nowhere to be, and I don't have to be up early tomorrow, so I can stay as long as you need. Or until Mr. D'Angelo comes home."

"That's right," I said. "He's due back here any minute. When he gets home, could you have him call my cell?" I offered Tiffany my business card.

She took it and said, "I will. And if Sunny comes back, I'll send you a text."

"Thank you, Tiffany," Gilley said. She was a sweet, earnest young lady. I could see why Sunny trusted her to care for Finley.

"And we'll call you if we find Sunny," I suggested.

Tiffany swiped at her phone and said, "What's your number? I'll send you a text."

We exchanged information and said our goodbyes.

Tiffany went back inside, and Gilley and I made our way to the car. "She's a sweet thing," he said.

"Yes," I agreed. "And she seems to really adore Finley."

Gilley glanced over his shoulder, back at the house. "I swear I've seen her before, though."

"She might live around here," I suggested. "And she's a runner. Maybe you saw her running."

He snapped his fingers and pointed at me. "That's it," he said. "I've seen her out running." As we reached the car, he asked, "Where did you want to start?"

"Gosh, I don't know," I said, my hand on the door handle, as I looked at him over the roof of the car. "Any ideas where she could've gone?"

In answer he said, "Was there anyplace that you liked to go when the boys were with their nanny and you needed a little free time away?"

I smiled, but there was a trace of guilt to go with it. "Target," I said. "I used to go there and just walk the aisles aimlessly for an hour or two. There was something so freeing and luxurious about walking around that huge space, free of the cries and grabbing hands of toddlers."

"Motherhood wasn't your strong suit, was it?" Gilley said with a chuckle.

"Those early days with twins were hard," I admitted. "Let's see, the nearest Target is in Riverhead."

"Ugh," Gilley said. "That's an hour away, Cat."

I glanced again at my phone. "And I think they close at ten, so they've just closed."

"She could be on her way back," he suggested.

"True. Let's do a simple search of the grocery store parking lot and a few of the restaurants that we know Sunny likes to frequent."

"What restaurants are those?" he asked.

"I was hoping you'd know."

He simply shrugged.

"Well, let's start at the grocery store and work our way out from there."

"Okay," he said.

We were just getting into the car when a set of headlights turned into the drive. I held my hand up to block most of the glare and heard Gilley say, "She's home!"

But as the car turned to park next to mine, I could see that it wasn't Sunny, after all. It was Darius.

He took note of the two of us standing next to his car and offered us a little wave before getting out and grabbing his gym bag. The man was soaked with sweat, and he smelled *ripe*.

I could tell that Gilley could smell it, too, because I saw him back up a little.

"Hey, guys!" Darius said, hoisting the gym bag to his shoulder. "Were you keeping my wife company until I got home?"

I closed my door and waited for Gilley to come around the car to stand next to me. He subconsciously waved his hand in front of his nose when he got a strong whiff of Darius, but luckily, he didn't comment on it.

"Hello, Darius," I began. "We actually weren't here to visit. We came to give Sunny some absolutely dreadful news, I'm afraid."

Darius blinked, and his expression turned serious. "Is her brother okay?"

It didn't surprise me that he assumed something had

happened to Shepherd. In the past two years, he had been shot twice and had ended up in the hospital both times. "Shepherd's fine," I said, quick to reassure him.

His shoulders sagged in relief, but then he asked, "What's happened, then?"

I looked at Gilley for a moment, trying to decide how to tell Darius about Yelena, but Gilley read that as a cue to spill it to him.

"Yelena was murdered," he said.

Darius blinked, his jaw fell open, and he took a step back, letting the gym bag drop to the pavement. "Yelena?" he repeated, his head shaking back and forth slightly as he took in the news. "Yelena *Galanis*?"

"Yes," I said.

Darius looked from me to Gilley and back again in disbelief. We both stood somberly while he absorbed the news. At last, he said, "When . . . How?"

"Tonight. It happened backstage, during the intermission of her show. She was stabbed by an unknown assailant," I said.

Darius stared at us with even more incredulity for a long moment, his jaw hanging open, and then he looked over his shoulder toward the house. "Did you tell Sunny?" he said hoarsely.

"No," I said. "She's not home."

He turned back to me again, his expression alarmed. "She's not . . ." Darius lifted his wrist to look at the time. "What do you mean, she's not home?"

I pointed to Tiffany's car. "Your sitter is here. Sunny went out around seven thirty, and Tiffany doesn't know where she went."

Darius shook his head some more, and I could tell he was trying to process everything that we'd just told him, and struggling to do so. He then looked over his shoulder at Tiffany's car, before swiveling his gaze back to me. "Did you call her? Did you call my wife and ask her to come home?"

"No," I said. "According to Tiffany, Sunny left her phone in the house."

Darius ran a hand through his hair and widened his eyes. "She *what*?"

I understood his shock. Sunny wasn't the type to leave her phone behind when she went out and left her toddler in the care of a sitter.

"She left her phone behind, Darius," Gilley said softly.

Darius's gaze pivoted to Gilley. "She would've noticed that she left it behind," he said. "She would've come back for it."

"Tiffany thinks Sunny came back to the house around nine so maybe she came in to look for it, couldn't find it, then went back out to see if she'd left it somewhere she'd already been."

That was the only scenario that even half made sense to me.

Darius placed both palms against his eyes, and I could tell he was trying to think and make sense of all the information we'd just given him. He then allowed his hands to drop, bent to pick up his duffel, then hoisted the strap over his shoulder again while also pulling out his phone. Tapping at the screen, he said, "I texted her when my plane landed to let her know I was gonna stop at the gym to get in a quick workout and I'd be getting in a little later than planned. I thought she was napping and that's why she didn't text back. She's been so tired lately."

"Do you know where she might be?" I asked, hoping he'd have some clue.

He started to shake his head again, but then he paused and looked toward the street. "She's been spending a lot of time at the garden of her yoga studio. She took charge of it when the yoga group came together."

"*Her* yoga studio?" Gilley asked.

Darius nodded. "She's one of five owners of a yoga studio in Amagansett. It's called Om Bliss." That was news to me. "Sunny's been working on the garden lately, trying to coax some life into it. Nobody else there cares about it, but it's one of Sunny's pet projects."

"Would she be there at night?" I asked.

Darius shrugged. "Sunny and I both like to unwind in our respective sanctuaries. For me, it's the gym, and for her, it's that garden at the yoga center. If she's not tending to it, she might be meditating or doing a little yoga by candlelight."

"We should head over and see if she's there," I suggested.

Darius nodded, but then he seemed to hesitate. "The only other place she might be is the park."

"Which park?"

Darius scratched at the widow's peak on his forehead. "It begins with an *H*," he said. "It's off of Newtown, in the center of downtown."

"Herrick Park?" Gilley said helpfully.

"Yeah," Darius said, snapping his fingers. "There. Sometimes she hires Tiffany to babysit for her while she drives over there to read for a while. She could've grabbed a book, gone there to read in her car, and nodded off, and that's why she's not back yet or worried about finding her phone."

"That makes sense," I said. Sunny always had a book handy, and I'd once seen her when she was quite pregnant doing just that—sitting in the public lot downtown, just reading in her parked car.

"Darius," I said next, "you go check out the yoga studio, and Gilley and I will try the park."

Darius nodded, then looked again toward the house; he seemed conflicted. "I gotta change," he said, pulling at his clothing. "And check in with the sitter to make sure she's okay staying with Finley."

We'd already done the latter but I understood that he wanted to check in on his son himself and change, which I was all in favor of because the man was a sweaty, stinky mess.

"Understood," I said to him before motioning to Gilley to get back in the car. "Tiffany has my business card. Send a text to my phone so that we can communicate, and if we find her, we'll text you immediately."

"Good," Darius said, opening the passenger door to pull out his carry-on and a guitar case. "I'll get on the road in the next couple of minutes."

I nodded, and Gilley and I left.

"That park isn't far from the office," I said as we got on the road.

"It's about three blocks, actually," Gil said.

I glanced at him, and he explained, "I go there sometimes for lunch when you're out with your man. It's peaceful. I like it."

"How come we've never gone together?" I asked.

"Because it's peaceful, and I like it," Gilley said, his eyelids drooping heavily.

"Ha-ha," I said just as dryly.

At that moment my phone pinged with an incoming text. Gilley lifted my phone from the cradle between the seats and read the text so that I could keep my eyes on the road. "It's Darius. He's on the road, heading to Ama-gansett."

"That didn't take long," I said. We'd left him less than five minutes earlier.

"He's as worried as we are," Gil said, putting the phone back in the cradle under the dash.

"I hope she's in one of the two places we're looking," I said. "I want to find her before she hears the news from someone else."

"Me too," Gilley said. "It's been a traumatizing night for everyone, I suppose."

"True that," I said. "It's not every day you're in close proximity to one murder, then stumble upon a second."

"What the heck was that all about, anyway?" Gilley said. "I mean, a mob hit in the back alley of a coffee shop just down the street from the theater where Yelena Gala-nis is murdered? It's too insane to be a coincidence."

"Or it's too insane not to be," I countered. "We've seen our fair share of mob hits around here, so another one wouldn't be so very surprising, other than the timing."

"True," Gilley said, shuddering. "I just want to find Sunny and get her home so that we can then go home. I need a hot bath and a big dish of ice cream to chase the blues away."

I was about to make a snarky comment when Gilley pointed ahead. "There, Cat. That's the parking lot for the park."

"Got it," I said, pulling into the lot.

As soon as I entered the lot, Gilley laid his hand on my arm and said, "Isn't that Sunny's Range Rover at the end?"

Only one car was in the lot, and it was indeed a silver

Range Rover, just like the one Sunny drove. I pressed the gas a little to get us to the SUV quicker.

"Can you see if she's in the car?" I asked as we approached. Gilley's eyesight was better than mine.

"No," he said. "It's too dark."

I parked, and we got out.

"Doesn't look like she's in the car," Gilley said.

I nodded and rounded to the passenger side, just to peer in, and that was when I let out a small gasp and shouted for Gilley.

"What?" he replied, rounding the Range Rover to come to my side. "What's wrong?"

Instead of answering him, I pulled on the handle of the car, but it was locked. I banged on the window, but Sunny, who was lying on her side, her torso spilling into the passenger seat, didn't stir. As I peered through the glass, I could clearly see that she held a prescription bottle in her hand. "She's taken some pills! And, Gilley, she's not moving!"

Gilley tugged on the handle, too, and shouted, "Sunny! Sunny, wake up!"

He then joined me in pounding on the window, but it was to no avail. I stepped back from the car and looked around for something, anything that might help us. "We have to break a window!"

Gilley stopped pounding on the window and flew to the trunk of my car. After pulling up the lid, he rummaged around for a moment and came up with a tire iron. He hurried back to Sunny's car and was about to shatter the passenger's side window when I shouted "No!" and caught his arm. "You'll spray her with glass!"

"Good point," he said. After stepping sideways, he brought the tire iron down on the rear passenger window, angling the blow toward the back of the car.

The glass didn't shatter so much as spider across the pane.

"Hit it again!" I urged.

Gilley beat the glass several more times, eventually carving out a small hole, and then he broke the rest down with a side-to-side sweeping motion. Reaching carefully through the window, he managed to stretch his arm behind the seat and tug at the rear passenger's side door handle.

When it gave way, he got in, leaned over the seat and unlocked the front passenger's side door. I pulled the now unlocked door open and leaned over Sunny, then felt along her body to find her still breathing but quite cold. "Gilley!"

"Is she alive?"

"Yes, but barely!"

"Should I call an ambulance?"

I was absolutely panicked, but I managed to devise the quickest way to help Sunny. "No," I said, waving toward the driver's seat. "Get in."

While Gilley ran around to the other side of the car, I got into the passenger seat and carefully lifted Sunny's body onto mine, pulling her legs away from the driver's side. "It'll be faster if we can drive her to the hospital," I told Gilley as he got into the car. "It's only about a half mile away."

Gilley settled into the seat and looked around the dash and on the floor. "Where's the key fob?" he asked.

"Don't worry about it! It's probably in her pocket. Just hit the START button!"

Gilley pressed the button to the side of the steering column, but nothing happened.

"Put your foot on the brake!" I snapped, the fear getting the best of me.

"My foot *is* on the brake!"

"Try again!"

"It's not working!"

"Then we need to call an ambulance!"

Gilley's hands were shaking. He jumped out, pulled his phone out of his pocket, and dialed 911.

While Gilley called for help, I shifted position, laid Sunny's head in my lap. Her hair felt damp but her skin was cool and dry. I looked her over and saw that she was barefoot and her toes and fingers were blue with cold.

Placing both hands on the sides of Sunny's cheeks, I patted them in an effort to get her to wake up. She didn't even flicker an eyelid. "Oh, God," I said, feeling tears fill my eyes. "Beautiful lady, what've you done to yourself?"

"Cat!" I heard Gilley say after he'd connected with a dispatcher.

"She's unconscious and breathing very shallow!" I yelled. There was, in fact, no need to yell, but I was now legitimately worried that Sunny might expire right in my arms. She felt painfully thin—even for her—which told me she hadn't been eating well enough. And she seemed so fragile.

"Cat!" Gilley repeated, more urgently this time.

"What?"

"Do you know what she's ingested?"

My gaze traveled to Sunny's palm, but the pill bottle had rolled out onto the passenger's side floor. "Hold on," I told him, moving awkwardly around Sunny's unconscious form to retrieve the prescription bottle.

After grabbing it and holding it up, I had to squint to see the small lettering. "Ambien," I said to Gilley and then reached across the seat to wave the pill bottle at him so that he knew to take it.

He repeated the information on the label to the dispatcher, and then he asked me, "Are there any pills left?"

The bottle was empty when I'd handed it to him, so I searched around the car, but there was no sign of any pills left. "No," I said, my voice hitching, as tears stung my eyes. Sunny had taken an Ambien around noon, so I knew she'd been in possession of the pills, but I had never thought she'd purposely overdose on them. "Gilley, tell them to hurry!"

I reached for Sunny's wrist and pulled it up from where it dangled over the seat. She was completely passive. Feeling for a pulse again I bit my lip when I found it faint and slow. Stroking her cheek I cried, "Sunny, please, please don't do this. Don't leave us, okay? Think of your son! Come on, honey, hang in there!"

The sound of a siren coming close let me know help was nearby.

"Yes, ma'am, I hear them," Gilley said. "Thank you for your help."

He hung up the phone and leaned inside the car's interior. "Oh, my," he whispered. "She's so pale!"

I nodded. Sunny's complexion in the glow of the overhead light was a ghostly white. Gilley and I both tore our glances away when a patrol car and an ambulance pulled into the small lot. An officer got to us first.

"What's going on here?" he asked.

"This is Sunny D'Angelo," I said to him. "She's our dear friend. We'd been out looking for her and found her here in her car, with an empty bottle of Ambien in her hand. She's unconscious and not responding."

He waved two paramedics over to us, and Gilley stepped out of the way while I got out of the car from the passenger's side. Gil came around to stand next to me while the paramedics worked on Sunny.

"We need to call Darius," I said to him.

"And Shepherd," he replied.

I bit my lip. "This is the last thing he needs to be dealing with right now. Maybe I should wait until after we know she's okay?"

Gilley placed the phone to his ear. "Cat, call him. If the worst happens, he'll be furious you didn't let him know in time to get to the hospital."

I nodded and turned away to place the call to Shepherd. The phone rang four times and went to voice mail, so I left him a lengthy message, told him to call me back, and added that I'd give him any updates I could.

After hanging up, I turned back toward Gilley in time to see them loading Sunny into the back of the ambulance. She was wearing an oxygen mask, and an IV had already been inserted into her wrist. Gilley took my arm and hugged it, as if clutching it for reassurance. I leaned my head against his. "She'll be okay," I whispered, but my voice hitched again, and my lower lip trembled.

The officer approached us. "Can you two join me over here so I can get some background information?"

My breath caught. I'd thought that Gilley and I could simply follow the ambulance to the hospital, and I didn't want to let it out of my sight should Shepherd call me and ask about Sunny.

"Officer, could we be interviewed at the hospital? We'd really like to follow behind the ambulance," I said.

"No, ma'am. I'm sorry, but I'll need to take your statement here." For emphasis, he looked meaningfully at Sunny's Range Rover, with its broken window.

"That's Detective Shepherd's sister," Gilley told him angrily. "We really should be with her."

The officer's brow furrowed, and he glanced at the ambulance, which was already pulling away.

"Well then, I'm definitely going to need you to stay right here with me and tell me what happened," he said.

I wanted to sock him. "I'm the detective's girlfriend," I said, hating the adolescent sound of the word. "We were at the playhouse this evening, and Shepherd asked us to find Sunny and tell her about Yelena Galanis."

He blinked at me for a moment, clearly surprised to learn that we'd been at the scene of a homicide as well as at the scene of an apparent overdose, but then he pulled out a small notepad and a ballpoint pen. After clicking the pen, he began to scribble. "Let's start with the basics," he said. "Like your names and addresses. . . ."

Chapter 6

We got to the hospital nearly an hour later. The stupid cop had taken his sweet time jotting down every single bit of information about us he could think of, and about the events leading up to our finding Sunny. He had finally released us after we'd repeated our story to him at least three times, and it had been all I could do not to simply turn my back on his pestering questions and head to the hospital before he could give me and Gilley the okay.

We arrived at the emergency room and found Darius pacing the hall, looking worried sick. Seeing us, he rushed over.

"Have you heard anything?" he asked us.

Gilley looked from me back to Darius. "We just got here."

Darius shook his head. He seemed unable to form coherent thoughts, he was so distraught. "Right. Right. I . . .

this whole night . . . she . . . Why?" he said, his eyes glistening with tears. "*Why* would she take all those pills? Why would she try to kill herself? Why?"

Hearing the words come out of his mouth hit me like a blow to the midsection. "We don't know anything other than she probably took too much Ambien, Darius. For all we know, Sunny could've taken the very last pill and it simply hit her too hard."

He shook his head. "The nurse came out to ask me about the prescription bottle found in her hand. It was mine. Sunny picked it up for me today because she knows how hard the jet lag hits me when I fly home from L.A."

"She took one this afternoon," I confessed to him. He pulled his chin back in alarm, so I was quick to explain. "She said she took only a half a pill, because she hadn't been sleeping herself. She called Tiffany and asked her to come watch over Finley while she got some rest. She wanted to be fresh when you got home."

Darius was shaking his head, as if he couldn't believe what I was saying. "No, no, no," he insisted. "She knows better than to take Ambien. *Why* would she risk that?"

"What do you mean?" Gilley asked.

Darius rubbed his eyes with his palms, and I could tell the man was exhausted both physically and mentally. "Ambien hits Sunny really hard. She's taken one of my pills before, right after Finley was born, and she went to sleep for about two hours, then woke up and started acting crazy. She got the ladder out of the garage and insisted that we needed to clean the gutters. The more I tried to talk sense into her, the crazier she sounded, and then she got so frustrated with me when I pulled the ladder out of her hands that she walked around the house and right into the ocean, fully clothed. I didn't see her until she was about neck-deep, and I had to swim like hell to reach her. When I did, she kept telling me that she was trying to catch a mermaid. I had to drag her out and lock all three of us in the bedroom together until she fell asleep again. When she woke up seven hours later, she had no memory at all of what she'd said or done."

"Oh!" Gilley said. "I've read about that. Some people who take Ambien fall into a sort of dreamlike state, where they can appear to be perfectly awake, but they're actually not. They can do all sorts of crazy things and never remember it."

Darius nodded. "I talked to my doctor about it, and he said the same thing. He said Ambien can affect women very differently than men, and for some women, it can be really dangerous."

I glanced down the hall toward the double doors of the ER, through which Sunny had, no doubt, been taken. "That would explain why Sunny didn't tell Tiffany that she was leaving and, if she in fact did come back to the house, why she left again without her phone."

"It could also explain why she took the rest of the pills," Gilley said. "She wasn't in her right state of mind."

Darius stumbled over to a chair and sat down heavily, his chin falling against his chest. "Jesus," I heard him say. "I should've picked up the prescription. If I'd known she was going to pinch one of the pills, I would've never let her pick it up from the pharmacy."

I moved over to sit down next to him. "This isn't your fault, Darius," I said. "Sunny was exhausted when I saw her this afternoon. She was probably so exhausted that she threw caution to the wind and simply gave in to the impulse."

But Darius didn't seem to hear me. He just sat there,

bent over, shaking his head back and forth, no doubt continuing to blame himself.

My phone buzzed, and I got up to answer it. Caller ID said it was Shepherd. "Hi," I said, not quite knowing how to begin.

"What's happened to Sunny?" he demanded, his voice sharp with emotion.

"I need you to brace yourself," I told him.

"Just tell me," he said quietly but firmly.

I took a deep breath and dove in. "She took an overdose of Ambien, and she's now at the hospital, where the doctors are working on her."

Shepherd was quiet on the other end of the line. He was probably stunned.

I thought it best to do the talking until he could compose himself to speak and ask me any questions he wanted. "Gilley and I went to her house, just like you asked, but when we got there, we were met by the babysitter, who told us that Sunny had gone out two hours earlier and that she hadn't taken her phone. We pressed her for more details, but she didn't really have any. As we were leaving, Darius showed up. He didn't know that Sunny had left the house."

"Darius is back already?" he said, and there was an icy note in his tone.

"Yes. He got in just a little while ago. When we told him what was going on, he was upset that Sunny had left the house without her phone. We split up to look for her in the two spots she likes to go when she needs some quiet time."

"The yoga place?" Shepherd asked.

"Yes. Darius headed there, and we headed to the park."

"What park?"

"Herrick Park. It's off Newtown."

Shepherd grunted. "What's her prognosis?"

"We don't know."

"Is Darius there?"

"He is. He's beside himself with worry."

Shepherd let out an audible sigh, and I could tell he was irritated with his brother-in-law, no doubt for leaving Sunny with all the duties of rearing a toddler when she was so obviously exhausted. "I'm on my way," he said and hung up.

"What'd he say?" Gilley asked me when I turned back to him and Darius.

"He's headed here."

Gilley widened his eyes. "That man has had one busy night."

Darius looked up and said, "He's the detective assigned to Yelena's murder, isn't he?"

"He is," I said. "And there was another murder that took place this evening right across the street from the theater."

Darius's brow furrowed. "You're kidding."

I shook my head. "No. I'm not. It appears to be a mob hit."

Darius's jaw dropped. "A *mob* hit?"

I nodded.

Gilley said, "There are more of those in this part of town than you'd think."

"Laney," Darius said, mentioning Shepherd's ex-wife, who was executed by a Mafia hit woman.

"Yes," I said.

Darius put his head in his hands. "This night is freaking surreal."

I moved over to sit next to him again and awkwardly patted him on the shoulder in an effort to comfort him. "For us too."

We had sat like that for a good ten minutes when Shepherd rushed into the ER, out of breath. I wondered if he'd run from the parking lot.

"Any news?" he asked, directing his question at Darius.

"No," Darius said. "They took her back over an hour ago, and they were gonna pump her stomach and give her some meds to counteract the effects of the Ambien in her system."

"How much did she take?" he asked next.

Darius's lower lip quivered slightly. "The whole bottle, Steve."

One look at Shepherd, as his face drained of color, told me how worried he was for his twin. I stepped forward and took his hand, then guided him over to the set of chairs opposite Darius and Gilley.

He sat down heavily. "Why would she take a whole bottle of Ambien?"

Darius's expression was a mask of guilt. "She picked up my prescription from the pharmacy today. I asked her to, because I was out of pills, and I always have trouble sleeping when I come back from L.A."

Shepherd's lip curled as he angrily regarded his brother-in-law. "Then you must almost never have trouble sleeping," he said meanly.

I bit my lip and watched as Darius dropped his gaze to the floor. "I gotta work, Steve. And it wasn't my choice to move back East."

Shepherd shook his head. I had the distinct feeling there was no love lost between the two men.

"Sunny took a half a tablet earlier today, Shep," I said softly.

His gaze slid to me, and his brow arched in question.

"I visited her just before noon. She looked exhausted and thin and at the end of her rope. She called Tiffany to come watch over Finley so that she could get some sleep, and she confessed to me that she took half a tablet so that she could be sure she slept until Darius arrived home. We think that even that small amount put her in a sleepwalking state, and she likely took the rest of the Ambien while she was in that condition."

Darius said, "Remember a couple of months ago, when I told you about how she'd tried to catch a mermaid?"

Shepherd nodded absently, his stare at the floor faraway and almost disconnected. At that moment his phone buzzed, and he pulled it out to look at the display. Muttering a curse under his breath, he got up from his chair and said, "I gotta take this."

Shepherd walked down the hall, and I could tell by the tense set of his shoulders that it was official police business, very likely about one or both of the cases he'd been working tonight.

Just as he made it through the double doors to the outside, a grizzled-looking man with a short, untidy beard, thick glasses, and a crooked nose came through the double doors. He was wearing scrubs and a lab coat. "D'Angelo?"

"Yes," Darius said, getting up quickly, his hands balled into fists, as if he was trying to brace himself for bad news. Gilley and I got up too.

"Are you Mr. D'Angelo?" the doctor asked.

"Yes. Darius. I'm Sunny's husband."

"Good. I'm Dr. Papageorgiou. I've been attending your wife."

"Yes?" Darius said, more a question than a statement.

I eyed the doctor with impatience. Why didn't he put all of us obviously anxious people out of our misery and tell us Sunny was fine?

"That was a very, very close call, Mr. D'Angelo, but I believe your wife will be all right."

Collectively, all our shoulders sagged in relief.

The doctor continued. "We'd like to keep her overnight for observation. Her breathing and heart rate are still a bit sluggish."

"Sure. Of course," Darius said. "When can I—"

"And I'd also like to set up a consult with an attending psychologist tomorrow morning," the doctor interrupted. "She'll need a psych eval before I'm comfortable releasing her."

"A . . . psych eval?" Darius asked.

Dr. Papageorgiou focused an intense look at Darius. "Your wife attempted suicide, Mr. D'Angelo. You'll need to come to grips with that and support any psychological counseling, therapy, and/or evaluation at a mental health facility."

We all audibly gasped at that.

"She didn't . . . ," Darius said, shaking his head vigorously. "Doctor, I swear, Sunny isn't suicidal."

The doctor's firm tone and level gaze never wavered. "She's severely underweight, dehydrated, and exhausted, not to mention that she consumed enough Ambien tonight to kill herself. And she very nearly succeeded. Those markers alone give me great cause for concern. Still, I'll hand over the decision to have her committed to my colleague tomorrow morning. We need to be sure she no longer presents a threat to herself or others, Mr. D'Angelo."

Darius simply continued to shake his head, and for the first time, the physician's expression turned compassionate. "There's nothing you can do for her tonight. I suggest you go home and get some rest yourself."

Darius stopped shaking his head and simply stood there with his jaw agape and a dazed look on his face. It was like he couldn't form the words to insist that it'd all been a big misunderstanding. That Sunny probably hadn't been in her right mind when she took all those pills.

But then it hit me: People who were suicidal weren't in their right minds by definition. What if Sunny *had* been fully conscious when she left to drive herself to the park? She'd taken only a half a dose, and that must've worn off by the time she woke up around seven thirty or eight to leave Tiffany and Finley behind, right?

"Hey," Shepherd said, causing me to jump. He'd come right up to me, and I hadn't even been aware. "Is there news? How's Sunny?"

Darius turned to him, a pained, astonished look on his face. He didn't seem capable of answering.

"And you are?" Dr. Papageorgiou asked.

"Detective Steve Shepherd," Shep said, pulling out his badge and flashing it for the doctor. "I'm Sunny's twin brother."

"Ah," the doctor said. "She's stable but has been moved to the ICU for further monitoring through the night."

"Thank God," Shepherd said after letting out a sigh of relief. "Can we see her?"

The doctor's gaze flashed to Darius, then back to Shepherd. "I'll allow one person to visit with her briefly.

Five to ten minutes only. She's stable, but I can't have her agitated or further exhausted until she's evaluated tomorrow morning."

"Evaluated?" Shepherd asked.

"I'll fill you in," I whispered to him.

Darius turned to us. "Thanks for coming, guys. I'll go back and see her. Steve, I'll call you tomorrow to give you an update."

Shepherd's brow furrowed. "I want to see her, Darius."

Papageorgiou rocked back on his heels. "As I said, I can allow only one visitor, gentlemen."

"I'm her husband," Darius said firmly.

"I'm her *twin!*" Shepherd countered. It was surprising to see him insist on cutting the line and getting in front of his brother-in-law. I was fairly certain that by way of their marriage, Darius's access to Sunny trumped Shepherd's.

"Do you have a medical directive or power of attorney?" Papageorgiou asked him.

Shepherd glared at the doctor, his lips a thin line of anger. "No, but I *am* an officer of the law."

"Is this a police matter?" the doctor retorted, and I could tell he was firmly on Darius's side.

Shepherd's jaw clenched and unclenched. "No," he finally admitted.

Papageorgiou turned back to Darius. "She's in room two-ten. Follow the green line to the elevators." Papageorgiou paused to point to a series of colored lines on the floor. "I'll let the ICU nurse know that you're cleared to visit with your wife for no longer than ten minutes."

"Thank you," Darius said in relief, and with one last defiant glance at Shepherd, Darius left us to head to the elevators.

When he and the doctor had both departed, I filled Shepherd in.

"That's ridiculous," he snapped. "Sunny isn't suicidal."

"How do you know?" I asked him, genuinely curious.

"What do you mean, how do I know?"

"I mean, Shep, that there was a time fifteen years ago when my sister was very, very depressed after a breakup, and she confessed to me later that she'd contemplated taking her life, and I never knew. There were no overt signs, other than she seemed sluggish and foggy every time I talked to her, and I always chalked it up to her being tired out because of her job."

"Her psychic work?"

"No, this was before all that. She worked at a bank back then, and there was a lot of pressure on her. Anyway, the point is that it never occurred to me that she was in such a perilous state."

"M.J. went through something like that when she was in college," Gilley said, breaking the silence. He was still standing next to me.

Shepherd and I looked at him in surprise.

He shrugged and added, "Her mom died when she was in fifth grade, and her dad started drinking right afterward. She never got therapy or counseling, and I think she pushed it all down for as long as she could, but when she was about twenty, it caught up to her, and there was a time when I made sure to stick close to her so that she didn't do anything stupid."

"How'd she pull out of it?" I asked Gilley.

"I finally convinced her to get some therapy at the university clinic, and she got on some antidepressants, which made a world of difference."

I nodded. "Abby too. She still takes them, I believe."

"Guys," Shepherd said, holding up his palms to us. "You gotta believe me, other than what happened with my parents five years ago, Sunny's life has been relatively gentle."

"Your parents passed away?" Gilley asked.

Shepherd nodded. "Mom died from ovarian cancer, and Dad passed away within six months of Mom's funeral. The strain on him through her sickness was too much for his heart."

"Did Sunny ever get counseling?" I pressed.

"Definitely. And she dragged me with her. Seriously, Sunny's on top of her mental health. Always has been."

"Maybe this time she was too quickly overwhelmed by insomnia and the duties of being a mother to a fussy toddler to recognize the oncoming depression," I suggested. "And don't forget how hard the pandemic was on everyone," I added. "I swear we're all walking around with a good case of PTSD."

Shepherd frowned and stared at the floor. "Yeah," he finally admitted. "That was kinda tough on her. Damn, I should've been paying more attention."

"We all should've," I told him. And then I reached out and took his hand. "It's not your fault, lovey."

He lifted his gaze to mine. "Then why do I feel so guilty?"

"Because that's what you do," Gilley told him. "You ride in on your white horse and save the day so often that this time it caught you off guard."

Shepherd slid a sideways glance at me. "Since when did Gilley get so wise?"

I chuckled. "Oh, trust me, Gilley is far wiser than he lets on."

Gilley beamed. "It's my side hustle," he said, adding a curtsy. "Now come on, you two. I'm exhausted, and there's nothing more we can do here. Let's get the three of us home."

Shepherd pulled me to his chest and kissed the top of my head. "I can't," he said to both of us. "I gotta get back to the scene." And then he paused a moment and added, "*Scenes*. Good God, this night is like a bad dream that just won't end."

"We'll walk you out," I said, hugging him tightly before taking both his hand and Gilley's to exit the hospital.

We parted in the parking lot, and walking to our car, I lagged behind Gil while I watched Shepherd's retreating form. He walked a little hunched over, like he carried the weight of the world on his back. I couldn't imagine being in his shoes, with so much responsibility and his own personal tragedies swirling in the mix.

"Cat?" Gilley called.

"Coming," I said absently and watched Shepherd for a few more seconds, feeling like I wanted to run to him and hug him tightly one more time.

Looking back, I really wish I had.

Chapter 7

The next morning, I woke up to the smell of coffee wafting up from my kitchen. And something else was flavoring the air with the scent of pastry and raspberries. After rolling over, I picked up my phone to check the time. It was six fifteen. On a Saturday.

I moaned and uttered a small curse under my breath, pondering if I should attempt to go back to sleep or head down to the kitchen to see why in God's name Gilley thought it a good idea to be up baking at this hour in *my* kitchen rather than his.

With a heavy sigh, I reasoned that Gilley got out the early morning baking tins like this only when something was troubling him. So, I did what any good friend would do—I rolled over and tried to go back to sleep, which worked for about fifteen minutes, or until exactly the point at which I was just starting to drift off when Gilley took his anxiety to a new level and began to loudly clang pots and pans together, creating an all-out ruckus in the kitchen.

With heavy-lidded eyes—and a glint of fury—I grabbed my silk robe from the knob behind the bathroom door and descended the stairs quietly while he kept up the racket.

I found him *literally* drumming the bottom of a saucepan with a wooden spoon, his back turned to me as he stared out the window.

"Catchy tune," I said.

Gilley jumped, then whirled around, holding the spoon like a weapon. *"Ahhh!"*

"Relax!" I said, putting up my hands. "It's just me."

"Oh," he said, immediately calming down.

A bit too quickly, I thought.

"Good morning, Cat. You're up early."

I plunked down on one of the barstools along the kitchen island. "Gee, Gilley, ya *think*?"

Gilley made a little moue face. "Couldn't sleep, huh?"

I stared dully at him. "No."

He nodded like he fully understood. "Me either."

I laid my forehead down on the island. "Why are you here, Gilley?"

"Your oven is more temperature sensitive, and I'm making a Gouda-apricot coffee cake, and the temp needs to be precisely one hundred and eighty degrees Celsius for twenty minutes, or it will overbrown."

I lifted my head to frown at him. "We have the exact same oven."

I'd personally made sure that Chez Kitty was equipped with top-of-the line appliances, just like at Chez Cat.

Gilley set down the spoon he'd been holding, and took up a dish towel. Fiddling with it, he said, "The lighting is better over here. And there's more room to spread out all the ingredients. And I was completely out of cake mix, but then I remembered you had a box in the pantry here."

"Gil?"

"Yeah?"

"Something troubling you?"

Gilley's shoulders sagged. "You know me so well."

I got up off the barstool and ambled around the island to the cabinet where I kept my French press. "Sit," I said to him. "I'll make us some coffee, and we can talk."

Gilley flounced over to a chair and took up a seat. I waited until I'd prepped the French press with fresh coffee beans and started the kettle, then set out twin mugs, cream, sugar, and two spoons before I spoke next to him. "Tell me what's on your mind."

"Michel left me a message this morning. I didn't hear my phone. I was in the shower."

I waited for Gilley to continue, but he'd paused, with a faraway look in his eyes, so I prompted him. *"And?"*

Gilley sighed. "He just said, 'I think we need to talk.'"

I winced. "Ouch."

Gilley's gaze locked onto mine. "That's bad, right?"

"Did you tell him about Spooks?" I asked, hoping that was all Michel wanted to talk to Gilley about.

"No," Gil said. "I was waiting for a good time to break the news."

I didn't confess to Gilley that I believed it was now past a good time, choosing instead to focus on a more optimistic approach. The kettle began to smoke with steam and I paused our conversation to pour the hot water over the beans in the French press. When that was done I said, "Maybe he just wants to tell you that he's booked another job and won't be home at the end of the month."

"He's already texted me that," Gilley said.

"When?"

"Yesterday, during your meeting with the count."

So much had happened in the past twenty-four hours that yesterday afternoon felt like it was ages ago. "Now I understand what led you to the Humane Society's home page."

Gilley gave me a crooked smile, but there was tremendous sadness in his eyes. "*Vogue* is going to stream fashion videos to its online subscribers. Photos of models will now become videos of models, and Michel is working to make that transition happen by teaming up with a documentary filmmaker in South Africa. He'll be gone all of October and most of November."

"Oh, Gil," I said. "I'm so sorry."

He shrugged and fiddled with his coffee spoon while staring at the counter. Sniffling, he whispered, "I really thought we'd make it."

It broke my heart to see him like this, and I quickly went around the counter to wrap him in a fierce hug.

I knew this heartbreak. It was more than simply the realization that you wouldn't spend the rest of your days with the person you'd married—it was the fact that in letting go of them, you had to let go of the dream of what you thought your life would be. The certainty of it and the comfort of that certainty were such tremendously difficult things to lose.

For a long time, I simply hugged Gilley, and I knew he was quietly weeping by the occasional sniffle and the small damp spot on the back of my shoulder that formed from his tears.

"I know, honey," I whispered to him.

I felt him nod slightly. He knew I knew.

The moment was interrupted by a bing from the timer over the oven. Gilley jerked out of my grasp and wiped his eyes. "The coffee cake is ready."

I stroked his hair and kissed his cheek. "Sit. I'll take care of it."

After moving over to the oven, I pulled out the scrumptious-looking cake and set it on the wire rack to cool. The mouth-watering aroma filled the kitchen with a heavenly scent.

"It needs to cool for about fifteen minutes," Gilley said.

I turned back to him, and he seemed more composed, although his eyes were wet and red.

"What can I do for you?" I asked him, and I wasn't talking about breakfast.

"I need a distraction," he said.

Pouring coffee into both of our mugs, I said, "We could take a day trip somewhere. Ooh! I know. We could head into the City and take a walk in the park. The leaves are just starting to turn, and I bet it'd be good for us."

Gilley sighed and shook his head. "I want to be close to home in case they call me about Spooks."

"Then how about a walk along the beach?" I pressed. Gilley needed fresh air and a little exercise. The weather had turned colder overnight, and it wasn't especially sunny out, with overcast skies, but at least it wasn't raining yet.

Gilley sighed again, as if he couldn't make up his mind. "I don't feel like it, Cat," he finally said.

"How about a Netflix marathon, then? We could stream some *Grace and Frankie*. You love that show."

"Because Jane Fonda is a living, breathing goddess,

and Lily Tomlin is a national treasure!" Gilley all but yelled.

We both laughed. That was his standard line every time I mentioned the show. It felt good to see him chuckle.

But then he sobered and said, "Yeah, I don't know that I'm in the mood for that, either."

"Did you want to call Michel?" I asked gently.

"No!" Gilley snapped. I pulled my chin back in surprise, and he quickly apologized. "I'm sorry. I didn't mean to bite your head off. I just . . ."

I reached across the counter and put my hand over his. "I know," I said. I'd put off having "the talk" with Tom until he cornered me in my home office and wouldn't allow me to escape it. I'd known what he was going to say, but those were words that couldn't be walked back, and I didn't judge Gilley one bit for not being ready to hear them just yet.

"What would you like to do, then?" I asked him after a moment.

"I want to visit Spooks," he said. "Even though he's not my dog yet, I keep thinking about how lonely he must be in that kennel, not knowing that he's going to be coming home with me."

"I love that idea," I said.

"Yeah?"

"Yeah. And we can ask the shelter if it's okay to take Spooks for a walk. Maybe along the beach?"

Gilley rolled his eyes. "You really want me to get some exercise, huh?"

I cut a slice of coffee cake for him and handed it over with a winning smile. "It'll do your mind some good, lovey," I said. "And I'm sure Spooks would love it!"

* * *

As it turned out, Spooks *did* love it. We got to the shelter shortly after it opened, and inquired about taking the adorably cute puppers for a walk. The shelter was thrilled that we'd come back to bond with Spooks, and made sure we had a leash and a portable water bowl for our walk along the beach. I pocketed two water bottles into my purse, and we set off. Along the way, Gilley asked if I'd take a video of him walking his soon-to-be pup, and I happily accepted his phone to shoot the video.

As I got ready to film, however, I made the same mistake I always did, and opened up his photo app instead of the camera, and I was shocked to discover a photo taken of me inside Sunny's SUV, holding her head in my lap and giving Gilley (and the camera) a panicked stare.

"Why did you take this?" I asked Gilley. The photo felt like a betrayal of Sunny's privacy, and I couldn't figure out why Gilley would take it.

He'd been leading Spooks away, and he had a hard time bringing him back to me to look at the camera, because the dog was much more interested in moving on to scents he hadn't yet fully investigated. Still, Gilley managed it and got close enough to squint at the screen as I held it up for him.

"Huh," he said when he saw the photo. "I don't remember taking that."

"It's in your photos," I said, nearly wincing at the accusatory tone that came out of my mouth.

Gilley's gaze flicked to me, his brow furrowed in confusion. "Cat, I didn't *intentionally* take that photo. I must've swiped left instead of up when I was trying to call nine-one-one. I was shaken up, seeing Sunny like that, and I must've accidentally taken the photo."

"Oh," I said, turning the photo back to me. "Sorry, Gil. I didn't mean to accuse you."

"It's fine," he said. "I understand."

Spooks had stopped tugging and sat down next to us to pant loudly. Gilley looked down at him and then asked me, "Hey, can you fish out one of the water bottles? I think he's thirsty."

"Sure," I said, lowering the phone to root around in my purse.

After I handed over the water to Gilley, he took the collapsible water bowl out of his back pocket and bent to offer Spooks a drink. "I'll delete the photo in a minute," he said, almost as an afterthought.

I felt guilty that I'd made him feel bad, so I merely shrugged nonchalantly and said, "Whatever."

While Gilley was squatting down to give Spooks his fill, I turned the phone back to face me because they looked very cute together that way and I wanted to take a photo of it, but I again tapped the stupid photo icon and had to look once again at the image of Sunny's prone body, her pale face, and my panicked expression.

"Gil?" I said as I stared at the screen.

"Yeah?" he said, distracted by his growing adoration for his new best friend.

I squatted down next to him and once again showed him the screen. "What's missing?"

Gil pulled his gaze away from Spooks and looked from me to his phone, then back again. "What?"

I wiggled the phone. "What's *missing*?"

"What do you mean, what's missing?"

I pointed to the screen. "There," I said. "See that?"

"See what? The middle console?"

"Yes."

"I don't see anything unusual or out of place," Gilley said.

"Exactly," I told him.

He sighed. "Can you just tell me what I'm supposed to not be seeing?"

I picked up the now empty water bottle at his feet and wiggled it. Then I watched Gilley's eyes widen. He looked again at the photo on the screen, then back to me. "How do you swallow an entire bottle of pills without any water?" he said.

"Exactly."

"Could there have been one in the driver's side door?" he said next.

"You got in on that side. Do you remember seeing one?"

Gilley closed his eyes to concentrate. "No," he said as he was imagining the scene. "I looked all around there for a key fob and there was nothing there."

I nodded. I remembered looking at the door when I pulled Sunny into the passenger seat and onto my lap. I hadn't seen it there either.

"Was it on the floor of the passenger seat?" Gilley asked. The photo allowed us to see both the driver's side floor mat and the passenger's floor mat, but parts of the mats were obscured from view.

I shook my head. "I remember looking down at the floor," I told him. "I was looking to see if she'd dropped any of the pills there, hoping she hadn't ingested the whole bottle. The floor mat was clean."

Gilley's gaze met mine. "So how did she get down an entire bottle of Ambien without water?"

"She could've simply forced the pills down," I said.

Gilley's expression was unconvinced. "Do you re-

member that the doctor said she was severely dehydrated?"

I let out a small gasp. "I do remember that."

"So, how do you swallow pills when you're dehydrated? It's hard enough when you're not thirsty. And
Ambien comes in a tablet, not a capsule, so that'd make it
even harder."

Gilley and I stared at each other until Spooks gave a
small woof. He was impatient to get back to the walk.

I handed Gilley his phone, pocketed the empty water
bottle, and we made our way down the beach trail in silence, each lost in thought.

"Should we tell Shepherd?" Gilley finally asked.

"Should we?" I replied.

Gilley bit his lip. "I don't know. On the one hand, you
know how suspicious he is, and how likely he is to make
something out of nothing, but on the other hand, how do
you explain Sunny's consumption of an entire bottle of
Ambien without any water?"

I continued to walk in silence next to Gil, thinking all
that over, before I finally stopped and said, "She could've
taken the pills when she came back to the house, Gilley."

"You mean when Tiffany thought she heard her while
she was on the treadmill?"

"Yes. I mean, it sort of fits, doesn't it? Tiffany hears
someone in the house, it takes her a minute to work up the
courage to investigate, and when she does, no one's there.
If Sunny had come back for the pills and enough water to
choke them all down, then it would've taken only a few
moments, right?"

Gilley handed me Spooks's leash and, after tapping at
his watch for a moment, used his now free hands to pan-
tomime opening a pill bottle, pouring out the pills into his

palm, which he then slapped against his mouth, then filling an imaginary glass with water and swallowing the
pretend mouthful with a loud gulp. Eyeing his watch
again, he said, "Seventeen seconds."

"Even if it was thirty, that'd be quick," I said.

"So, not so unusual that there was no water in the car,"
Gilley said.

I nodded. "And it explains what Tiffany heard. Sunny
did very likely come back to the house to take the pills."

I let out a sigh of relief, but it was somewhat forced.
Thinking about Sunny willingly ingesting an entire bottle
of Ambien wasn't something to be relieved over. It was
something to be very, very concerned by.

We walked Spooks for another thirty minutes or so,
with not a lot of conversation between us. I could tell that
the facts of Sunny's overdose were troubling both of us
tremendously.

When we got back to the car, with a very happy and
somewhat tuckered-out pup, Gilley said, "Maybe you
should call Shepherd and ask him how Sunny's doing?"

I nodded. "I was just thinking that."

I called Shepherd using the car's Bluetooth so that
Gilley could listen in.

"Hey, beautiful," he said when he picked up the call,
his voice a little gravelly from lack of sleep.

"Hi, there," I said, smiling at the warm tone. "Gilley's
with me in the car. We want to know how Sunny's doing."

Shepherd blew out a breath. "It's not good," he said.

My grip tightened on the steering wheel, and Gilley
looked at me in alarm. "What's happened?" I asked.

"Her psych eval was troubling," Shepherd said.

"What does that mean?"

"It means that the shrink thinks she should spend some time in a mental health support unit."

My eyes widened. "At the hospital?"

"No. Darius is having her committed to the EHPC. And before you ask, that's the East Hampton Psychiatric Center."

"Oh, my," I said. "For how long?"

Shepherd's voice became flat, almost void of emotion, which, I'd come to learn over the past year, meant he was struggling to keep his emotions in check. "We don't know. Until they can be assured she's no longer presenting a danger to herself or others."

I put a hand to my mouth. I'd never dreamed that Sunny was in any state to actually be committed. "So, she *did* attempt to harm herself?"

"Yeah. Darius told me she confessed to him this morning, and the hospital shrink confirmed it."

"She was aware of what she was doing, then," I said, trying to make sense of it all.

"They think so," Shepherd said, and there was a slight crack in his voice, and I knew his effort to flatten out his emotions wasn't working.

"I'm so, so sorry, Shep." I didn't know what else to say.

There was a pause, and then Shepherd said, "She's in good hands at least. And she's safe. And awake, but she's still a little groggy."

"Did you talk to her?"

"Not yet. Darius is with her. He said the shrink doesn't want her upset, and he's worried that confessing to me about what she'd done last night might trigger her in the wrong way."

I wanted to cry. I knew how close Sunny and her brother were, and this had to be killing him.

"What can we do for you?" Gilley asked.

Shepherd sighed in a way that revealed just how exhausted he was. "Nothing, Gil, but thanks. I'm just trying to focus on this case, which, thankfully, I now have a break on."

"You have a lead in Yelena's murder case?" I asked.

"I do. In fact, you guys, I gotta run. The judge is about to sign my arrest warrant, and the suspect is a flight risk, so I want to nab him before he has a chance to sneak off."

I wanted to ask him for details, but I knew that he'd likely not share much with me until after he'd made the arrest. Plus, asking him would only delay him further. "Of course," I said. "We'll chat later, okay?"

After we'd disconnected, I turned to Gilley. "That was fast."

"You know how Shepherd loves to make a quick arrest," Gilley said, with a crooked smile.

I made a face at him, but it was all too true. My boyfriend was known to flash the handcuffs first and ask questions later. "Hopefully, we'll learn all about it tonight."

Gilley twisted in his seat to look back at Spooks. "He's super adorable, isn't he?"

I eyed the pup, now fully spread out on my back seat, sleeping away, and grinned. "He is, Gilley. I'm so glad you two found each other."

When we got back to the shelter, Gilley was reluctantly about to hand over the leash to the staff worker when she grinned broadly at him and said, "Why don't you go ahead and keep that?"

Gilley's brow furrowed for a moment, but I understood exactly what she meant. Leaning over, I gave Gilley a fierce hug. "Congratulations, Papa!"

"What?" Gilley said, still confused.

"It's a dog!" I said, pointing to Spooks.

Gilley's eyes instantly welled up with tears. "I can keep him?"

The staff member nodded and clapped her hands. "Your application has been approved!"

Gilley sank to the floor and hugged Spooks, who kissed him all over and seemed to know the moment was special.

Chapter 8

A bit later Gilley, one excited pooch, and I were in the car, heading toward Spooks's new home. We'd left the shelter with a "new pawent" gift bundle that included a soft plush squeaky toy, a day's worth of dog food, a tag for a collar with Spooks's name and Gilley's cell phone number, and a certificate of adoption, which Gilley swore he was going to frame and hang above the mantel.

At Gilley's insistence, we stopped at a large warehouse-like store called the Pet Palace, where Gilley began shopping like he was in one of those *Grab and Go* game shows.

By the time we got home, it was well after lunch, and Spooks was alert and busy sniffing every corner in Chez Kitty, while Gilley and I hauled in the huge bundle of things he'd purchased for his new little buddy.

"Does he really need four separate beds?" I asked, lugging two plush, oversized doggy lounge beds, while Gilley jammed two more that were even bigger through the door behind me.

"Yes!" Gilley's muffled voice replied.

"Where do I put these?" I asked, dropping both in front of me.

"One next to the couch and one next to the kitchen counter," Gil instructed.

I set the beds where he'd instructed, while Gilley waddled to the back of the cottage with the other two beds. I then went about filling up Spooks's water dish and placed it against the wall near a side table, where it wouldn't get knocked over. I then moved over to the bags we'd already brought in from the car, and put those up on one of the kitchen chairs, where Gilley could sort through them at his leisure. I didn't think he even knew the full extent of what he'd bought, but I wasn't going to criticize. The poor pup probably hadn't been spoiled the whole time he was at the shelter—if he ever was spoiled at all.

"Sebastian," I said, pulling out another chair to plop myself down on.

"Yes, my lady?" my AI butler replied.

"Please take note that we have a new permanent resident in-house. His name is Spooks, and he'll probably set off all the motion sensors when Gilley and I are out of the residences."

"I've made a note, my lady. Your lunch has been delivered and is viewable on the front steps of Chez Cat."

I leaned sideways to look out the window toward my house, where I could clearly see the to-go order I'd placed while Gilley was being checked out at the pet supply store.

"Excellent, Sebastian. Thank you."

At that moment, Gilley came out with a satisfied look on his face. "He's all set up," he said, stopping short when he saw that Spooks had hopped up on the couch and was staring at Gilley with heavy-lidded eyes but a wagging tail.

"Spooks," Gilley said, placing his hands on his hips before pointing to the dog bed next to the couch. "Not on the furniture. You need to sleep on your brand-new bed."

The dog's gaze drifted to the dog bed, then back up to Gilley, and his short tail thumped even harder.

I held in a snicker and got up to head to the front door. "I'll bring our lunch in while you lay down the law with our newest family member."

After retrieving the bags from the front porch, I came back inside to find Gilley sprawled out on the dog bed and Spooks still firmly ensconced on the couch.

Pausing in the doorway, I said, "Yep. That's about how I thought that would go."

Gilley hopped to his feet. "I was just showing him how comfortable it is."

I glanced meaningfully at Spooks, who eyed me in return and, I swear to God, flashed me a big ole doggy smile. "He seems convinced."

Gilley made a face. "He'll get there. It's a new space. He's still getting the lay of the land."

"Uh-huh," I said.

After making my way over to the counter, I pulled out our twin Caesar salads and set us up at the table before looking back over to Gilley, who was again lying on the doggy bed, pretending to sigh contentedly and make some snoring sounds.

Spooks was also making some snoring sounds, but his were real.

"Yo, Gilley," I said softly. "Come to the table like a good boy."

Gilley scowled and struggled to get up from the dog bed. Upon arriving at the table, he pulled out his chair, and in a commanding voice, I said, "Sit!"

"Ha ha," he said woodenly.

I giggled. It was too easy.

We chatted for a bit about Spooks. Gilley was anxious to begin training his new four-legged companion, and he waxed on for a good ten minutes about the vast and varied dog collars, hats, and sweaters he'd found on Etsy, and I had a feeling Spooks would be decked out in rhinestones, glitter, leather, and feathers before too long.

At last, Gil seemed to have worn himself out from talking excitedly about Spooks's wardrobe, and I took the opportunity to say, "We should probably get some work done this afternoon."

"Work? Work on what?" Gil asked.

I shrugged. "I don't know. Maybe prep some notes for Leslie Cohen. I'm scheduled to meet with her on Monday, right?"

"Uh," Gil said, moving his eyes side to side, like he was looking for an escape. "She canceled."

"She did?" I asked, surprised. "Did something come up?"

"Don't know," Gilley said.

"When is she rescheduled for?"

Gilley avoided my gaze. "She's not."

"What do you mean, she's not?"

"She feels she's gotten all she can out of your weekly meetings," he said, so softly I had to lean in to hear him.

"Are you serious?" I asked.

Leslie was a mess. She'd graduated from Georgetown Law, only to discover she hated the thought of being a lawyer and had no idea what direction to head in next. She'd been sponging off her parents for the past two years, doing little other than socializing with friends and shopping online. She'd come to me only when her mother had insisted on it—having heard of me from one of two articles written about my practice—and had threatened to cut her daughter off financially unless Leslie met with me and redirected herself toward getting a job and making her way in the world like a responsible adult.

We'd had only three sessions together.

"Unfortunately, Cat, I am serious. The email arrived late last night, and it pretty much said exactly that."

I pressed my lips together. "I bet she comes back when her mom finds out she's no longer coming to see me."

Gilley cleared his throat and squirmed in his chair. "Mrs. Cohen was the one who sent the email."

My jaw fell open, and heat rose to my cheeks. I was embarrassed and irritated; I'd worked hard for Leslie.

"Well, I hope Leslie lives up to her potential," I said stiffly.

Gilley forced a smile and looked at me with sympathetic eyes.

"Who else is on my calendar for next week?" I said, moving on.

Gilley's forced smile turned to a grimace. "Just Chrissy," he said, referring to my longest-running client to date.

Chrissy was on her fourth marriage, and that was also headed for splitsville. She was an absolute pain in the tokus: needy, uncooperative, argumentative. And she rarely listened to my advice, much less took it. I'd been working with her for six months, and we'd made very little headway. I'd tried to fire her three times, but she had always managed to cause such an emotional scene that I'd allowed her back.

"What about Esther?" I asked, referring to one of my elderly clients.

"She and her husband are on vacation in Greece next week, remember?"

"Yes," I said. "What about Virginia?"

"She and her husband are going with Esther."

I blinked in surprise. "They are? I didn't even realize they were friends."

"They weren't until they both started seeing you."

"Wait, what?" I asked.

"Esther met Virginia while both of them were waiting on us to arrive the day that I accidentally overbooked them for the same appointment, remember?"

"Oh, yes. I do remember that. Bad day for us, being late and double-booking them."

"I've apologized a bajillion times, Cat," Gilley said moodily.

"I know, lovey. And I've accepted that. I was merely commenting on the memory of that day."

"Well, maybe it wasn't so bad, because Virginia and Esther are now buddies."

"So, nobody else is on the books?" I asked, a bit panicked. My business was an ebb-and-flow kind of deal, and truth be told, I'd seen a lot more ebbs than flows.

"Not unless Aaron Nassau wants to schedule another session."

"Did you follow up with him?"

"Not yet," Gilley said testily.

I smiled and tried to convey that I wasn't being critical. "Why don't we reach out now?" I said. "I'd like to know how he's coping after such an emotional time yesterday."

Gilley whipped out his phone and scrolled through it before finding Aaron's number, pressing CALL, and putting the phone to his ear.

A moment later he said, "Aaron? Gilley Gillespie, Cat Cooper's assistant." Gilley paused, and his expression registered concern.

"What?" I said softly.

Gilley caught my gaze and simply handed me the phone. "Something's wrong," he whispered.

I placed the phone to my own ear and heard quiet whimpering. "Aaron?" I said. "It's Catherine Cooper. I'm calling to check on you. How're you doing?"

There was loud sniffling on the other end of the call. "Not well, Catherine."

"Oh, my, Aaron. I'm so sorry. Are you still upset about our conversation yesterday?"

"I take it you don't read the papers," he said.

My brow furrowed. "Actually, I do. And if memory serves me, the markets are all up this morning, and the forecast for the rest of this year looks promising."

"Oh, I don't give a fig about the markets right now," Aaron said, his voice hitching on a small but unmistakable sob.

And then, like a big old light bulb turning on in my mind, I put two and two together and actually gasped into the phone. "Ohmigod, Aaron . . . Yelena Galanis. She was your ex, wasn't she?"

The sound of Aaron weeping absolutely gutted me. "I . . . can't . . . believe . . . she's gone!" he sobbed.

I bit my lip and realized that Gilley was staring at me

with his mouth agape. I could see the sympathy in his own eyes for poor Aaron.

"I'm so, so sorry," I said to the count. "This must be such a blow."

His weeping intensified.

I looked at Gilley, absolutely pained by the fact that this poor dear man was sobbing his heart out and I was helpless to comfort him other than to speak a few words of sympathy. "What can we do for you, Aaron?" I finally said.

He didn't answer. He simply wept.

By now, Gilley had gotten up from his chair and moved to the kitchen. He brought back a pad of paper and a pen, and then he wrote out a note. It read, *Should we go to him?*

I nodded. That was exactly what we needed to do.

"Aaron," I said gently, "Gilley and I are coming over. You shouldn't be alone right now. You can expect us in twenty minutes or so." I didn't know where Aaron lived, but most people in the Hamptons were at most fifteen to twenty minutes away from each other no matter in which direction you drove.

"Okay," Aaron squeaked, and he hung up.

I got up and gathered my purse as Gilley knelt down next to Spooks and whispered in his ear. The dog's short tail tapped against the couch cushion, but he didn't move as we headed out the door.

"Do you think he'll be okay?" I asked Gil while he pulled the door shut.

"Spooks or the count?"

"Spooks."

"He'll be fine. His paperwork said he was a super-calm pup, with no obvious signs of separation anxiety."

"Good," I said, and we hurried to the car. After we got in, Gilley tapped on his phone again, then plugged Aaron's address into the car's navigation system while I backed out of the driveway.

When we got on the road, Gilley said, "He's in Amagansett, near Indian Wells Beach."

"I told him we'd be there in twenty minutes."

"We'll have a little time to spare, which is why I think we should stop and get him something to eat. He'll need nourishment and liquids."

"Great idea. What'd you have in mind?"

"How about Faye's Pho?" Gil suggested. "Pho is the ultimate comfort food. And it's fast."

"Agreed. Put in an order, will you?"

Gilley tapped at his screen some more. "Done. And I put in an order for us too. We can heat it up for a snack when we get home. That Caesar salad didn't fill me up."

After picking up the takeout, we were soon in Aaron's neighborhood, which was a particularly tony part of East Hampton.

The estates were enormous, and I was a bit jealous that they each had such a deep lot with a large section of private beach.

"Wow," Gilley said as we wound along a particularly curvy road. "This is even nicer than your neighborhood."

"It is," I said. "But probably fitting for a Danish count, right?"

"If he lives around here, he's definitely got money," Gilley said. "Big bucks."

The turn-by-turn directions pointed us to Bluff Road, and I pulled the car into one of the drives off that road. The driveway was long and sloped upward under a canopy of tall trees. At last, we stopped at a rectangular-looking structure with narrow windows and consisting of two levels, which looked like they were made of poured concrete. No, scratch that. The place looked like a prison.

"Not the friendliest-looking home," Gilley said as we came to a stop at the front door.

"No. It's not. But we're not here to criticize. We're here to offer support and comfort."

Gilley reached behind him for the carryout bag from Faye's, and we exited the car and approached the two front steps leading to the door. Gilley motioned for me to go in front of him, so I was the first to press the doorbell.

It gonged loudly from inside.

Gilley rocked back on his heels a few times while we waited.

And waited.

And waited.

"Press it again," Gil said, nodding toward the doorbell.

It had made such a loud sound before that I was a hesitant to ring it again. "What if he's indisposed?"

"What if he was out back and didn't hear it the first time?"

"He knew we were coming over." I didn't want to be one of those guests who pressed the bell like an impatient pedestrian at a crosswalk.

Gilley sighed dramatically, then reached around me to press the bell himself. It gonged for a second time, and I cringed at the thought that Aaron was somewhere inside, irritated that we weren't a little more patient.

Gil and I continued to wait in silence for another minute or two, and I'll admit that I was now a bit worried that neither gong had produced the count at the door.

"You're sure you got the right address?" I asked Gil.

He eyed me with heavy lids.

"Okay, okay," I said. "Sheesh, you don't have to yell."

Gilley chuckled. "I mean, please, Cat. You've known me for how long and you still second-guess my internet sleuthing skills?"

"Right. Shame on me," I said, but I was a little distracted, as I was looking around the drive for any signs that Aaron might be outside.

Seeing no sign of him, I glanced next at my phone and noted the time. "Where could he be?"

"Honestly, why isn't there a maid or a butler to answer the bell?" Gilley said. He then handed me the carryout bag and turned to walk back down the steps.

"Where're you going?" I asked.

He pointed toward the side of the yard, and when he disappeared around the corner, I hustled down the steps to follow him.

A concrete pathway led us to the back of the house and a narrow lap pool. The scrubby backyard fell away from the house in an open slope that allowed a spectacular view of the ocean.

"Nice," Gil said, pausing to admire the view.

I glanced at it but then focused on the pool area. There was nothing but a few patio chairs, the pool, and a grill set against the house. No sign of Aaron.

Gilley stopped admiring the view and walked right up to the twin sliding-glass doors. I squinted toward them but couldn't see anyone inside.

That, of course, didn't stop Gilley from moving right up to the doors and cupping his hands to peer inside.

I gasped. "Gilley, stop that!"

He continued to peer inside, so I hustled up to him and gave him a firm pat on the shoulder. "I'm serious!"

Gilley stepped back from the doors, clearly impatient

and annoyed. "We've been out here waiting for him to answer for hours," he complained.

"Three minutes," I corrected. "But yes, I agree. It's far too long for our arrival to go unanswered."

After handing him back the carryout bag, I lifted my phone and began to tap at the screen while retracing my steps along the pathway toward the front of the house with Gilley trailing behind me.

"Who're you calling?" he asked when we reached the front of the house again.

"Aaron," I said. I put the phone to my ear and listened through the five rings. Then it went to voice mail. "Aaron? It's Catherine. Gilley and I are at your door, and we rang the doorbell twice. If you're not up for company, I totally understand, but would you at least let us know if you're all right? I'm worried."

I hung up the call and stared at my phone, waiting for a message or a call or *something* from Aaron to let me know that he knew we were there but wasn't up for visitors. After another minute or two, I took up tapping at my phone again.

"Now who're you calling?" Gilley asked.

"Shepherd," I said, then raised a finger to my lips when I heard him pick up the line.

"Hey," he said, as if he were in a rush. "I'm a little busy. Can I call you later?"

"Actually, I'm calling with a concern, and I may need an officer of the law," I said.

Shepherd's tone turned crisp with focus. "What kind of concern?"

"Gilley and I are at a client's home. We're checking on him because he's having a difficult time, emotionally speaking. And we confirmed that we'd be over within twenty minutes or so, but now he's not answering the doorbell or my calls."

"How difficult a time, emotionally speaking, are we talking?"

"Enough for me to be a tiny bit panicked that he's not answering the bell."

"I'm on it," he said. "I'll get a uniform over to do a wellness check. What's the address?"

"Actually, we're in Amagansett," I said, remembering that this town wasn't in Shepherd's jurisdiction.

"Huh," he said. "I was just in that neck of the woods, and I've got a crew headed out there now too."

"You were? You do?"

"Give me the address and I'll call over to APD and have them send a uni," he said.

"Six-one-seven Bluff Road."

There was no acknowledgment from Shepherd, so I said, "Shep? You there?"

"I'm here," he said. "Your client wouldn't be Aaron Nassau, would it?"

My eyes widened, and I pulled in my chin in surprise.

Gilley, staring at me intently, mouthed, *What?*

"Yes. Yes, that's him," I told Shepherd, getting a bad feeling. "How did you know?"

"Your client is fine," Shepherd said. "Well, relatively speaking. He's about to be charged with murder."

My jaw dropped, and I shook my head.

"What?" Gilley said. "Cat, *what!*"

"What do you mean, he's being charged with murder!" I yelled.

I hadn't meant to screech at Shepherd; it was just too preposterous to contemplate. My sweetheart was a wonderful man; however, he had one very bad habit of arresting first and asking questions later.

"Cat, listen, I can't talk about this right now. I gotta prep for the interrogation. I'll fill you in later."

"Interrogation?"

"Interview," Shepherd said with a chuckle. "I meant interview."

I said nothing for a moment, my mind racing furiously, while Gilley continued to look at me in earnest. And then my eyes narrowed, and I said, "Is Aaron's lawyer there?"

It was Shepherd's turn to be quiet for a moment. "No," he said softly. "He hasn't asked for one yet."

"Gotta go!"

"Cat! Wait! Don't you dare get invol—"

I hung up by pressing my finger angrily against the red button at the bottom of my phone and immediately flipped over to my contacts list.

"Let me guess," Gilley said when I placed the phone at my ear for a third time. "You're calling Marcus."

I put a hand on my hip and ground my teeth. "Damn straight I'm calling Marcus!"

Marcus Brown was the best defense attorney in all of Long Island. He'd represented me when Shepherd arrested me for murder (which I hadn't committed), and he'd also represented two other friends of mine when they'd been hauled down to the station by my overzealous main squeeze.

Marcus had easily won a dismissal in each of those cases. Shepherd's circumstantial evidence was no match for Marcus Brown in a courtroom.

"Catherine Cooper," Marcus purred, picking up the call on the first ring. "To what do I owe this unexpected pleasure?"

"Hello, my friend," I said, warmed by his greeting. "I need you."

"Personally or professionally?"

"The latter."

I heard the crinkle of paper, and I imagined Marcus turning to a fresh page on his legal pad. "Talk to me."

I told Marcus about Aaron and how Shepherd had just arrested him.

"That man never passes up an opportunity to arrest first and ask questions later," Marcus said with a sigh.

I stifled a chuckle, as I'd already thought that same thing. "Right?"

"Whose murder is he about to be charged with?" Marcus asked.

"Probably Yelena Galanis's," I said. "Shepherd was on the case last night, right after it happened."

Absolute silence filled the connection.

"Marcus?"

"I'm here," he said. But then he said nothing more.

"Are you all right?" I asked, because it was such an odd reaction.

"Fine," he said quickly. "Catherine, are you willing to Venmo me for the initial hour with Nassau? I can reimburse you once he retains me, but should he refuse my services, I won't be able to represent him in this matter."

"Of course, Marcus. I'll send that Venmo right over."

"Perfect. I'll call Shepherd and insist that he cease questioning Mr. Nassau until I get there."

"Wonderful. Thank you."

I hung up with Marcus and handed the phone to Gilley. "I need to know what a Venmo is and how to make a payment for an hour of Marcus's time," I said.

Gilley smirked.

"Stop smirking!"

Gilley's smirk turned into a giggle. "You're the mother of teenagers. How is it you don't know this stuff? Like, doesn't it ever come up in casual conversation?"

"I'm the mother of teenage *boys*. They don't talk to me. They grunt."

"Ah. Fair point."

Gilley did some stuff on my phone, tilting the screen toward me so that I could watch, but truly my mind was elsewhere, and I was simply happy when he announced, "Done. Marcus has been retained for the hour."

"Perfect," I said, beginning to walk away. "Come on," I called over my shoulder.

"I'd ask where we're going, but I already know our next stop will be to the East Hampton Police Department."

"Damn straight," I growled, balling my hands into fists.

"Cool," Gilley replied. "I love a good fireworks show."

Pulling open the driver's side door, I snapped, "Just get in!"

Gilley opened his door, placing his free hand over his mouth to suppress a giggle. "And the light show has already started!"

Chapter 9

As we turned back onto the road, retracing our way to East Hampton, Gilley remarked, "Kind of amazing that in the twenty-five minutes it took us to get here, Shepherd arrived and arrested Aaron."

"We always did have fabulous timing," I muttered.

"Are you mad at Shepherd?"

"Of course I'm mad at Shepherd!" I yelled, angrily gripping the steering wheel.

"May I ask why?"

I glanced sideways at Gilley, wondering if he was teasing me, but he had an earnest expression, which confused me. "Because he arrested an innocent man. *Again!*"

"Did he?" Gilley asked. I leveled a look at him, and he added, "I'm just playing devil's advocate, Cat, because you know Shepherd's going to give you the same argument."

"Yes, he's innocent," I said firmly. "You met Aaron. Do you think he'd be capable of murder?"

"Cat, it's been my experience that human beings are capable of anything. Even the nice ones can commit murder."

I mulled that over for a few minutes. "No," I said at last. "Yelena was stabbed to death. That method of murder requires a certain personality type, Gilley. Someone capable of snapping in absolute fury, and Aaron didn't show any sign of that. If Yelena was the woman he was still pining for, then he must have been aware of her reputation—and her show—and yet when he came to see me, he was distraught not over what she might say about him from the stage but about not having her in his life. There was no hint of jealousy or anger over being made fun of. He simply wanted her back in his life.

"Plus, you didn't hear the heartbreak in his voice when I called him earlier. He was destroyed, Gilley. Just absolutely, heartbreakingly destroyed. And it was obvious, even to you, when he picked up the line that he was distraught. How could he have faked that if he wasn't crying before we called?"

Gilley nodded slowly. "That's all true," he said. "Great point."

I smiled and squared my shoulders. I knew I was right. Aaron simply wasn't a killer. I could feel it in my gut, and my sister always said that one should always trust one's gut feelings.

Fifteen minutes later we pulled into a parking space right next to Marcus, who was just getting out of his car. He looked devilishly handsome in a tan suit with bright orange tie and cream-colored dress shirt. He lowered his sunglasses to mid-nose to stare at us over the rims after

Gilley and I got out of the car, and I swear Gilley practically swooned with the cool silhouette Marcus cut.

"Catherine. Gilley," he said with a nod.

"Hello, Marcus," I said, adding a small wave.

"Hello, gorgeous," Gilley said.

I eyed him sharply, but Marcus covered his mouth to
hide a chuckle.

"I mean, he *is* gorgeous, right?" Gilley said to me.

"He's quite handsome," I agreed, joining in the banter.

"And that suit!" Gilley added, waving at Marcus's
duds. "Perfection!"

Marcus dropped his hand to give in to that chuckle,
and I could tell he was pleased by the compliments.
"Thanks, Gilley," he said, running his fingers along his
lapel. "It's an art."

We gathered in a half circle, and I made a sweeping
motion toward the door. "Shall we?"

"Whoa, whoa," Marcus said, holding up a hand to stop
us. "What's this 'we' business?"

"Cat wants to yell at her boyfriend," Gilley said.

I glared at him, and he stared insolently back at me.

"No one's going to yell at anybody, at least not until I
find out what the facts are," Marcus said.

"The facts are that Shepherd has *once again* arrested
an innocent man," I said.

"Do you know what evidence he might have against
Nassau?" Marcus asked.

"Uh . . . no," I said. "Whatever it is, it's probably flimsy."

"But you don't know that for sure?"

"Well, no. I don't."

"Okay, listen, Catherine, I know you mean well, but if
Nassau agrees to retain me to represent him, then your

going in there to yell at Shepherd could jeopardize my case."

I took up a stubborn stance with my hands on my hips. "How could that jeopardize your case?"

I wasn't trying to be contrarian. I simply wanted to yell at my sweetheart.

"Well, for starters, say Shepherd engages you in an argument. And say he begins to question you about your client. Did you know about the relationship between Mr. Nassau and the deceased?"

I opened my mouth to answer, closed it for a moment to think, then said, "Well, yes. But not right away. He told us that he'd dated a woman who'd dumped him flat and he was distraught over it."

Marcus nodded. "Uh-huh. When did he tell you this?"

"Um . . ." I said. "Yesterday."

"Mm-hmm," Marcus hummed. "So, the day of the murder, Mr. Nassau was agitated. Is that fair to say?"

"Upset," I corrected. "He was upset."

"I see. Thank you for that clarification. So, on the day of the murder, you saw Mr. Nassau upset at the fact that Ms. Galanis had broken up with him and was seeing other men? And that Mr. Nassau was very likely aware that Yelena Galanis had a hit show running at the local theater, where her material was comprised entirely of her dating escapades and likely featured Mr. Nassau as one of the unnamed twelve angry men. Do I have that correct, Ms. Cooper?"

I could see what he was doing from a mile away, and I hated that I'd been naïve enough to believe I could simply barge on over here, yell at Shepherd and, in doing that, assist Aaron in his situation. It was a ridiculous assumption, and one I was feeling very embarrassed for having.

"Marcus?" I said after a long, thoughtful pause.

"Yes?"

"Do give Mr. Nassau our best and tell him to reach out, should he wish to talk, once you've gotten the charges dismissed."

"Let's hope that's as far as this gets," Marcus said. "But I hear you. I'll pass on the message."

"Will you call us later with an update?" Gilley asked.

"Sure, but I'll speak to you only about what the police have on Nassau, nothing about what he tells me."

"Attorney-client privilege," I said.

Marcus nodded.

"All right. Thank you, Marcus. We'll look forward to your call."

With that, I took Gilley by the elbow, and we left Marcus to his job.

Gilley and I drove in silence for much of the ride home, until finally he said, "So you're really not going to ask Shepherd about what he was thinking arresting Aaron?"

"I can't," I said. "You heard Marcus. If I do, I could open Aaron to incrimination."

"But what if Shepherd asks you?"

I shrugged. "He can ask all he wants, but I'm not going to tell him a thing unless he calls me in for an interview, and even then, I wouldn't go without Marcus." And then I looked at Gilley, knowing he had overheard my entire first meeting with Aaron. "You have to promise not to say anything, either."

Gilley lifted a dainty pinky. "Pinky swear. And if he hauls me in, I'll call Marcus to the rescue."

"Good," I said.

Gilley jumped at the sound of his phone ringing and pulled it out from his back pocket. After glancing at the display, he simply allowed the phone to continue to ring.

"Are you going to answer that?"

"Probably not," Gilley said.

"Who is it?"

"Michel."

I raised my brow in surprise. "Ah," I said.

Gilley's phone rang one more time and then stopped. He pocketed it again, and we drove the rest of the way home in silence.

Several hours later Gilley and I were just finishing up the dinner dishes when my phone rang. Thinking it was likely Shepherd, I was actually surprised to see that it was Marcus.

"Hello, Counselor. Calling with good news, I hope?"

"Afraid not, Catherine," he said somberly.

"Tell me," I said, grabbing Gilley's arm to alert him that there was trouble.

Marcus sighed heavily. "Shepherd has some pretty damning evidence against Mr. Nassau."

"Like what?"

"Like the murder weapon for one."

"They found the knife?"

"It's a letter opener with the Danish royal family crest on it, and although the handle was wiped mostly clean, EHPD was able to lift a partial thumbprint that matches Mr. Nassau's."

"Oh, dear," I said, while Gilley's brow furrowed as he looked at me.

"There's also video footage from Ms. Galanis's doorbell camera, showing Mr. Nassau arriving at her home shortly after she left for the theater yesterday. It was around five, which was a half hour after she left for the theater. The video shows him peeking into her windows and trying the door handle."

"Oh, my," I whispered.

What? Gilley mouthed. I could only shake my head and hold up a finger, telling him to wait.

"And there's a recording on Ms. Galanis's voice mail of Mr. Nassau telling her that he can't stand to live without her, and he might do something drastic if she doesn't take him back."

"Oh, Aaron, what were you thinking?" I whispered.

"What? Cat, *what*? What was he thinking?" Gilley pleaded.

I didn't answer him, because Marcus was continuing to talk.

"And, if that weren't enough, Shepherd has video footage from a gas station two blocks from the theater where Aaron stopped to purchase a bottle of water just ten minutes before Yelena's intermission break."

I put a hand over my eyes. This was terrible. "Are you going to take the case?"

"Of course I'm going to take the case," Marcus said. "And the first thing I'll do is contact the Danish embassy to see if I can secure sovereign immunity for Mr. Nassau."

"Sovereign immunity?" I repeated.

"Yes. Since he is a member of the Danish royal family, I might be able to get Mr. Nassau an exemption from prosecution of a criminal act. He's already got it for civil acts, but I'd push for it, and if granted, he'd have to leave the country immediately, but at least he wouldn't face a murder one charge."

I took that in, struck by how much it felt like justice was being cheated in light of all the evidence that Marcus had just revealed to me. "But, Marcus . . . what if he's guilty?"

Marcus didn't answer me right away, and I felt in that moment before he spoke that he was weighing what he'd say against how I might view him. "It's not my job to determine his guilt or innocence, Catherine. It's my job to represent him legally and keep him out of jail—any way I can."

"You're right," I said. I'd almost forgotten. Still, it didn't sit well with me. "Thank you for filling me in, Marcus. I very much appreciate it."

"Have a good night, Catherine," he replied, and I swear I detected a note of relief in his voice.

When I got off the call with Marcus, I filled Gilley in.

"So, Aaron *did* murder Yelena?" Gilley said after I'd finished.

I thought about it for a long moment before I answered him. "What I can't figure out is why Aaron would leave my office yesterday, so desperate for my help in getting him to move on from the love of his life, and then, within hours of that pained confession, commit premeditated murder."

"I don't know that I'm following you," Gilley said.

"What I mean is, if you're going to kill the woman who left you, the woman you're clearly still so in love with, why would you set up an appointment with a life coach?"

"To cast doubt on your actions," Gilley said. "Maybe Aaron knew you'd testify in court to his frame of mind a few hours beforehand."

I nodded. "Agree. However, did anything about Aaron's pained session with me yesterday strike you as false?"

It was Gilley's turn to take a moment to consider that. Finally, he said, "If I'm being totally honest, Cat, no. Nothing about his manner or his story or his professed love for his ex seemed contrived. He genuinely looked and sounded heartbroken."

"Exactly," I said. "He sounded the same on the phone with me earlier. And he also said something that stuck out to me when I first asked why he was so upset."

"What?"

"He said, 'I take it you don't read the papers.'"

"The papers? You mean *newspapers*?"

"Yes."

"So, you think Aaron learned about Yelena's murder through the newspaper."

"Yes. He didn't say, 'Watch the news,' Gil. He said, 'Read.'"

"Why is that important?"

"Aaron sounded like he'd just learned of the news, but we know that Yelena's murder was the lead story on all the local news programs both last night and this morning. So if he'd been faking, he would've said, 'You don't *watch* the news,' not 'Read the news.' When we reached out to him today, he truly sounded like he'd just learned of Yelena's death, which means he'd read about it when he opened up his paper today, and not before."

Gilley nodded and pointed a finger at me. "It's a subtle distinction that lends more to truth than to fakery," he said.

"Exactly."

Gilley and I were both silent for several moments

while we each contemplated what we thought of Aaron's guilt or innocence.

Finally, I said, "Say, Gil, what would you think about—"

"Yes," he said, cutting me off.

I blinked. "You didn't even let me get out my question."

Gilley rolled his eyes. "Oh, please. You were about to ask me if we should poke around a bit into Yelena's murder and do a little sleuthing of our own."

I blinked again. "How did you know that was what I was going to ask?"

Gilley grinned and reached over to tap my temple. "Because I live inside your head."

I laughed and knocked his hand away. "Whatever. Where should we start?"

"Probably with her act, don't you think? We should figure out who the lovers were in *Twelve Angry Men*. That'd at least give us eleven other suspects to focus on."

I snapped my fingers and pointed at him. "Exactly! Gilley, that's exactly where we should start." Tapping at my lip, I thought for a moment and said, "Tucker McAllen was Lover Number One, right?"

"That's the general consensus," Gilley said. "I think Joel Goldberg was Lover Number Four."

My brow furrowed. "Lover Number Four. Remind me again, what were the clues?"

"The guy who introduced her to a girl's best friend, and then she waggled that big tennis bracelet, remember?"

"Ah, yes. Now I remember, and didn't Reese tell you that the rumor was that Goldberg was Lover Number Four?"

"He did. He heard it from a woman who said she'd

seen Goldberg and Yelena canoodling at a café next door to one of his jewelry stores."

Goldberg was a familiar name. His jewelry stores were very high end and dotted every town in the Hamptons.

"Thank God for your bat-like hearing," I said. I hadn't heard much other than murmurs during the show.

"Comes in handy," Gilley said, moving over to the couch to plop down next to Spooks, who had just finished his bone treat and was busy licking his paws. As Gilley put his feet up on the ottoman, Spooks got up, turned around on the couch cushion, then settled himself with his big silver head in Gilley's lap.

"Awww," I said, moving over to sit next to the pair. "He knows he's home."

Gilley stroked one of the pup's ears. "I hope so. I never, ever, ever want him to feel abandoned again."

Pointing to the dog bed in front of the couch, I said, "So, you've given up on the rule of no dogs allowed on the furniture already?"

Gilley shrugged. "I still have the receipt. We can take the beds back to the Pet Palace tomorrow."

I chuckled, then got serious again. "Okay, so do we know any of the other lovers?"

"By *we*, I'm assuming you mean *me*."

"That's what I like about you, Gil. You're so perceptive."

Gilley rolled his eyes but allowed himself a playful grin. "I got the feeling that Lover Number Five was in the navy."

"The 'six gold stripes' line?" I asked. Yelena had made a crack about Lover Number Five being cheap, saying that the only gold he paid for were the six gold stripes on his sleeve.

"Yeah," Gilley said. "She also said he was a three-star guy in a two-star suit. The gold stripes mean length of service, if I'm not mistaken, and the stars indicate rank."

"What would three stars make him?" I asked.

"Don't know," Gil said, then he pointed to his tablet, which was on the coffee table. "Would you mind?" he asked, indicating that if he bent forward to get it, he'd disturb Spooks.

I smirked but got up to retrieve the tablet and handed it to him. Gilley balanced the tablet on his lower thigh, cracked his knuckles, wiggled his fingers over the keyboard, and dove in. I waited patiently, stroking Spooks's head and smiling when the dog sighed contentedly.

"Aha!" Gil said.

"You found out what rank three stars is?"

Gilley eyed me first in confusion, then in impatience. "No. I mean, yes. That's the first thing I looked up, along with the stripes. Lover Number Five has at least twenty-four years in service, and he's a vice admiral."

"Wow. An admiral? Yelena dated a naval vice admiral?" I had no idea what a vice admiral did, but it sounded impressive.

"No, Yelena dated a Coast Guard vice admiral."

"How do you know it's the Coast Guard and not the navy?"

"Because I found out who she dated. The only vice admiral anywhere near the Hamptons is this guy . . ." Gilley swiveled his tablet around so that I could see the photograph of a very handsome man with chiseled features, black hair that was gray at the temples, and a big, beautiful smile. He was dressed in a dark blue uniform with six gold stripes on his sleeves and three gold stars near his shoulder.

"He's pretty," I said.

Gilley swiveled the tablet back toward himself. "Right?"

"Yeah. I can see why she'd be attracted to him."

Gilley tapped the corner of his tablet and said, "Meet Vice Admiral Liam Leahy. He has a place on Shelter Island."

Shelter Island was to our north. It was a medium-sized island for these parts, sandwiched between Sag Harbor and Greenport—the two end prongs of Long Island.

"Huh," I said. "Would a vice admiral throw away his whole career out of revenge for a former lover making fun of him onstage?"

Gilley shrugged. "I'd say maybe if I hadn't heard all of that part of Yelena's act. Of all the lovers she mentioned, he was kind of the most boring."

I nodded. "Yeah. Number Five got the fewest laughs."

"So, there really wasn't anything salacious about him," Gilley said. "And a vice admiral is second in command in the Coast Guard. He's way up there in rank."

"Is he married?" I asked, thinking that if Leahy was married and he had an affair with Yelena, that could definitely end his career.

"Nope," Gilley said. "He's a divnk. Just like Shepherd, actually."

"A divnk? What's a divnk?"

"Divorced, no kids."

I blinked. "Then what am I?" I asked.

Gilley smirked. "The envy of divorcées everywhere."

I laughed. "Come on, Gilley, I'm serious."

"So am I," he insisted. "You're divorced, with two kids in boarding school, a sexy boyfriend, and all the money a person could want. You're a divrahah."

"What's a divrahah?"

"Divorced, rich, and happy as hell."

I rolled my eyes. "You make it sound like I'm happy that my sons are at boarding school."

"Oh, please, Cat. They were here the second half of the summer and had dinner with us, what? Four times?"

"Eight," I said and offered Gilley a chagrined smile. "I counted."

"Exactly my point. They were at the beach or the skate park way more than they were here."

I sighed. "I'd still rather have them home than away at school."

"But can you deny you're happy as hell?"

"No," I said. "No, I'm pretty happy."

"Exactly my point. And thank your stars you're not a mankatbed."

"A . . . *what*?"

"Mankatbed."

"What the devil is that?"

"Married, no kids, about to be divorced."

"Oh, you're right. That would be bad. Who do we know that's a mankatbed?"

Gilley eyed me expectantly.

It took me longer than I'd like to admit to realize he meant himself. "Oh, come on," I said. "Gilley, you are not!"

"Aren't I?" he said, his lower lip quivering just a tad.

I moved in for a hug, disturbing Spooks, who moaned slightly in protest. When I let go, I kept my hands on Gilley's shoulders. "I'm here for you. Day and night. Whatever you need."

Gilley nodded and pointed to his tablet. "Shall we get on with it?"

"Yes," I said, sitting back again. "Where were we?"

"Talking about Mr. Leahy. Who's divorced, no kids, and the apparent mark of a very clever, albeit very dead, lady."

"Yes, that's right," I said. "Do we know if he was recently divorced? Maybe he had an affair with Yelena and that ended his marriage, and he killed her in revenge."

"He's been divorced for six years," Gilley said, scrolling through his tablet. "At least according to my public records search."

"Let's put him on the list of suspects, anyway. We want to be thorough in our investigation."

"Agreed," Gilley said.

"Okay, so that's three out of eleven, and it's not even nine o'clock yet."

"We are good," Gilley said.

"Okay, so how do we identify the rest—especially the ones we didn't get to hear about during the second act?"

"I wish we could talk to Sunny," Gilley said. "I'm sure she'd know every guy in the show."

I shook my head. "I don't think so. She told me yesterday, when I went to pick up the tickets, that Yelena was planning to name names that night, and she gave me the impression that she didn't know who Yelena would publicly identify. She also said she hadn't yet seen the act."

"Hold on," Gilley said, swiveling to me with wide eyes. "Yelena mentioned that she was going to name names?"

"Yes," I said. I didn't know why Gilley was so excited by that. "She told Sunny when she gave her the tickets that she was going to drop a few names at the end of the show."

"Sugar," he said, "way to bury the lede."

"You think if Yelena told Sunny she was going to

name names then maybe Yelena also told other people and it got back to the murderer?"

"Uh, *yeah*," Gilley said, like it should've been obvious.

"Don't be mean," I told him.

"Sorry," he said. "You're right. That was rude."

I shrugged and let it go. "How do we find out if Yelena told other people her plans for the evening?"

"We hunt down the twelve angry men and grill them about how much they knew about Yelena's show."

I nodded. "I like that. But how are we going to grill them exactly, Gilley? We don't know these men, and we wouldn't have any reason to walk right up to them and start asking them personal questions like that."

"Hmm," Gilley said. "That's true. We'll need an excuse."

We both stared at the floor while we thought about an excuse good enough to approach any of the men we identified.

"I've got nothing," I finally said.

Gilley sighed. "Me either. But not to worry. I'll think of something."

Headlights outside flashed across the room through the open blinds. I looked over my shoulder.

"Who's here?" Gilley said.

I got up and went to the front door. Spooks must've heard whoever it was outside approaching, because his head popped up and he jumped off the couch to run over to me and place himself between me and the door.

"Woof!" he barked. The sound was like a low rumble of thunder. Definitely not a bark to be messed with.

"Gilley?" we heard through the door.

Gilley had gotten up and was next to me. "Hey, Shepherd," he said through the still closed door.

"Is that a dog in there?"

"Woof!" Spooks barked in reply.

Placing a hand on the doorknob, I looked pointedly from Gilley to Spooks and back again. "Best hold on to him, Gilley. He's never met Shepherd."

Gilley knelt down next to Spooks and hugged the pup to him.

I opened the door, and Shepherd stood on the first step, hesitantly. "When did you get a dog?" he said by way of greeting.

"This is Spooks," Gilley told him. "Spooks, meet Shepherd."

Spooks had his hackles raised, and although he wasn't growling, we all understood that Shepherd needed to be on his best behavior until Spooks could approve his arrival.

"Hey, buddy," Shepherd said, kneeling low to get on Spooks's level. "He's a good-looking guy. Did you get him from the shelter?"

"We did," Gilley said, allowing Spooks to move forward toward Shepherd. "We picked him up today."

Shepherd nodded and waited for Spooks to inch forward and sniff at him. "Hey, guy," Shepherd said and very carefully lifted a hand to stroke the dog's ear. "How ya doin'? Huh? Who's a big boy? Huh? Who's a good buddy?"

I put a finger to my lips to suppress a bubble of laughter. Shepherd had completely melted at the appearance of a dog, and it was adorable.

Spooks, it seemed, had also allowed his protective heart to melt, and his stub tail was wagging back and forth furiously as he pushed his big head into Shepherd's chest. Then he had a sudden thought and bolted inside again to retrieve a squeaky toy and bring it over to Shepherd, who played tug with him for a bit out in the driveway while Gilley and I eyed each other knowingly.

At last, Shep came inside himself, still pulling on the squeaky toy while Spooks dug his heels in and tried to coax his new friend to continue playing. "Man, I love dogs," Shepherd said.

"You do?" I asked. "I never knew that about you."

Shepherd nodded. "I had a bunch of dogs growing up, three, sometimes four at a time, and they were all rescues. Rescues make the best companions. They've seen the darker side of life, and they're grateful for any love they get."

"Agreed," Gilley said, moving to the kitchen counter, where he dug through one of the bags we'd brought inside after our trip to the Pet Palace. When he produced a large Kong, he said, "Spooks! Hey, Spooks! You want some peanut butter?"

The dog cocked his head at Gilley, the squeaky toy dangling out of his mouth. Gilley chuckled and headed into the kitchen to fill the Kong with a yummy treat. Spooks dropped the toy and padded after him, leaving me alone with Shepherd.

"How come you don't own a dog now?" I asked, feeling a sudden tension in the air between us.

"No time," he said, looking wistfully at Spooks's departing form. "I spend too many hours at the station to be a good parent to a pooch."

"Ah," I said.

"Yeah," he said.

I tried to think of another thing to say to fill the awkward silence that followed, but Shepherd beat me to it. "Thanks for butting into my case today, Cat."

My shoulders sagged. "Is that what this is?" I said, pointing to the door, then to Shepherd. "You came over here to give me a lecture?"

"Oh, come on. You knew I would," he said.

"I didn't butt into your case, Shep. I merely recommended an attorney for my client—whom you arrested based on flimsy evidence."

"It ain't flimsy, honey," Shepherd said, and his tone was dead serious. "Yelena was murdered with a letter opener that belonged to Nassau."

"How do you *know* it belonged to Aaron?" I asked.

"It has the coat of arms of the Danish royal family on it," he said easily.

"A letter opener with a coat of arms of the royal family on it can probably be found in any tourist gift shop in Denmark," I argued.

Shepherd chuckled. "I doubt a tourist gift shop sells a fourteen-karat gold letter opener with the official coat of arms inlaid with sapphires, yellow diamonds, and rubies."

My mouth fell open. "Whoa," I said. "That has to be worth a pretty penny."

Shepherd nodded. "Our best guess is that it's worth fifty to sixty grand. Probably more."

"Probably a lot more," I said. "Which begs the question, why would Aaron use it to commit murder?"

"Because it was handy," Shepherd said, moving around me and over to the couch, where he collapsed in a tired heap.

"Do you want something to eat, Shepherd?" Gilley called from the kitchen.

"Whatcha got?"

"I made a sweet potato and chickpea curry over bas-
mati rice."

Shepherd sniffed the air. "That must be what smells so
good. Yeah, Gilley, a plate of that would be great."

"Coming right up," Gil said, and he got to work
pulling the leftovers out of the fridge.

"Where did you find this letter opener?" I asked next,
wanting to continue the conversation.

"At the scene. One of the techs found it under the
dressing table."

"What was it doing there?"

"I dunno, Cat. Maybe Nassau threw it there after he
got done stabbing my victim to death."

I looked at him crossly. "Shep," I said, "why would
Aaron leave behind the most incriminating piece of evidence and not take it with him if he did in fact kill Yelena?"

"I think he panicked," Shepherd said.

"How convenient," I said drolly.

"It happens," Shepherd said.

"What did Aaron say about it when you asked him?"

"You mean, what did Marcus Brown allow him to say
when I asked him?"

I pursed my lips in an effort to keep them from spreading into a small grin.

Shepherd rolled his eyes and said, "Nassau claims that
he has no idea how it got in Yelena's dressing room, but
he suspects she stole it the last time they were together."

"She stole it?"

"That's what he says. That's not what I believe."

"Why would she steal something worth so much
money?" I said, as if Shepherd hadn't even spoken. "I

mean, stealing anything over ten thousand makes it a felony, right?"

"It does," he said. "But Nassau was quick to say that if she had taken it, he wouldn't have pressed charges, because he still loved her, and as far as he was concerned, she was welcome to anything of his that he owned."

"And you don't believe him," I said.

"Of course I don't believe him. He had to add that last bit to take away the motive for murder."

"I'm missing that. What motive?"

Shepherd shrugged. "Nassau discovers his extremely valuable letter opener is missing, suspects Yelena has stolen it, heads to the theater to confront her about it, finds it, and stabs her with it when he finds the proof of her larceny."

"Why wouldn't he have simply called the police?" I asked next. "If he'd suspected that Yelena had stolen the letter opener, why wouldn't he have simply filled out a police report?"

"You'd have to ask him that," Shepherd said.

"But does that really make sense to you?" I pressed. "I mean, you're a seasoned detective. Does it make sense that a man would stab his former lover with the very object he suspected she stole, only to then throw it under a dressing table as he ran out the door?"

Shepherd rubbed his tired eyes. "I don't know what was going through his mind at the time of the murder, babe. All I know is that your guy did it. I had him set up to confess it, and then you stuck your nose into it, and now what was almost a slam dunk means I gotta work triple hard to prove my case."

"Here you are," Gilley said, handing Shepherd a steaming bowl of the delicious curry. "And here you also are," he added, pulling out a pint bottle of chilled pale ale from under his arm.

"Gilley," Shepherd said with a grin as he took the bottle from him, "you really know how to spoil a guy."

"I've had some practice at it," Gilley said, clearly pleased, as he shuffled over to a nearby chair and plopped down himself.

Shepherd tucked into his dinner, and we waited in silence for him to take a few bites. "Oh, man," he said, hovering his fork over the meal. "Gil! This is good!"

Gilley's grin widened.

"Any word on Sunny?" I asked, suddenly thinking of her.

Shepherd stopped chewing. In fact, he froze in place for a beat or two, but then he seemed to recover himself. "Nothing new," he said. "I stopped by their house on my way here. Darius had his hands full with Finley. He says that Sunny is kind of out of it. They've got her on some heavy sedatives to keep her calm until they can figure out what might've triggered the episode."

"Did you get a chance to see her?" Gilley asked.

Shepherd stared at his food and shook his head. I could see the tense line of his shoulders and knew he was terribly worried about his twin. "Darius is the only one allowed to see her right now, and he said even his visits are kept short. They don't want her upset, and they're worried that seeing me might make her upset."

"Why?" I asked.

"I don't know, Cat," Shepherd said, his voice suddenly hard. "Maybe because I'd lose it if I saw her locked up in some mental ward."

I bit my lip, regretting the fact that I'd pressed him on the point. "I'm sorry," I whispered.

He shook his head, set his fork in the curry, and reached over to squeeze my hand. "It's not you. It's this whole situation."

"Understood," I said.

We let Shepherd continue to eat his dinner in relative silence, but then he looked up at us and said, "I'm getting self-conscious with you two watching me eat. Somebody say something."

"How's that other case going?" Gilley asked.

Shepherd grunted and chewed the bite he'd taken for a moment before answering. "That one's a puzzler."

"Do you still think it was a mob hit?" I asked.

Shepherd shook his head, then shrugged. "I don't know what to think of it. I assigned the case to Santana—"

"Santa?" Gilley interrupted. "Are his eight tiny reindeers also on the case?"

Shepherd leveled a look at him. "Not Santa, Gil. *Santana*. He's the department's new detective. A hotshot out of Queens, he asked for a transfer here ''cause he likes the sea.'" Shepherd used air quotes for that last part, and he added an eye roll. "Anyway, he's worked enough homicides that I figured he could probably handle this one, and I'm keeping tabs on it 'cause I'm not ruling out that there's a link to Yelena's murder, but everything Santana's reporting back to me so far only adds to the mystery."

"Like what?" I asked.

"Well, like the fact that we were only able to identify the vic by using the key fob in his pocket to locate his car, which was in the same parking structure where you guys were parked. He left his wallet in the car, along with his phone and anything else that might identify him, and although he was wearing a women's size-ten raincoat, stuffed with two hundred thousand dollars—"

"Two *hundred thousand?*" Gilley and I both gasped.

Shepherd nodded and continued, as if we hadn't interrupted him. "In the lining. Labretta found the car. The plates were registered to a guy named Mark Purdy, and when we searched the car, we found a wallet and phone in the glove box. ID matching the vic identified him definitively.

"Purdy's on no one's list for organized crime. He's a retired estate attorney, lived in a condo overlooking the bay in Sag Harbor, and the ME says that he doesn't think the murderer used a knife to slit Purdy's throat. He thinks it was piano wire."

"Oh, God," Gilley said, his face a mask of horror. "I thought they did that only in the movies."

"Nope," Shepherd said. "They do that in real life too. It's quick and effective, and it sends a clear signal."

"So, you really do believe this was a mob hit," I said.

"For sure. What I can't figure out is the money. None of the bills are counterfeit, so why the hit man didn't take it with him is a puzzler."

"Maybe the hit man didn't know that it wasn't counterfeit," Gilley said.

Shepherd sighed and rubbed his eyes again. He seemed utterly exhausted. "Maybe," he conceded. "Santana's digging into Purdy's financials to see if he can trace the money or find any hints of a connection to organized crime."

"I don't know whether to hope for a connection or not," I said. "On the one hand, it would be a relief to know there wasn't some crazed serial killer type roaming the streets, looking for victims, and on the other hand, it'd be yet *another* Mafia hit entering our lives in a terrible way."

"How is this entering your lives?" Shepherd asked, and he was giving me that look like I'd better not even think about getting involved in an amateur sleuth kind of way.

"Well, Gilley and I *did* discover Purdy's body," I said quickly, while Gilley avoided making eye contact with Shepherd.

"Uh-huh," he said, clearly still suspicious. Wagging his finger at us, he added, "Do *not* get involved in this, you two."

"Wouldn't dream of it," Gilley said.

"The thought never entered our minds," I said.

Shepherd continued to stare at us like he knew we were big fat fibbers. Which, hello . . . we were! But no way was I going to confirm that.

Shepherd finally let up and tried to stifle a huge yawn. "Man, I am beat."

I stood up and took his hand. "Come on," I said. "Let's get you to bed."

"I'm staying over?" he asked as he got to his feet, and there was the sweetest bit of hopefulness in his voice.

"Of course you're staying over," I said, wrapping my arm around his waist and guiding us toward the door. "I'm not about to let you drive home in the state you're in."

"What state am I in?"

"Tired and suspicious."

Shepherd grinned down at me. "It's like you know me."

Chapter 10

The next day, I spent the whole day in the city with my sons. Monday morning, however, I went straight to Chez Kitty. I wanted to pick up where Gilley and I had left off on Saturday night.

Letting myself in, I called out to him, but he wasn't anywhere in the house. And neither was Spooks. There was, however, a note on the table that said that he and the pup had gone for a walk, and that I should make myself comfortable with some coffee and have the slice of quiche Florentine he'd set aside for me.

I smiled as I unwrapped the plate. Gilley was always taking care of me, and as much as I was heartbroken that he and Michel seemed to be headed for a split, I was grateful that Gilley wouldn't be leaving me anytime soon.

After polishing off the quiche and the coffee, I

straightened up the living room, tossing Spooks's various squeaky toys into the toy basket, doing a bit of light vacuuming and dusting, and before I knew it, I'd also organized Gilley's spice rack.

"Where the devil could he be?" I muttered to myself when I glanced up at the time. I'd been at Chez Kitty for well over an hour.

As if on cue, the front door opened and in came Gilley and Spooks, but leaning on Gilley and hobbling forward was none other than Tiffany—Sunny's babysitter.

"Oh, my goodness!" I said in alarm when I saw that the poor girl was sticking her right foot out in front of her in an effort not to have it touch the floor. "What happened?"

"She rolled her ankle," Gilley said, guiding Tiffany to a nearby chair.

The young woman's face was contorted in pain, and I hurried to pull the ottoman over so that she could lift her foot onto it. She winced and hissed out a breath as she very carefully placed it onto the cushion.

After hurrying to the freezer, I pulled out a cold compress and came back to the chair to see Gilley very gently putting another pillow underneath Tiffany's ankle to give it more support.

Kneeling down, I said to Tiffany, "This is going to hurt, sweetie, but we have to try and slow down the swelling."

A tear leaked down Tiffany's lovely face, and she nodded. Then she hissed a few breaths through her teeth as I slowly, slowly lowered the compress onto her ankle. "Ohmigod, ohmigod, ohmigod!" she cried as the coldness spread across her injured foot. Gilley held her hand and rubbed her fingers.

"I know it hurts," he said. "Try to hang in there for a few more seconds, and it'll get easier."

She nodded as more tears slid from her eyes. I wondered if she hadn't broken the ankle.

When Tiffany seemed a fraction less uncomfortable, I said, "What would you like for us to do, Tiffany? Is there someone we can call? Or should we take you to urgent care immediately?"

"I smashed my phone," she said, her voice hitching on the words.

Gilley produced the phone out of his pocket. The screen was smashed and dark. "I can't get it to turn on," he said. "And she can't remember her parents' numbers."

"They're just in my phone, you know?" she said. "I never have to think when I call them."

"How about where your dad works?" I tried. "If you can think of the company, maybe we could call his office and ask for him."

"He's at home today," she said miserably, and I knew that it was useless to push her for details. Her mind was clouded with pain, and she might even be in a bit of shock.

"Okay," I said gently, rubbing her arm. "Should we take you straight to urgent care, then? Or would you like us to drive you home and your parents can take you?"

"H-h-home," she sputtered, wiping the tears from her face, but more tears simply followed. The poor love was so distressed. Waving to her foot, she cried, "I can't believe I did that! I'm supposed to run the New York City Marathon this year!"

Tiffany stared at her ankle as if it'd betrayed her, and I couldn't tell if the tears were from pain or from disappointment that she'd be missing the race. Perhaps they were from both.

"Maybe it's not so bad," I said, even though her ankle was clearly swollen and turning a frightening shade of blue.

I glanced at Gilley, and he was staring at her injured foot like he was afraid some alien creature might burst out and attack him.

"We'll let you sit for a bit, and then we'll help you to the car," I told her. "Gil?"

He tore his eyes away from Tiffany's foot and looked at me with wide, almost panicked eyes. "Yeah?"

"I believe I've got a set of crutches in the garage from when Matt had that calf strain last year. They'll be short for Tiffany, but at least they'll allow her to maneuver under her own power."

"Uh-huh?" he said, not understanding what I was getting at.

"Why don't you go see if you can find them while I make room for Tiffany in my car."

"Yeah, okay," he said, and then he bolted for the door.

"Spooks," I said to the pup, who'd lain down right next to Tiffany's chair to stare up at her with worried eyes. He sat up when he heard his name. "Stay," I said, pointing to him.

He replied with a soft snort and placed his head on Tiffany's thigh.

I nodded to him. "Good boy." Then I squeezed Tiffany's shoulder and said, "We'll be right back."

She didn't respond or even acknowledge that I'd spoken. Instead, she stared into space and petted Spooks's head.

I left the pair of them and headed out to move the seats in my car so that we could ease Tiffany in without forcing her to put any weight on her foot.

Fifteen minutes later the four of us were on our way, headed northeast, and before too long we were turning into a subdivision off of Hither Lane.

"It's that one on the left," Tiffany said, pointing to a lovely French country home with neatly tended gardens and a circular drive.

I turned into the drive and pulled as close to the front door as the pavement allowed. "Gil," I said, unbuckling my seat belt, "I'll ring the bell while you help Tiffany out, okay?"

"Got it," he said.

After hurrying out of the car and up the steps, I rang the bell, and the door was opened right away by a woman with white-blond hair, big blue eyes, and a round face, who was just about my height.

"Hello," I said. "I'm Catherine. I'm a friend of Sunny D'Angelo, and we met your daughter the other night, when she was babysitting Finley."

The woman eyed me with confusion until she noticed what was happening behind me. She gasped as I was quick to explain. "My friend Gilley found Tiffany hobbling along after she rolled her ankle. We drove her home because she'd smashed her phone when she fell."

"Oh, my goodness!" Tiffany's mother exclaimed. "Charles! *Charles!* Come quick!"

I stepped aside just before Tiffany's mom rushed past me down the steps, and stayed to the side as a tall, broad presence emerged from the hallway and approached the front door.

Tiffany's dad was a surprise. He was African American, with a beard and a belly, but he stood at least six feet five. Possibly taller, as he literally had to duck his head to come outside. "What's happened?" he asked.

"Your daughter rolled her ankle on her run. We brought her home because she smashed her phone when she fell and couldn't remember your phone numbers."

Charles barely acknowledged that I'd spoken, and he hurried down the steps to join his wife while Gilley helped to prop up Tiffany, who was now out of the car.

Bending at the waist, Charles simply picked his daughter up in his arms like a rag doll and carried her up the steps and inside with ease. Gilley stayed by the car, next to Spooks, who was sticking his head out the window, and I waited for Tiffany's mother to pass me on the stairs before I made my exit, but she paused on the landing and said, "Thank you! Thank you so much for bringing her home."

"We almost took her to urgent care," I admitted. "But deferred to Tiffany about where she wanted to go."

"No, she definitely should've come home. Charles is an orthopedic surgeon."

My brow lifted in surprise at how fortunate that was for Tiffany. "Oh, good," I said. "Who better than her dad to immediately assess her injuries?"

Tiffany's mom stuck out her hand. "I'm Brenda."

"Catherine Cooper," I said, shaking her hand.

"Would you like to come in for a minute? I'm sure Charles would like to thank you for helping our baby girl home."

By now, Gilley had sidled up next to me, and, tapping his chest, he said, "Gilley Gillespie."

Brenda nodded and shook his hand. "Brenda Blum."

"We don't want to be a bother," I said.

"You're not," Brenda insisted. "Please, come in for a moment, won't you?"

I smiled and nodded, and we followed Brenda inside.

Charles had taken Tiffany to the kitchen, and she was sitting on the island, with her father kneeling down to inspect her foot as he eased her running shoe off.

Poor Tiffany cried out as the shoe came loose, and Charles looked pained as he glanced at his daughter. "Sorry, baby. I have to get a look at your foot, okay?"

She nodded, and I noticed the tears were sliding down her cheeks again. Tiffany held her breath, and we did, too, as Charles slipped off her sock. I winced when I saw how purple her whole foot was.

"Can-can I still run the marathon?" Tiffany whimpered.

Charles looked up at her again, his face sympathetic but firm. "No," he said. "Tiffy, you're going to be sidelined for the next two to three months, depending on any damage to the tendons. I'll take an X-ray at the hospital, but it looks like you've got broken second and third metatarsals."

Tiffany burst into tears, and Charles stood to hug his daughter.

I laid a hand on Brenda's arm. "Brenda, thank you so much for asking us in, but I really think it's best if we leave you to tend to your daughter."

She nodded, tears welling up in her own eyes. "You're right. I'll walk you out."

We turned and headed out the way we'd come, but at the front door Brenda said softly, "This is just one more terrible thing to happen this week."

That was when I remembered that Sunny had told me that Yelena had recommended Tiffany to her for babysitting, and that Yelena had been friends with Tiffany's parents. "Oh, Brenda, of course," I said. "I nearly forgot that you were friends with Yelena Galanis, correct?"

Brenda blinked in surprise and said, "Yes. We knew her well. It was such a shock to find out that she'd been murdered. I'm still reeling from the news."

"I totally understand," I said. "And you have my deepest sympathies."

"Did you know her too?" Brenda asked.

"No," I said, declining to mention that we'd been at the show the night of the murder. "We'd never met, unfortunately."

Brenda nodded, and then she opened her mouth to say something, seemed to think better of it, but then whispered, "Yelena was Tiffany's birth mother."

Next to me, I heard Gilley gasp, and I knew I'd sucked in my own breath in surprise.

"She was?" Gilley said.

Brenda put a finger to her lips. "Tiffany doesn't know. We'd planned on telling her this year, because she's known Yelena her whole life. It was part of the arrangement of the adoption, actually. Yelena promised never to tell Tiffany the truth. She said she'd leave it up to us to decide if that was appropriate, and while Tiffany was in Europe this summer, Charles and I made up our minds to tell her. Yelena was supposed to come over for dinner tonight so that we could all tell her together."

I bit my lip. "I'm so, so sorry," I said.

Brenda nodded, and her eyes welled again. Glancing over her shoulder, she said, "She's been training so hard for the past three years to get fast enough to run the marathon, and she was lucky enough this year to get a lottery number. I don't even know how she'll be able to deal with the hard stuff now that she can't run. It's her coping mechanism, and it was how she got through her senior year, during the lockdowns."

Gilley and I nodded, and I thought we both sensed that Brenda was confessing all this to a pair of strangers because it was easy to confess such things to people she didn't know. It was safer to say something personal to two people you'd likely never meet again.

"If we can be of any help to you or to her, would you let us know?" I asked, reaching into my purse to pull out a card. I handed it to Brenda, then squeezed her arm in sympathy and turned to go.

"You're a life coach?" I heard her say.

"I am," I said, glancing over my shoulder. "So . . . if you or Tiffany needs someone to talk to, please think of calling me, okay?"

Brenda nodded and offered us a small smile before waving goodbye.

When we were safely back in the car and on our way back home, Gilley said, "*That* was a twist I didn't see coming."

"Right?" I said. "That poor girl, though."

"Exactly," Gilley said. "She gets a ticket to the New York City Marathon and rolls her ankle six weeks before the race *and* will soon learn that her birth mother—whom she's known her whole life but didn't know was actually her mom—was murdered three nights ago."

"I do not envy the Blums," I said, thinking of Tiffany's poor parents and the task before them of comforting their daughter through three heartbreaks.

"Do you think they'll tell her?" Gilley said.

I eyed him in surprise. "Of course. Why wouldn't they?"

Gilley shrugged. "Would it be more painful for you to think that your birth mother was some stranger out there and was never named, or that she was a woman who'd been murdered the week before the confession could be made and you would've gotten the chance to form a whole new relationship with her?"

I frowned. "I see your point."

"I wonder if Sunny knew," Gilley said next.

Again, I glanced at him in surprise. "Gosh, I don't know, Gil. She didn't give any hint about it to me, but then, she could've been protecting Yelena's privacy."

"Sunny and Yelena . . . Their history as friends goes back to college, right?"

I nodded. "That's my understanding."

"How old do you think Tiffany is?"

"Twenty. Maybe twenty-one."

"The timing fits," Gilley said.

"It does," I admitted. "Still, what does it matter now?"

Gilley sighed. "I guess it doesn't."

"How did you stumble upon Tiffany, anyway?" I asked.

"I took Spooks for a walk all the way to Indian Wells Beach, and he had a great time splashing in the waves. On the way there, we passed Tiffany going in the opposite direction. I waved at her, but I don't think she remembered me, 'cause she just kept on truckin'." Gilley laughed. "Anyhoo, when we were about a quarter mile from home, we found Tiffany on the ground, near a big ole pothole. She'd fallen in, rolled her ankle, and couldn't walk."

"The poor thing! How long was she like that?"

"She said she was there only a few minutes, and nobody stopped to help her, which is simply unacceptable, but what're you gonna do?"

"Well, *you* stopped and helped."

"I did. She said she was doing a fifteen-mile loop

around East Hampton when she took a sip of water and didn't see the pothole."

"I don't know whether I'm more pained hearing that Tiffany fell into the pothole or that she was doing a fifteen-mile run!"

"My thoughts exactly. Runners are weird."

"Candice is a runner," I said, referring to my sister's best friend and business partner, whom Gilley knew well.

"Abby's Candice?"

I nodded.

"It figures. That woman is superhuman."

I laughed. Candice was a formidable woman in every respect. I had been a member of her posse once or twice and genuinely respected her, even if I didn't necessarily want to spend a lot of time with her, because she was pretty intimidating.

"Abby says Candice is running the Vermont One Hundred next year."

"What's the Vermont One Hundred?"

"One hundred miles, mostly uphill."

Gilley blanched. "My God, *why*?"

"No idea, but I agree with you. Runners *are* weird."

We both fell silent then, lost in our thoughts, and I continued to wind my way in the direction of Chez Cat.

Breaking the silence after an idea struck me, I said, "You know what, Gil?"

"What?"

"Well, I've been trying to figure out how we can learn more about Yelena's angry men, and I think I've come up with something clever."

"Do tell," Gilley said, turning to look at me expectantly.

"Well, you know how theater people love to gossip, right?"

"I do," Gilley said.

"I'm wondering if anyone at the theater might've overheard some gossip about the identities of some of Yelena's lovers."

Gilley's grin was slow to spread, but it was ear to ear when he finished thinking about my idea. "That is brilliant!" he said. "And we know that Shepherd isn't asking them about the other men, because he believes he's got the right man in jail."

"Exactly," I said. "It's bound to be an untapped resource for suspects."

Gilley pointed to the road ahead. "The theater's three minutes away. Shall we?"

"You want to go there now?"

"I don't think we have a moment to spare. If there's anyone left at the theater who worked on Yelena's show, they'll probably be nearly finished putting away the old set and getting ready for the new act, which most definitely would've been booked in a hurry."

"You think there's a new show there already?"

"If not already, imminently," Gilley said. "A theater can't make money off of empty seats, and I'm sure they would've booked a new act ASAP."

"That just seems so . . . cold," I said.

Gilley lowered his lids, stuck his nose in the air, and adopted a British accent. "It's the theater, dahling. The show must go on!"

* * *

We arrived at the theater just a few minutes later. I parked down the street, well away from the theater's entrance.

"We passed, like, six other parking spaces," Gilley remarked. "Why are we so far away?"

"I don't want Shepherd to see my car if he decides to come back and take another look at the scene of the crime," I confessed. "He'll be miffed at me if he knows we're sticking our noses into his case again."

Gilley chuckled. "I love how adorable you are when describing Shepherd's reaction to us snooping around." Using his fingers for air quotes, Gilley said, "'Miffed.' Ha! He'll be atomic."

"You're not making me feel better . . ."

"Nuclear!"

I glared at him.

"Apocalyptic!" And then he made a popping sound and mimed his head exploding.

"Will you stop!"

Gilley giggled. "I'll try. But they come so easily to me. Sometimes it's hard to hold back."

We got out and put some money in the meter, then headed toward the building. "I hope we can get inside," I said as we neared the entrance.

"We'll go around to the back," Gilley said. "Employees are always knocking on the back door to be let in. Just follow my lead."

I trailed behind Gilley as he led the way to the back of the building, and we were both surprised to find the backstage door propped open with a chair. Gilley gallantly stepped forward, pulled the door open wide, and bowed. "After you, m'lady."

"Why, thank you, kind sir," I said, stepping through the entryway into a darkened corridor. It took a moment for my eyes to adjust, and I felt, rather than saw, Gilley step in next to me, and then we both paused to get our bearings.

"This way," Gilley said, stepping over a bundle of electrical cords. I followed after him, lured by the sound of hammering.

We passed no one on our way toward the sound, but we could hear two men chatting away with each other about the Yankees.

As we rounded a cluttered corner of discarded theater odds and ends, I could see that we were entering back-stage right, and on the stage were two men in overalls—one guy on a ladder, one on the floor—working to take down Yelena's backdrop. They stopped abruptly when they spotted us.

"You can't be back here," the man on the floor said. His tone was sharp, and it rattled me. I paused on my way toward them.

Gilley, however, was unfazed. Smiling, with the air of authority, he said, "Forgive the interruption, gentlemen, but we're from the Sharp Group."

The two men stared blankly at him.

"The personal insurance agency for the theater," Gilley said, like they should've known. He then surprised me by producing a card from the inside of his blazer pocket and extended it out to the man holding the ladder, who made no move to walk toward us to retrieve it.

"You can't be back here," the guy repeated.

Gilley swiveled his head to regard me, folded his arms, and rolled his eyes. Turning to the two men again, he said, "As investigators into the pending lawsuit brought by Ms. Galanis's heirs, we in fact, *can* be back here."

They continued to stare blankly at him, but I did notice that their aggressiveness had migrated to surprise and a look of uncertainty.

Gilley pocketed his card and folded his hands in front of him, like he was preparing to give a speech. "Now, a few questions for the two of you," he said, stepping toward them. I followed. "Were you both here the night Ms. Galanis met her . . . ?"

Gilley's voice trailed off, and both men appeared confused.

"Death?" the guy on the ladder said.

"Unfortunate end," Gilley said, adopting a tight smile.

"We were," said the man on the floor. "We were onstage, behind the main curtain, changing out the backdrop for the second act."

"And prior to intermission?" Gilley pressed. "Where were you?"

The man on the ladder pointed to just behind where we were standing. "There," he said. "In the chairs."

I looked behind me and saw the two cane chairs side by side, with a small table set between them, and on the table was a deck of playing cards. That must've been how they passed the time during Yelena's act.

"Excellent," said Gil. "And your names are?"

"Gus Webster," said the first guy; then he pointed to his buddy on the ladder. "And that's Donny Cass."

Gilley nodded, then paused before asking them his next question to size the two gentlemen up.

Rather than simply standing there, looking stupid, I decided to assist Gilley with the ruse and dug into my purse for a small notebook that I used to make shopping lists and a pen. After extracting both, I flipped to a fresh page. "Gus Webster and Donny Cass," I said, scribbling their names in the notebook.

"Gus," Gilley said, with a nod toward the man. "And Donny."

They nodded back.

Gilley placed his hands behind his back and began to walk a few paces to and fro—à la Inspector Clouseau—while peppering the men with questions, such as, Did they see or hear anything suspicious the night of the murder? Did they notice anyone who didn't seem to belong backstage? Did they personally know Ms. Galanis? Did they see anyone come into the theater after the murder to snoop around, perhaps looking for discarded evidence?

The answer to all Gilley's questions was no, save the last question, which Gus answered, "Just you two and the police."

"I see," Gilley said, as if Gus's statement was telling.

Gilley then pointed toward the direction he and I had come from. "I noticed that the backstage door is propped open with a chair," he began, and for the first time the men's demeanor changed. They became noticeably nervous. "Is that a typical practice for you two here at the theater?"

Donny looked at Gus, his eyes wide and somewhat panicked. "The door sticks, and it's easier for us to get tools and supplies out of our trucks if the door's propped open."

"Ah," Gilley said, his tone disapproving. Pursing his lips, he said, "And was that door propped open the night of the . . ."

"Murder?" Donny asked in a squeaky voice.

"Unfortunate incident?" Gilley finished.

Donny backed his way down the ladder, then turned once he'd gotten to the floor, to look meaningfully at Gus.

Gus's lips flattened into a thin line. "I don't remember," he said.

"Of course you don't," Gilley said. "But here's the thing, Gus. If you're knowingly lying to me right now, and I catch you in it, then I'll name you as a codefendant in the lawsuit, and you'll be subject to the same penalties and damages that our agency will be."

Gus gulped.

Gilley continued. "Your pension, your savings, your retirement, your house, all those things could be in play."

Gus turned pale.

"Of course, as an employee, I'd like to protect you, Gus. But only if you come clean with me. On the night of the . . ."

"Unfortunate incident," the two men said in unison.

Gilley smiled sharply at them. "*Murder*, was that door propped open?"

"It may have been," Gus admitted. And I could see he was well and truly terrified of losing his life's savings to a fictional lawsuit.

Thinking Gilley might be being unnecessarily cruel, I stepped in. "Thank you for that admission, Gus. It's an important detail that we can try to mitigate by suggesting that you had no idea that Ms. Galanis could've been in danger from one of her lovers, correct?"

Gus shook his head vehemently. "No! I swear. I had no idea the lady had anybody wanting to hurt her."

"Me either," Donny was quick to point out.

I nodded and tapped Gilley on the shoulder. "I told you they were perfectly innocent of all liability, Simon."

Gilley grinned. I could tell he liked the fake name I'd given him. "You are right again, Felicity."

I smiled too. Felicity was such a pretty name.

"Still!" Gilley said, spinning to pace away from me again. "I'm troubled that they saw no one backstage at the time of the . . ."

"Unfortunate incident?" Donny tried.

"Murder?" Gus said.

"Violent homicide of Ms. Galanis," Gilley said. "How could someone simply sneak past the two of you if you were backstage during the entire first act?"

The men stared at Gilley, as if dumbstruck.

Gilley pointed behind us. "The corridor coming from the backstage door leads directly to here. If you two were sitting in the wings, waiting to assist with the set change for the second act, how could someone possibly slip past you?"

Donny also pointed to the area behind us. "Through the secret door," he said. "It's painted black to keep it hidden. You'd miss it if you didn't know it was there."

Both Gilley and I swiveled to look behind us.

"There's a hidden door back there?" I said, thumbing over my shoulder.

"Yep," Donny said. "It's just inside the backstage door. Like I said, you'd miss it if you don't know it's there."

"And where *exactly* does it lead?" Gilley asked.

"To the dressing rooms and the hallway behind the curtain leading to stage left," Gus explained.

"Huh," I said, looking back over my shoulder again. "I totally missed that."

"If it's just inside the door, then we definitely would

miss it," Gilley said. "Especially if we were coming in from outside. Remember? Our eyes needed to adjust to the change in light."

"But it was evening the night of the murder," I said softly, reminding Gilley of that one crucial detail.

"Which would've made the door all the harder to see," Gilley said, and I had to nod in agreement. He was absolutely right.

"Is that door ever locked?" I asked, just out of curiosity.

Gus nodded. "Sometimes, but never during a show."

"Is it locked now?" Gilley asked.

Gus turned red. "Uh, I don't think so."

Gilley nodded again. "Excellent. Gentlemen, we would like to thank you for your time. Please carry on with your work, and we'll be in touch should we need any further information from you."

With that, Gil turned on his heel, grabbed my elbow, and we walked away.

"I take it we're headed to the hidden backstage door?" I asked.

"Duh," Gil said, bringing out his phone.

I wondered why until we reached the door, which was indeed hard to see, and Gilley snapped several photos of it with his phone. He then tried the handle, and the door opened freely. With another gallant bow, he said, "Felicity?"

"Thank you, Simon," I said with a smile and walked through into the pitch dark. "I can't see a thing in here."

The area lit up quite suddenly with a bright light when Gilley switched on the flashlight of his phone. Upon locating the light switch to my right, he flicked it, and the hallway was illuminated.

It was a wide hallway, filled with framed playbills from previous shows and more backstage clutter.

We walked down the hallway without speaking, taking in the space, and stopped abruptly at a door with crime-scene tape across it and a placard in the shape of a star at eye level that read MS. GALANIS.

I stood back from the door and looked it up and down, and that was when I realized there were rust-colored droplets on the floor near the door. I stepped back quickly, pointing to them so Gilley could see. He made a face and also stepped back.

We both surveyed the floor—we couldn't help it—and the macabre scene unfolded as even more droplets dotted the wood planks on the floor in a gruesome series of polka dots. I followed their trail and was even more stunned to see that they weren't limited to the floor but had also stained the doorframe and the opposite wall, and then my gaze landed on the outline of a bloody handprint on the floor just beyond the door—as if Yelena had reached out for help beyond the opening but had died in the effort.

I put a hand up to cover my mouth, realizing for the first time how violent her death had been. "Good Lord," I whispered when I felt I could speak again.

Gilley's expression was equally horrified. "She must have been attacked just inside the door," he said, pointing to the arch of rusty drops.

"What a terrifyingly horrible way to die," I said.

The more I looked at the scene, the more convinced I was of one thing: Aaron Nassau did not murder Yelena Galanis. This was done by someone who was filled with rage—not heartbreak.

"Should we go in?" Gilley asked me.

"You're kidding, right?" I said, pointing to the crime-scene tape and the large sticker covering part of the door and the doorframe.

"There's no way they'd know we were the ones that broke in," Gilley said. He pointed to the ceiling covering us and the hallway. "No cameras."

I shook my head. "All Shepherd would have to do is ask Gus or Donny if we broke in, and they'd give us up in a heartbeat."

"You mean they'd give up Simon and Felicity," he said. "From the Sharp Insurance Group." Gilley reached inside his pocket and withdrew the card he'd offered Gus. It was his card from my office. He'd gambled that Gus wouldn't come forward to take the card from him, and it'd worked.

"Clever," I said. "However, me thinks Shepherd would tweeze out the truth in a hot second, so no. We are *not* breaking in. Besides, what would be worth seeing other than more grisly remnants of the crime scene?"

"Dunno. Which is why I say we should break in."

"No, Gilley," I said firmly.

With a sigh, he said, "Fine. But let's check out the rest of this backstage area."

I nodded and waved for him to proceed.

We moved away from Yelena's dressing-room door, then continued down the hallway past several more dressing rooms of various sizes. All were empty of anything but vanity tables and chairs.

At last, we came to the end and a tight corner, around which we could once again hear Gus and Donny, who were hammering away and continuing to talk about the Yankees' chances of winning a pennant this year.

Gilley peeked his head around the corner, then motioned for me to follow. I kept close to him as we rounded the corner and came into a large backstage left area. We were very much in shadow, so I wasn't worried that Gilley and I would be seen by Gus or Donny, but we were quiet as mice all the same.

After a cursory look around, I motioned to Gilley that we should head out, and he paused next to a small desk and a short stack of paper.

Let's go! I mouthed.

He nodded, took up the stack, and we were on our way.

We didn't speak until we had left the backstage area and Gilley had hit the light switch on his way out.

Once on the sidewalk and headed to the car, I pointed to the sheets of paper. "What's that?"

"Yelena's script," he said.

My brow shot up. "Her script?"

"Yep," Gilley said, breaking into a crocodile smile as he waved it at me. "And you know what it's filled with?"

"What?"

Gil bounced his brow. "Clues."

Chapter 11

"This is a gold mine," I said, flipping through the pages once we were home again, this time at Chez Cat, sitting at my kitchen island, sipping tea and perusing the script.

"I know, right?" he said. "Neither one of us got to see the second act, so from that standpoint alone, it's a treasure."

I read through the lines, which had felt so spontaneous coming from Yelena's lips, and marveled that she hadn't sounded rehearsed when she'd delivered all those zingers. It read exactly as it'd sounded, like a monologue—a train of thought, one lover following another through all twelve men.

"I'd really like to know who Lover Number Two is," I said.

"The legislator?"

"Yes. What we don't know is if he's a local rep or a national one."

"He'd be national. No way would Yelena date someone in the state legislature. And I'd put odds that it's a senator and not a congressman. She'd be after someone with stature."

I giggled with mirth and shook my head. "I doubt Yelena had an affair with Chuck Schumer."

"Who said it was a New York senator?" Gilley said. "*Lots* of politically powerful people have homes here in the Hamptons."

"Good point. Which widens up the field again."

"As if it weren't wide enough with eight unknown suspects," Gilley mused.

"Don't you mean nine? We only know of McAllen, Goldberg, and Leahy."

"I'm assuming Aaron is in this script somewhere," Gilley said with a sigh.

"Oh, that's right. We'll need to look for him in the script just to confirm though," I said.

After setting the script on the counter, I laid my hands flat on top of it. "We need to go through this page by page with a fine-tooth comb."

"Agreed," he said, tugging at the corners of the pages until I let him have them. He then turned several pages, stopped on one particular page, and turned it toward me. "Did you see that?"

I squinted at the page but couldn't see what had caught his attention. "What?"

Gilley tapped the bottom left corner. "See that note?"

I blinked. I'd missed it on my cursory look through the pages. "I can't make it out. Can you?"

Gilley turned the page back toward him and moved his

finger to the bottom paragraph, marked *Lover Number Eight*. "See that arrow?" he said.

I did see it. It was faded, because it'd been written in pencil, but I could make it out. "You think the note is in regard to Lover Number Eight?"

"I do," Gilley said. "Her handwriting is terrible, but I believe the note says, 'Call Gene,' and then I believe that's a dollar sign."

Gilley pointed to the squiggly symbol, and I nodded. "I think you're right. So do we both agree that Gene is very likely Lover Number Eight?"

"We do," Gilley said.

"And that she was calling him for money?"

"She was."

"Like, for what? Support? Or something more nefarious, like blackmail?"

"That thought had crossed my mind," Gilley said.

"So who's Gene?"

Gilley shrugged. Then his eyes lit up. "Hold on," he said, pulling out his phone and tapping at it madly.

I refilled both our cups with more tea, waiting him out.

At last, he exclaimed, "Yes!" and then he turned the phone to face me. "Gene Bosworth."

"Gene Bosworth," I repeated as I looked closely at the screen. Then I read aloud. "Gene Bosworth, of Southampton and Manhattan, real estate developer, philanthropist, and patron of the arts, passed away on Wednesday, December twelfth, from complications of COVID-nineteen. He is survived by his sister, Kennedy June Bosworth-Murdock, and his brother-in-law, Eric Murdock, and his two nephews, Tad and Theo."

I stopped reading and frowned at Gilley. "This can't be the same Gene, Gilley. He's dead. He died last year."

Gilley nodded but then flipped through the script to the page on which began Yelena's monologue about Lover Number Eight. Holding the script up, he began to read. "'Lover Number Eight has decided to permanently social distance himself from the rest of us—except, of course, for his dear, beloved sister, or as I like to call her, his one true love. It took me far too long to realize how much she and I look alike, and why he once called out her name in bed like a gasp for the caress of a summer's day.'"

"A bit poetic," I mused.

"No, Cat, don't you get it? 'Summer's day'?"

"Clearly, I don't," I said.

Gilley rolled his eyes. "His sister's middle name is *June*."

"Okay, that's a bit of a stretch."

As if challenged, Gilley went back to tapping at his phone again, and with a triumphant "Aha!" he turned it toward me.

I leaned in to stare at it and saw that he'd pulled up an image of a woman in the center of a group of people who bore a striking resemblance to Yelena. The caption under the photo read *Eric Murdock and his wife, June; Chris Fitzpatrick and his wife, Winnie; Bill O'Dowd; and Ritvik Patel at the Spring Fling Festival in Westchester.*

"She goes by June," Gilley said. Then he pointed to the script again and said, "'He once called out her name in bed like a gasp for the caress of a summer's day.' Yelena was speaking in code. She was referring to June."

"Ew," I said.

"Right?" Gilley agreed, making a face.

"But are we really sure, Gilley? I mean, couldn't that all be a coincidence? And why would Yelena write a note to call Gene about money if he died in December? It's September—nine months later."

"I don't know. But I definitely know I want to do a little more research in this direction."

I nodded. "We should absolutely explore that angle." Then I grabbed the script and said, "Come on, I've got a scanner upstairs in my office. We can scan this in and make a copy so that we can both study it for clues."

An hour later, Gilley and I were back at my kitchen counter, having both read our copies of the script. Setting mine down, I waited for Gilley to earmark a page before I asked, "Did anything speak to you about the identity of the other lovers?"

"Number Eleven is Aaron," Gilley said. "She said the word *count*, like, fifteen times."

It was a little less than that, but I smiled at him and added a nod. "Agreed."

I got up and went to the whiteboard I'd propped up near the sink, and I wrote in Aaron's name next to the number eleven that I'd written beforehand, when Gilley and I had first come downstairs and had decided to keep track of the lovers using my whiteboard.

"So," I said, pointing to the list. "We know that Lover Number One is Tucker McAllen, the real estate developer; Lover Number Four is Joel Goldberg, the jeweler; Lover Number Five is Liam Leahy, the vice admiral; Lover Number Eight is Gene Bosworth; and Lover Number Eleven is Aaron Nassau."

"Which leaves Lovers Number Two, Three, Six, Seven, Nine, Ten, and Twelve to identify."

"Right," I said, pacing in front of the whiteboard. "Should we tackle this one by one, starting with Lover Number Two?"

"I have no clue who he could be," Gilley said. "I did a cursory search of any members of Congress that live here in the Hamptons and could find only this guy." Gilley turned the screen of his phone toward me, and I gazed at the picture.

"Oh, yeah," I said. "I voted against him in the last election."

"Me too," Gilley admitted.

"Still, he's about the same age as Yelena," I said.

"He's also got four kids, ages three to thirteen, a gorgeous wife, and a place in Eastport."

"That's a bit of a hike."

"It is. Plus, Cat, if a guy like this stepped out with a woman like Yelena, it'd be gossip central. I just don't see it."

"What do you mean?"

"I mean, if he cheated on his wife and the mother of his four kids with Yelena, no way would she not hear about it."

I tapped my chin. "That's true."

"I'm gonna do some more digging, of course, see if I can't get a handle for the representative's schedule, to see if he was even in town the night of the murder, but my gut says this ain't our guy."

I sighed. "Okay, then we'll leave Lover Number Two blank for now. Let's move on to Lover Number Three."

"Three is curious," Gilley said, lifting up the script to flip to the section on Lover Number Three. Quoting from the page, he said, "'Lover Number Three is all about the clothes. He wears them like a mask, making you think he plays for one team, when he really plays for the other.'"

"Someone in the closet," I said, guessing.

Gilley set down the script and pursed his lips. "Maybe," he said, in a way that didn't convey that he was convinced of my conclusion. He lifted his phone and began to tap at it.

"What're you thinking?" I asked.

"Yelena's dress for the show was an absolutely gorgeous creation, no?" he said.

"Oh, my God, yes," I agreed. "Stunning. And she was flawless in it."

"Custom," Gilley said. "Right?"

"The way it fit her like a second skin? Had to be."

Gilley pivoted his phone around so that I could see. It was Yelena's Instagram page. "Like this number, right?"

The photo in question showed Yelena dressed in a burgundy, sparkling, floor-length pantsuit that flared widely at the bottom and had a slit from neck to navel, allowing her ample décolletage to practically spill out. The pants were tight and tapered, and the overall silhouette of the suit and the padding of the shoulders gave her a particularly powerful look. It was absolutely a tailor-made cut and fit.

"Indeed. They look like they definitely could've been designed by the same person," I said.

Gilley scrolled to the next photo. "And here," he said.

The photo showed Yelena dressed in a rose-colored gown that fit her shape like a glove. The photo was obviously taken during the pandemic, because she was wearing a face mask made of the same material as her dress, but it was studded with Swarovski crystals.

"Yes. Another custom outfit. And I love it on her."

Gilley nodded. "When her show started causing a stir, I began following Yelena on the gram, and I remember scrolling through these, loving her style. She wears a lot of Vivace."

"Vivace?"

"Antonio Vivace. He's starting to catch fire in the fashion world. Michel is a big fan, and he's been pushing Anna's team to feature some of Vivace's designs in *Vogue.*"

I smirked at the way Gilley casually dropped the name of Anna Wintour, like he was on a first-name basis with her. Though, to be fair, his husband likely was.

Gilley was silent for a moment as he continued to scroll through the photos, until he came up with what he seemed to be looking for. Turning his phone around to me again, he said, "That's him."

An impeccably dressed man with an olive complexion; a long face; big, brown, soulful eyes; and tendrils of silver hair pooling onto his shoulders stared out at me. He had the most sensual lips, set in a Mona Lisa smirk as he commanded the attention of the photographer. Meanwhile, three bare-chested male models were draping themselves over him, fawning in a way that suggested he was their *objet de désir*.

"You think he's who Yelena is referring to?" I asked Gilley.

"I do. The gown she wore for her act is obviously from him. He has a certain style that celebrates a voluptuous woman's curves that's hard to get right. You see Christian able to do it well, and maybe Zac, but the list of truly talented designers creating clothes for the Rubenesque crowd is appallingly small."

I resisted the urge to ask Gilley if he meant Christian Siriano and Zac Posen, because I knew it would only give him pleasure to say, "Duh. Who *else* would I be talking about, Cat?"

Instead, I directed the discussion back to the topic at hand by pointing to the script and saying, "So, Vivace is what . . . ? *Not* closeted and not even gay?"

Gilley shrugged. "Professionally, it would be to his advantage to be seen as someone on the LBGTQ spectrum, leaning heavily toward the G, but he could also be bi or pansexual. I've never met the man, so it's hard for me to tell."

"What other clues from the script fit?"

"Most of it," Gilley said, picking up the pages again. "I mean, if you understand that she's referring to Vivace, it makes sense. She calls him a silver-haired fox with a passion for women, wine, and walkways."

"She was a clever girl," I said.

"Indeed."

I turned and uncapped my marker. "Okay, I'll add him to the list, but we'll need to dig a little more into him as a possibility, because her clues are cryptic enough that we could be wrong."

"Agree, agree, agree," Gilley said.

"Okay, so let's look at Lovers Six and Seven and see if they offer up any clues," I said.

"Lover Seven *definitely* offers up some clues," Gilley said, and the expression on his face had me quite curious.

"What clues?"

In answer, Gilley began to read directly from the page. "'Lover Number Seven was made entirely of chocolate. Dark, bitter, gorgeous chocolate—'"

"He was black," I said, reading between the lines.

"That would be my guess," Gilley said; then he got

back to the script. "'Willing to sell his soul for a dollar, he'd stand up for any white collar. He didn't care if you were guilty, as long as you could pay.'"

I felt the color drain from my face. "An attorney."

Gilley held up a finger and continued to read. "'Generous in bed, certainly the second best of the lot, but unwilling to be seen putting caviar on a toast point of white bread.'"

"What does that mean?"

"I think it means that he didn't like to be seen in public with a white woman."

"Understandable," I said, feeling my defenses go up. I had a very niggling feeling that Yelena might be referring to someone I knew and cared about, and it worried me for every reason I could think of.

Gilley continued. "'When I got tired of his song and dance, I tossed him right back in the harbor.'"

"Oh, no," I said, as my suspicion was all but confirmed. "Are we both thinking the same thing?"

"Uh, that Marcus Brown fits every cryptic descriptor, including being tossed back in the 'harbor,' which is code for Sag Harbor?"

I nodded. It would explain why, when I'd called Marcus to beg him to represent Aaron, he'd been silent when I mentioned that Yelena had been murdered.

"Okay, so we're both thinking it's Marcus. Gilley, what do we do?"

"I think we need to call Marcus," he said.

I blanched. "And say what, exactly?"

"Oh, I dunno, Cat. Maybe start off by asking him how his day is going and then drift into asking him if he was the one who *murdered* Yelena Galanis?"

I made a face. "Or perhaps something more tactful."

Gilley set down the script. "I suddenly don't like this project."

With a sigh, I reached for my phone. In my heart of hearts, I didn't believe for a second that Marcus Brown had killed Yelena. But I thought it was important to ask him about her, given the fact that he was currently defending a man she had also dated, and was now accused of murdering her. To me, it was a gigantic conflict of interest, and something I was convinced would make Aaron quite vulnerable at trial.

"Catherine Cooper," Marcus said, picking up the line.

"Hello, Marcus," I said, trying to regulate my tone to something casual and breezy. "I've got you on speakerphone, and Gilley is also here."

"To what do I owe this pleasure?" he said amiably.

"Well . . ." I began collecting my thoughts hurriedly and was still unsure how I would proceed. "Gilley and I were considering helping you with the case against Aaron."

"You were, huh?" Marcus asked. "In what way?"

I cleared my throat and dived in. "This morning we took a little trip to the theater and discovered Yelena's discarded script. We've been going through it, attempting to identify the twelve angry men, you know, to give you a pool of suspects to help cast doubt upon the killer being Aaron."

"Nice," he said. "I'd like a copy of that when you get a moment."

"Of course," I told him. "While we were—"

"And I'd like to hear who you've identified when you get a decent number of names."

"Sure thing," I said. "We've made excellent progress so far."

"How many names do you have?"

"Including Aaron, we've got six," I said.

"Possibly seven," Gilley told him, eyeing me meaningfully.

"Let me guess, you got to Lover Number Seven and determined it was me?"

Gilley and I exchanged a look of surprise. "Uh . . . yes," I said.

"Is it you?" Gilley asked.

"It is," Marcus said. "I dated Yelena very briefly eighteen months ago. I thought we ended things amicably, but I might've been mistaken. I've heard through the vine that her portrait of me isn't exactly flattering."

My brow furrowed. How could he not see the problem here? "Marcus," I said, "why did you agree to represent Aaron when you're also featured in Yelena's act? Isn't that a *huge* conflict of interest?"

"No," Marcus said, without elaborating.

"Why not?" Gilley pressed.

"Because I didn't murder Yelena."

Gilley rolled his eyes and tossed up his hands. I couldn't have agreed more.

Marcus probably sensed our frustration and finally elaborated. "Listen, on the night that Yelena was murdered, I was at a poker game hosted by Judge Andrew Cordite—a New York Supreme Court justice. Also there were two other judges and a former attorney general. I was with those gentlemen all evening, from seven p.m. to two a.m., so I have about as airtight an alibi as you can ask for."

I felt my shoulders relax in relief.

But then Gilley said, "You could've paid someone to do it."

"Certainly," Marcus said. "But that could apply to any one of Yelena's lovers. Remember, she dated only the wealthy and powerful."

I shook my head, still a bit bothered by it all. "Marcus, Yelena calls you one of the angry men. If you had feelings for her, and in your investigation of this case against Aaron, you became convinced that he did it, wouldn't that compromise his defense?"

Marcus actually laughed. "Catherine, I didn't develop feelings for Yelena. She and I never had a romantic relationship of any kind. We were lovers. That was all. We didn't date, have dinner together, or spend quality time with one another on the weekends. We simply got together for a physical relationship about once every two weeks for two months or so. And while I'm saddened that she was murdered, since I broke things off with her, I honestly haven't given her another thought."

"Wait, *you* broke up with *her*?" Gilley asked. "That's not what the script says."

"I'm well aware that Yelena claims to have tossed me back in the harbor," Marcus chuckled. "I held no grudge against her for wanting to salvage her ego after our split."

I eyed Gilley in a way that silently asked him what he thought. He shrugged and nodded his head. I nodded mine too.

"Thank you, Marcus," I said. "We both appreciate your honesty. But maybe you should also come clean to Aaron. Just so that he's aware that his attorney had a prior relationship with the woman he was in love with."

"I've already done that, Catherine," Marcus assured me. "It was the first thing we talked about."

"And he was still willing to hire you?" Gilley asked.

"He was."

I said, "Okay, well, if it's good enough for Aaron, then I suppose it's good enough for—"

"Have you told Shepherd?" Gilley suddenly asked.

There was a pregnant pause on Marcus's end of the call, then, "No."

"Don't you think you should?" Gilley pressed.

Marcus sighed. "No," he said. "Not yet."

"Why?" I asked, thinking it could only help the situation if Marcus were completely forthcoming.

"Because if I can't arrange for sovereign immunity for Mr. Nassau, then I'll be using my brief affair with Yelena as a defense tactic. Mr. Nassau could hardly be considered the only suspect worth investigating if the police didn't even bother to question me—a person also featured in her act."

"Oh, that is clever," Gilley said.

"Thank you," Marcus said, with a hint of good humor. "And now I need to ask you two not to mention my relationship with Yelena to Shepherd, either."

"We won't," Gilley said quickly, but I didn't respond right away.

"Catherine?" Marcus asked.

"I'm here," I said.

Meanwhile, Gilley stared at me and mouthed, *What?*

"It's just . . . ," I began.

"Tell me," Marcus said.

"I don't want to lie to him, Marcus. We're in a committed relationship, and I feel like I'd be betraying him if I lied to him."

"I see," he said. "So you consider the act of omission a lie."

"No," I said, trying to clarify my own feelings as I spoke out loud. "But if he asked me if I knew anyone else who might've had a relationship with Yelena, I'd feel compelled to tell him."

"Well then," Marcus said, "let's hope he doesn't ask you."

"Yes," I said. "Let's."

Chapter 12

Gilley and I spent another hour going over the script, and we thought we identified two more possible names, beginning with Lover Number Six. There were multiple double entendres for football in his section of the script, and Gilley was able to cross-reference some of Yelena's social media posts to events attended by both her and an NFL legend, Brad Bosch, who had a house near Hook Pond, a stone's throw away to our west.

Bosch had played for the Giants from 1988 to 1999 and was now a featured commentator on ESPN. I'd seen him several times on the local news, discussing football with the station's sportscaster. Everything fit for a Brad/Yelena romance once we researched his background a bit.

And then we studied Lover Number Nine, in a weird coincidence, when we moved on from Brad to local news anchor Ike Chipperfield, from the very station where Brad would often make his appearances.

"She could've met Ike if she ever escorted Brad to the station for an interview," Gilley mused.

"Agreed. There's even this line, Gilley," I said, picking up the script to quote from it. "'Lover Number Nine and I were definitely behind the scenes, away from the camera and the jealous eyes of the quarterhack.'"

"'Quarterhack,'" Gilley said. "You know, I thought Yelena was deliciously clever, but now I'm wondering if she was really just cruel."

"The latter," I said.

Gilley eyed me suspiciously. "Did you really have a headache at intermission, or did you just not care to see Yelena's second act?"

"Yes," I said, winking at him.

Gilley chuckled, but then he sobered and eyed the whiteboard, where I'd just filled in Ike's name for Lover Number Nine. "What's interesting about all this is that we haven't drawn any obvious connections to the man who was murdered in the alley. . . . What was his name again?"

"Purdy," I said. "Mark Purdy."

Gilley's brow bounced. "Good memory."

"Thanks, but it's less skill than it is the fact that you're not likely to forget the name of a man you encountered minutes before he was murdered."

"I wonder if Shepherd's team has made any progress on that front."

I sighed wearily and came around to sit in the chair next to Gilley again. "I have no idea."

"Do we think he could've been one of the remaining lovers?" Gil said next.

I glanced at the whiteboard. "Well, there're only three names left, right? Lovers Two, Ten, and Twelve."

"Two is the legislator," Gilley said.

"Yes, so Purdy's out as a candidate for Lover Number Two. No history of running for office that we could find."

Gilley nodded and held up his script to read. "'Lover Number Ten treated life like a racetrack, circling the field and going nowhere fast.'"

"Does that describe a retired estate lawyer?" I asked.

"Nope. That describes a race-car driver."

I snapped my fingers. "Yes, Gilley! That's *exactly* who that would describe. Are there any local race-car drivers around these parts?"

"No one comes to mind. I'll do some research later."

"Good," I said. "But back to Mr. Purdy. That leaves only Lover Number Twelve as a possibility."

Gilley flipped a few pages and again read from the script. "'Lover Number Twelve, you know who you are. The best of the Lovers. You had my number from the beginning, and you never failed to call. You're the son of a queen, a dreamer. A wisher. A maker of promises. But all your wishes are empty, all your promises lies, and you sit in your castle and look down your nose, and who are you really? Just another pretty face with a well-practiced line.'"

"Ouch," I said.

"She gets even meaner," Gilley said, making a face while he flipped through the last three pages. "She calls him a commitment-phobe and a lazy playboy."

"Well, she was mean about Marcus after he dumped her. Maybe Lover Number Twelve also dumped her."

"That'd be tough on someone like Yelena. Getting dumped by the two best lovers she's ever had," Gil said.

"Yeah. Which also means that Number Twelve definitely isn't Purdy."

"Why do you say that?" he asked me.

"I would've put Purdy in his late sixties to early seventies. And he was frail in stature and likely four inches shorter than Yelena. I doubt he could've kept up with her on a walk, much less between the sheets."

"In other words, we can assume that Purdy doesn't connect to Yelena's act."

"Not that I can see. Assuming all our guesses are correct, of course," I said.

Gilley frowned. "Which means both his appearance in the coffee shop and his murder in the alley weren't related to her."

I stared at the whiteboard without replying to Gilley for a long moment. "I'd agree if it weren't for two things that don't make sense."

"And they are?"

"The blood on his hand before he was murdered, and the size ten ladies' raincoat."

. Gilley's eyes widened. "Yelena was probably a size ten," he said.

"That's what I was thinking. The coat was far too big for Purdy. He stumbled on the hem when he entered the coffee shop."

"Maybe he needed the extra length to fit in all the money," Gilley said.

I considered that but then said, "How thick would a stack of two thousand bills be?"

"That's right," Gilley said. "Shepherd said the two hundred thousand in cash on Purdy was all in hundred-dollar bills." After picking up his phone, he tapped at it and said, "A thousand one-dollar bills measures four-point-three inches high."

"Roughly eight-point-six inches of bills to pack into the lining of a raincoat," I said.

"Yep," Gilley said, tapping again at his phone. "A woman's raincoat is roughly one-point-eight meters of fabric."

I got a measuring tape from the drawer in my kitchen where I kept various odds and ends. Measuring it out on the counter, I said, "Even with stacks a half inch thick, he would've had plenty of room with a coat half that size."

"So, he didn't need an oversized coat," Gil concluded.

I stood back and rewound the measuring tape. "No."

"Then why was he wearing it?"

"Maybe so Yelena could walk out of the theater without drawing attention to herself while carrying a suspicious looking duffel bag stuffed with money—assuming the money in the lining of the raincoat was for her, of course."

Gilley eyed me intently before he nodded. "Do we think Purdy actually killed Yelena?"

I shook my head. "You saw all that blood on the floor backstage, Gilley. Whoever murdered her would've been covered in blood. Only Purdy's hand was smeared with it."

"Could he have been a witness?" Gilley asked next.

I pressed my lips together, thinking that through. Finally, I nodded. "If he walked in while Yelena was being murdered, he could've fled the scene in a panic, which would explain the fear I saw in his eyes when he entered the coffee shop. He might've known or assumed that the killer was in pursuit, and probably thought he was safe sneaking out the back."

"But he wasn't," Gilley said. "And if the killer was

covered in blood, he couldn't have entered the coffee shop to go after Purdy without a bunch of witnesses seeing him."

"But he could've entered a darkened alley and waited for Purdy to take the side street to the parking garage, only to watch him appear in the alley itself."

"Why didn't Purdy call for help, though, if he witnessed the murder?" Gilley asked.

"He didn't have his phone on him, remember? He left it in the car," I said.

"But why didn't he ask to use the coffee shop's phone? Or even your phone, for that matter, when he bumped into your table?"

"If he was carrying two hundred thousand dollars on his person, meant for the murder victim, and his hand was smeared with her blood, I doubt he would've wanted to call attention to himself by playing the role of witness."

"Good point. Especially if he was still a licensed lawyer. Paying off someone blackmailing you probably wouldn't sit too well with the New York licensing board."

"So, what did Yelena have on Purdy?" I asked.

"Don't know," Gilley said, once again eyeing the whiteboard. Then he pointed and said, "Hold on. What about Lover Number Eight?"

I eyed the board myself. "Gene Bosworth?"

"Yeah. Remember? The note in the script said to call Gene for money."

"You're thinking Purdy handled Gene's estate, right?"

"I am."

"It'd be good to know that for certain and be able to put that puzzle piece in its place."

"You could call Shepherd and ask him to look into it," Gil suggested.

I cocked an eyebrow at him. "You're joking, right?"

"Yeah, I knew it was a no-go the second it was out of my mouth."

I snapped my fingers. "But you know who might be able to access that information and who would actually appreciate our super sleuthing?"

Gilley grinned. "Marcus Brown."

"Exactly. If court papers for Gene's estate were filed, Marcus could call up the county clerk and get that information easily."

Gilley waved at my phone on the counter. "What're you waiting for? Call him!"

I did just that, but instead of telling Marcus all about our theory over the phone, I set up a meeting for the three of us for the end of the day.

"And I'll be bringing a whiteboard," I told him.

"A whiteboard?" he said. "I have one here, Catherine. You can use mine."

"No, mine has a list of names on it that I think you'd be interested in, Marcus."

There was a pause, then, "In that case, by all means, bring the whiteboard."

An hour and a half later, I had changed into a pair of black skinny jeans, black Louboutin pumps, a matching Chanel sleeveless turtleneck and had topped the entire ensemble off with a pair of chic Oliver Peoples square-rimmed sunglasses.

When I breezed through the door of Chez Kitty to collect Gilley, he waved his hand up and down in my general direction and said, "Ooh, Catwoman. I like it."

I grinned. "I love that you get me."

Gilley then looked down at himself and said, "I'll change. Be with you in a jiff."

"Hurry," I called as he dashed down the hallway toward the bedroom. "We're supposed to be there in thirty minutes."

A mere four minutes later, Gilley emerged wearing tight-fitting black jeans and an equally tight-fitting T-shirt with a logo that read BAD TO THE BONE. Completing the ensemble, he wore a studded leather bracelet on his left wrist and a big gold ring on his right hand.

"Biker?" I asked.

"Badass," he countered.

I nodded approvingly. "It works. Let's roll."

I donned my sunglasses, he put on a pair of aviators, and we were off to the races.

Luck was with us as far as traffic was concerned, and we arrived at Marcus's office building right on time. The structure was interesting, made up of three stories of bright white brick standing starkly against the dull brown buildings surrounding it. Part of the first floor wasn't actually a floor, but a parking area for tenants and visitors. A set of large pylons supported the second and third floors above, giving the parking area shelter from the elements.

We parked in one of only two available spots and headed toward the main entrance. Coming through the doorway, we were greeted by a security guard.

"Who are you here to see?" he asked.

"Marcus Brown," I said.

"Names?"

Gilley and I exchanged a look. The guard held no clipboard or anything to refer to, so I wondered how he'd know we had an appointment.

"Catherine Cooper and Gilley Gillespie," Gilley said.

The guard spoke into the mic at his shoulder. "Cooper and Gillespie here to see Mr. Brown."

There was a pause, then a garbled reply that sounded like "Granted."

The guard stepped to the side and pointed to the elevator. "Third floor. Suite three-oh-two."

We nodded our thanks and proceeded to the elevator, which opened before we'd even had a chance to hit the button. What was even weirder was that when we got in the car, the button for the third floor lit up all on its own.

"That's creepy," I whispered to Gilley.

He nudged my shoulder and pointed toward the upper right corner of the elevator. A camera was aimed down in our direction. "Someone's watching us closely."

We got off the elevator and proceeded to the suite marked 302. The door had a unique design compared to the others lining the corridor—made of black walnut that had been shined and polished to really show off the beauty of the wood, it was broader than the other doors and probably quite a bit thicker.

Gilley began to reach for the latch, but the door opened on its own, swinging inward slowly so that we could enter.

After crossing the threshold, we came into a bright white room with an edgy abstract sculpture, which I thought might be a representation of Lady Liberty. She sat on the far wall, directly opposite the door, in the mid-size lobby that we found ourselves in. The area was decorated with overstuffed gray couches and a few Eames side tables, but otherwise the place was fairly minimalist.

I looked around but didn't see a receptionist, or a receptionist's desk, for that matter. However, as Gilley and

I exchanged *Now what?* glances, a door opened to the right of us, and a woman dressed in charcoal-gray silk stepped forward, extending her hand.

"Ms. Cooper," she said smoothly, shaking my hand, before turning to Gilley and greeting him by name as well. "I'm Jasmine Taylor, Mr. Brown's paralegal. May I ask if you'd like a cappuccino or an espresso before I take you back to meet with him?"

Gilley turned to me. "Okay. I'm impressed."

I couldn't help but grin. "Two cappuccinos would be lovely," I said, speaking for the pair of us.

"Perfect," she said. "This way, please."

She led us through the door and down a hallway with two office suites off to the side. Two hard-at-work people—one woman, one man—sat at the desks within, hovered over their laptops, and didn't even look up as we passed.

At the end of the hall was a closed door, and we could hear Marcus's voice from inside. It sounded like he was wrapping up a call.

Jasmine knocked softly. There was a pause; then Marcus called out, "Come in, Jaz."

She opened the door as Marcus was saying his goodbyes. He pocketed his phone and stepped forward to greet us. "Catherine," he said, smiling wide and taking my hand.

It always gave me a little thrill when Marcus radiated warmth at me. He was a gorgeous man, powerful, in that he exuded confidence. He was someone I always hoped to have on my side.

"Marcus," I replied just as warmly, feeling a small blush touch my cheeks. I'd never, ever tell Shepherd this, but I had a tiny crush on Marcus.

As Marcus and I basked in the glow of each other's company, Gilley shoved his hand into the mix and practically shouted, "Hi, Marcus!"

Gilley's crush on the counselor *might* be a teensy bit bigger than mine.

"Gilley," Marcus said with a chuckle. Then he looked from me to Gilley and back again. "Are you both coordinating your outfits again?"

"We are, and aren't you a dream for noticing," Gilley said, swishing his hips and looking coyly at Marcus.

Marcus chuckled again and waved us over to his desk and the two chairs in front of it. "Come, sit, and tell me about this whiteboard, which, I see, you didn't bring."

"I took a picture," I told him, holding up my phone. "It was easier to get in the car."

Marcus grinned. "Excellent. Mind texting it to me?"

I did just that, and he opened the text to survey the board. "You two *have* been hard at work," he said, and I could tell he was impressed. Gilley looked over at me and bounced his eyebrows.

While Marcus reviewed the names on the list we'd compiled, I took in his office, and I found it interesting that there were no shades of gray to soften the stark contrast of the bright white walls and the dark wood tones of the furnishings.

I'd once read that the law wasn't written in black or white, but in subtle shades of gray. I thought it telling that Marcus largely surrounded himself with back-and-white tones. His view of the world seemed more pronounced and assured in that regard. Either something was right or it was wrong, and his confident assurance in one or the other no doubt helped juries to decide in his favor more often than they didn't.

Marcus set his phone down and eyed us with interest. "This list is very helpful. Thank you," he said. "How sure are you about the names on the list?"

"For most of them, we're probably eighty-five to ninety-five percent certain," I said.

Marcus nodded. "And which names are you unsure about?"

"Mark Purdy," I said.

Marcus's brow furrowed, and he picked up his phone again to glance at the list. "I don't see his name here. Which one is he? Two, Ten, or Twelve?"

"None of them," Gilley said. "Which is another reason we're here."

Marcus set his phone down. "Enlighten me."

Between us, we filled Marcus in on what we knew about Mark Purdy, including the backstory of my encounter with him on the night of Yelena's murder.

Marcus waited patiently throughout the explanation, and he didn't interrupt us once. When we finished, he said, "I heard there was a murder in the area near the theater, but I hadn't yet learned that it was timed so soon after Yelena's."

"We think there's a connection," I reiterated.

"Yes," he said. "I'm thinking there must be, especially in light of the women's size-ten coat."

"We think Purdy was paying off Yelena," I said.

"For whom?"

"For Gene Bosworth. Or rather for his estate."

"You said Purdy was an estate attorney, yes?" Marcus said, pulling up the lid to his laptop to type on it while we answered.

"Yes," Gilley said. "We think he handled the estate of Gene Bosworth." Gilley then produced his copy of the script—the original—and handed it over to Marcus. "On page twenty-eight there's a handwritten note in the bottom left corner, where Yelena wrote, 'Call Gene,' and then the dollar sign."

"Since Gene Bosworth died last December," I said, "we think Yelena wasn't saying to call Gene so much as she was reminding herself to call the trustee of Gene's estate to ask for money."

Marcus set down the script and pursed his lips in thought, and then he swiveled to type on his laptop for a few moments, before his eyes darted back and forth as he read the screen. "Purdy retired right before the pandemic got bad," he said.

I nodded. "That makes sense."

Marcus picked up his phone and hit a button. "Jaz, I know it's late, but if you call right away, you can catch the clerk's office. I need you to find out who the attorney of record was on a Mr. Gene Bosworth's estate. Good. Thank you."

"Yelena indicated in her script that she suspected Gene had the hots for his sister," I said.

Marcus's eyes went wide. "Really?"

"Yes, really," Gilley said.

Marcus again picked up the script and flipped through the pages. He stopped when he got to Lover Number Eight and read the lines while we waited. His phone buzzed, and he picked up the receiver. "Yes?" he said. Then, after a moment, he added, "You're sure?" Another moment passed, and he finished with, "All right. Thank you. I'll have a research project for you tomorrow regarding Mr. Purdy, so see me first thing when you get in, okay? Good. Good night, Jaz."

When Marcus hung up the phone again, Gilley said, "It was Purdy, wasn't it?"

"No," Marcus said.

"*No?*" Gilley and I repeated in unison.

"It was Albert Finch."

"Who's Albert Finch?" Gilley asked.

Marcus shrugged. "I'm not familiar with many estate attorneys. You don't run into them in the criminal defense law circles."

"Ah," Gil said. And then he muttered, "I really thought we were onto something there."

"You may be," Marcus said. "I'll have Jasmine check around and see who Purdy's clients were. Maybe there's another name on the list that he's attached to."

Gilley and I both perked up. "Ooh, yes," I said. "That must be it. If Yelena was looking for cash from Gene, she probably was looking for cash from at least one or two others, right?"

"She was," Marcus said, in a way that suggested there was more to the story.

"Did she try to extort you?" Gilley asked.

"She did," he said. "Not overtly, but she did call me and suggest that she was launching her one-woman show, and if I wanted to remain anonymous, I might want to think about making a charitable donation."

"Whoa," I said. "What did you say?"

"I told her that extortion was a crime punishable by up to twenty years in prison, and she hung up. I had hoped that I'd scared her off the tactic, but obviously, I hadn't."

"We should talk to the other names on the list and see if she tried that trick with them," I said.

"How?" Gilley asked me. "Do we just call them up

and say, 'Hey there! Your ex-girlfriend was brutally murdered. She wasn't by chance trying to extort money from you, was she, Suspect . . . I mean Lover Number Five?'"

Marcus chuckled. "No, we'll have to be more subtle than that."

Gilley snapped his fingers. "I know!" he said. Turning to me, he said, "Cat, what if we threw a party and invited all these guys, and once they've had a chance to imbibe a little truth serum, we ask them about Yelena?"

"Truth serum?" I asked.

"Vodka."

"Ahhh," I said. "You know, that's actually not a bad idea. The problem is, how do we get them to show up? I don't know any of them, and they'd likely decline an invite to a random stranger's party."

Gilley frowned. He'd thought he was really onto something.

"What you need is a lure," Marcus said.

We both looked at him. "A lure?" I said.

"A party honoree," he said. "Someone well known, with status."

"Like a celebrity? We don't know any celebrities," Gilley said.

Marcus shook his head. "Gilley, here in the Hamptons, celebrities are a dime a dozen. What you need is somebody rich." Pointing his finger back and forth between us, he said, "Who's the wealthiest person you know?"

"Catherine Cooper," Gilley said immediately.

I blushed and laughed. "Oh, Gilley, I am not."

"Uh, yeah you are," he insisted.

Marcus wore an amused smile on his face, and I felt my blush deepen.

"What about the Entwistles?" I said.

"Oh," Gil said. "Yeah. I forgot about them. They're definitely richer than you."

I laughed lightly and looked again at Marcus, but his amusement had turned to seriousness. "You know the Entwistles?" he said.

"Yes," Gilley and I both said in unison.

"*Julia* Entwistle?" Marcus stressed.

"Yes. And her grandson Willem," I said.

Marcus sat back in his chair and held his hands up in surrender. "Catherine, Gilley, if you could make either of them your honoree, you'd have one of the hottest tickets in town."

"Really?" I said, looking at Gilley to see what he thought. He seemed as surprised as I was. "I mean, we've been to their home, and we know they must be very comfortable, but neither of them socializes very much, Marcus. How could they be so attractive to our guests?"

"Julia Entwistle is one of the wealthiest women on Long Island, Catherine. Her money and pedigree go way back. She's blue blood, and nothing brings out the ever-social-climbing Hamptons crowd like a billionaire blue blood in attendance at a social gathering. Plus, you're right. Julia hasn't been to a social event in a decade. If you could score her appearance at your gathering, you'd get all your suspects to accept in a hot second."

I frowned. The last time I'd seen Julia she'd been bound to a wheelchair, and she'd looked quite frail. I didn't want to do anything to put stress on her. "Would Willem Entwistle be an equally appealing draw?"

"He might," Marcus said. "He stands to inherit everything, I assume, so that's a definite plus in his favor, but his influence over some of the more powerful players here in the Hamptons is far less than that of his legendary grandmother."

"How do you know all this about the Entwistles?" Gilley asked.

Marcus grinned. "It's my business to know who's who around here, Gilley. Defending big names takes big money, and I like that about practicing law in the Hamptons."

"Would you also be looking to score an introduction?" Gilley said.

Marcus's grin widened. "I wouldn't ever say no to meeting the legendary Julia Entwistle. Or her grandson."

"We'll make sure you get an invite," Gilley promised.

"Excellent," he said. "What else do you need from me?"

I raised my hand slightly and said, "Did Yelena try to extort Aaron?"

"He says she didn't," Marcus confessed.

"Why don't you look like you believe him?" I asked, reading Marcus's expression.

"Because I don't."

"He'd lie to you?" Gilley asked.

"He's still in love with her ghost," Marcus said. "He's trying to protect her."

"The poor man," I said. "How's he doing overall?"

"Not great. The odds for sovereign immunity in this case are long, and my colleague at the Danish embassy says it doesn't look good."

"When will you know?" I asked.

"Within a few days."

"What can we do for him?" I asked next.

Marcus waved his hand casually in our direction. "You're doing it. You've given me a list of eight other suspects to focus on, and you're going to throw a party where we can casually question at least a few of them. This will really help his defense."

"And don't forget about the Purdy angle," Gilley said. "If Purdy was delivering a payoff to Yelena, and if we can prove that, then that's motive pointing to one of these other guys for sure, right?"

"It is," Marcus said. "I'll know more in the next day or two about him and his client list, and I'll call you with any updates."

"Perfect," I said, getting to my feet. Extending my elbow out to Gilley, I said, "Come along, Mr. Gillespie. We have a party to plan."

Gilley bounced to his feet and looped his arm through mine. "Marcus," he said, dipping his chin demurely. "Always a pleasure."

Marcus grinned. "It is, isn't it?"

Gilley laughed, and with a wave goodbye, we left to head home.

Chapter 13

The first thing we did when we arrived back at Chez Kitty was to order dinner and feed Spooks. The dog always gulped down his food like he was afraid someone else would steal it.

"The poor thing," I said, watching him eat.

"I know," Gilley said. "He eats every meal like it's going to be his last. I read in one of the pamphlets they sent home with us that dogs who've experienced intense abuse and hunger can act like that. I'm hoping that with time and regular meals, he'll realize that he'll always get enough to eat here. Oh, and I've got to order one of those special bowls that forces him to slow down, because eating that fast isn't good for him."

"You didn't already buy it at the Pet Palace?" I said, giving his shoulder a playful knock with my own.

"That was the only thing I didn't buy."

Gilley's phone rang, and he took it out to read the display. After declining the call, he stuffed the phone back into his pocket and cleared his throat. "Spam," he said, avoiding my gaze.

"You'll have to talk to your husband sometime, lovey," I said.

"I know," he sighed. "But I just can't right now, Cat."

"Does he know that you're this worked up over the prospect of a talk?"

"I keep sending his calls to voice mail, so I'm thinking yes."

I sighed. "Okay. It's your marriage."

Gilley bent low to hug Spooks, who had finished his meal and had come over to thank Gilley for it. I watched the two of them play tug until Sebastian let me know that our dinners had been delivered and were waiting on the front steps to Chez Cat.

"Here or there?" I asked Gilley.

"Here or there what?" Gil replied, pulling hard on the other end of a braided rope, which Spooks was inching out of Gilley's hands.

"Where would you like to eat?"

"Oh, um, here is fine," Gil said. "Less to move," he added, indicating the dog bed by the couch.

"I don't know why you think we'd need to move that just to bring Spooks over. He never uses it."

"Yes, but I want him to," Gilley said.

"Do you?" I asked. I suspected that Spooks was cuddled up to Gilley at night on the bed, and I imagined that my dear friend rather liked being cuddled on the couch too.

Gilley waggled his fingers at me. "Shoo, fly. Shoo! And bring us back some dinner."

We ate our meal over talk of the party. By the end we had a wonderful idea to create a sort of *Dancing with the Stars* theme, as I really wanted to have the affair outside if the weather would cooperate.

"This weather pattern is supposed to hold for the next ten days," Gilley said, checking his phone.

"That's encouraging," I said. "Do you think next weekend is pushing it a little fast?"

"Not really," he said. "But first, you need to see when and if Willem can make it."

"Ach," I said, getting up to retrieve my purse, where I kept my phone. "I'd completely forgotten that we needed to reach out to him."

After placing the call, I waited several rings until a rather hoarse voice answered. "Catherine?"

"Willem!" I said. "Hello, my friend! How are you?"

"This is a nice surprise. I'm well, and you?"

"I'm very well. Thank you. But you don't sound well. Are you coming down with a cold?"

Willem chuckled. "No, nothing like that. You just woke me, that's all."

I looked at the clock. It was ten past eight. "I'm so sorry," I said. "I didn't realize you went to bed so early, otherwise I never would've disturbed you."

"I actually went to bed late, and you're calling early. Chanel and I are in Thailand."

"Thailand?"

"He's in Thailand?" Gilley asked, scooting his chair close so that he could hear more of the conversation.

"Yes," Willem chuckled. "We eloped!"

I gasped and stared with wide eyes at Gilley.

"What? What?" Gilley said.

"Willem and Chanel eloped!"

"Ohmigod!" Gilley squealed and grabbed the phone right out of my hands. "Willem! Congratulations! This is such amazing news!"

I pulled the phone out of his hands and laid it on the table, then pressed the speaker function.

Willem was in the middle of an explanation, it seemed. "Planned on coming here for vacation, and we had a layover in Vegas, of all places, and when we were there, I just kind of stood on my tiptoes and popped the question."

Gilley and I let out a peal of laughter. Willem was a little person, and he thought nothing of making light of his dwarfism. His new bride was a former model. She was tall and lithe and completely smitten with Willem. They made an adorable couple.

"What did your grandmother say?" I asked him. Julia Entwistle couldn't have been happy to hear the news that her grandson hadn't invited her to his wedding.

"She's fine. She's throwing us a reception when we get home," Willem said. "I'm sure you two will be getting your invites soon."

That reminded me about the reason for my call. "When will that be?"

"The reception?"

"Yes, but more importantly, your return home?"

"Save the date of October twenty-third, if you can," Willem said. "And we'll be home on the tenth."

Since it was well past September tenth, I took that to mean he wouldn't be home for another three weeks. After hitting the MUTE button, I quickly asked Gilley, "Should we wait?"

"For what? For them to get home and attend our party

before attending their reception, all in the span of a week?"

I frowned.

"Guys?" Willem said. "You there?"

"Sorry, Willem. I didn't realize I accidentally touched the MUTE button," I said. "I'm so thrilled and happy for both of you, and we will definitely be attending your reception."

"Awesome," Willem said. "But was there something else? You guys called me. What's up?"

Gilley and I shrugged at each other, and then Gilley made the executive decision and said, "We were calling to invite you to a party, because we needed your help."

"My help? Help with what?"

"Cat and I are up to our old tricks," Gilley said, then added a laugh, like investigating a murder was such fun!

"Are you messing with the mob again?" Willem sounded worried.

"No," I was quick to say. "But we are attempting to help another client of mine, who seems to have gotten himself into some trouble."

I then took several minutes to explain everything to Willem. He was silent for a moment after I finished. "I think my aunt knows the count," he said.

"She does?" I said, surprised, but then not.

"Yeah. I think they've even had dinner together once or twice. My great-grandmother was Danish, and if memory serves me, Grams would be a distant cousin of Aaron's through her mother's family."

"Wow," I said. Even Gilley seemed impressed.

"Have you called her yet?" Willem said next.

"No," I admitted. "I'm hesitant to get her involved. She seemed so frail the last time we saw her."

"What's it been? Like, a year?" Willem asked.

"A year and a half," I said.

"Well, you should see her now, Catherine. She's a whole new woman. She started the RBG workout routine right after my curse was broken, and she's found herself a personal trainer, who comes to the house four days a week, and she's even ditched the wheelchair and walks three miles a day on a treadmill."

"You're kidding," Gilley said.

"No, I'm serious. She's a new woman."

"That's amazing! I'm so relieved to hear she's doing so well," I said.

"You should call her and tell her what you're up to," Willem insisted. "She'd want to help. And throwing a party in her honor would really make her happy. Every time we talk, she keeps complaining about how bored she is."

"You really think she'd come?" I asked.

"I do," he said. "And you could even throw it in honor of her eighty-fourth birthday, which is at the end of this month. Chanel and I never would've skipped out on her birthday, but Gram bought the trip for us as a surprise and she insisted we go, so we couldn't say no."

"Ooh, I would *love* to put together a birthday celebration for your grandmother!" Gilley said, clapping his hands rapidly together.

"You'd actually be doing me a favor," Willem said. "I was starting to feel guilty about being separated from her on the thirtieth, and the only thing I could think of to do was to send her a personal chef to cook her favorite meal, but if you two want to throw the party, I'd like to insist on paying for it."

"Done," Gilley said before I could politely decline. "What's the budget?"

I stared at him in disbelief. Was he crazy? We would be using Julia as a means to an end, and because of that, we owed it to her to pay for her party.

"Start at fifty, but if you have to go up, do it. And save the receipts. I'll reimburse you as soon as I'm home."

My eyes were blinking so fast while my mind tried to take in the quick exchange between Gilley and Willem that I forgot to even protest. And before I knew it, Gilley was saying, "Perfect. I'll keep you apprised of our progress. Shoot me your grandmama's deets and we'll reach out ASAP!"

"Great. Bye, Gilley! Bye, Catherine!"

"Will—" I began, but Gilley cut me off.

"Bye, Willem! Give Chanel a kiss from us!" And with that, Gilley hit the END button and swiveled in his chair to look at me with glee.

"Why would you agree to that?" I demanded.

"What? Allow him pay for the party?"

"Yes!"

"Because I know how it feels to be away from your mom on her special day, and how you wish someone close by could make her feel special, because you can't."

I softened immediately. "When was your mom's birthday?"

"The first of April. We didn't get our second dose of vaccine until April fifth, so I couldn't go to Savannah, and I felt guilty and sad about it all day."

"Why didn't you tell me?"

"Because that was the day Shepherd surprised you with flowers and a candlelight dinner, and you were so happy. I didn't want to bring you down."

I rubbed his arm. "Oh, Gil. I'm so sorry. We'll fly to

Savannah next year to surprise her on her birthday, okay?"

"Yeah?" he said hopefully.

"Absolutely," I vowed. "Now, let's call Julia and see if we can't arrange to make her birthday memorable."

We called the number Willem had sent Gilley in a text, but Julia didn't pick up, so Gilley left her a sweet voice mail. "She's probably gone to bed," Gil said, eyeing the clock. "It's just about nine o'clock."

I got up and stretched. "Okay, then," I said. "I'm headed home. I'm exhausted too."

"Lightweight," Gilley giggled.

I stuck my tongue out at him but couldn't keep down a little chuckle myself. "Good night, Gilley," I sang.

"Good night, Cat."

Spooks got up when I opened the door, and came trotting over to me. I bent to hug him and nearly asked Gilley if I could take him to Chez Cat for the night, but I knew Gilley needed Spooks's company more than I did.

"Take care of him, okay?" I whispered to the pup.

He gave me a kiss on the cheek, and I left to head to bed.

The next morning, when I entered Chez Kitty, Gilley was saying goodbye to someone on the phone. I waited for him to hang up before I asked who it was, although I was secretly hoping it was Michel and they'd worked things out.

"Perfect," he said, sounding happy. "Okay, love, I'll give you a call in the next couple of days, okay? Wonderful. Bye now." Gilley blew a kiss into the phone before hanging up, and my heart lifted with hope.

"Michel?" I asked, pointing to the phone.

Gilley let out a mirthless laugh. "No, that was Julia. She called me twenty minutes ago, and I told her all about our super sleuthing, and she is totally on board!"

"She is?" I asked, blinking in surprise.

"She is!" Gilley sang, his voice going up a few octaves. "And she's *thrilled* to attend a birthday celebration in her honor!"

"Ah, now I know why you're so giddy. You get to plan a party with a giant budget and no one to tell you no."

"Exactly," Gilley said, grinning ear to ear. "We should get started on the guest list right away," he said, hurrying to the kitchen to retrieve a pad of paper and a pen. After sitting down at the table, he began to scribble. "We'll invite all the suspects, of course, and Marcus and Shepherd and—"

I sucked in a sharp breath and clamped my hand onto Gilley's arm.

"Ow!" he said, tugging on his arm. "You know I bruise like a peach! What gives?"

"Shepherd," I said softly, letting go of him. "Gilley, *what* am I going to do about Shepherd?"

"Why is this a problem?"

"I can't invite Shepherd *and* all the men who'd dated Yelena and were featured in her show. He's bound to catch on when I start asking these men all the same questions about their relationship with Yelena."

"Just point him toward the guests and tell him to mingle. What's the big deal?"

I stared at him for a long moment before I said, "Gilley. It's Shepherd. The man who hates people, especially chatty people in fancy clothes whom he's never met before."

"Oh, yeah," Gilley said, but then he eyed me like he took me for a simpleton. "Sugar," he said next, "you *have* to invite him. He'll be ten times as suspicious if you don't. But here's the trick. If you ask him to come, he'll want to get out of it, because snobby parties, fancy clothes, and people in general aren't his gig, and then you'll pick a fight with him that he's not supportive enough, and if he tries to apologize, you just continue to make a big deal out of it until he tells you in a huff he's not coming."

"You know," I said, tapping the table, "that is actually a terrific plan." Shepherd would definitely react the way Gilley had described, and picking a fight with him was easy.

It was the making-up part that might prove problematic, but I could worry about that later.

"Okay, Gilley," I said, with new resolve. "Let's plan this thing!"

The rest of the week went by in a whirl of details, emails, phone calls, texts, mad dashes to various boutiques and restaurants, and always another thing to do. Luckily, Shepherd was so busy working his case against Aaron that he wasn't available for much time with me. I missed him, but I didn't relish the impending fight I was supposed to instigate.

"Can we stop at the mailbox on Chestnut?" Gilley asked as we got in the car, ready to knock out the final errands for the party. "I have a card for Mama to mail out, and their last pickup is at four."

"Of course," I told him, making a right at the stop sign, instead of the left that typically took us to town. The mailbox was almost directly across the street from Sunny's house, and I felt a pang when I thought of her. I missed her and wished that she'd be released from the hospital. Shepherd had visited her a couple of times, and each time he had come away unsettled, telling me only that Sunny remained in an agitated state, but nobody could pinpoint why.

We pulled up in front of the mailbox, and Gilley fished around in his messenger bag, hunting for the envelope he needed to mail out, and I looked across the street at Sunny's beautiful home. Gilley got out of the car and headed to the mailbox while I waited. After mailing his letter, he trotted back to me and opened the car door and got in just as a big Range Rover pulled past us and turned abruptly into Sunny's driveway.

I didn't know why, but Gilley and I continued to watch from the car as Darius emerged from the driver's side of the Range Rover and walked around to the rear passenger seat, where he got Finley out of his car seat. Then he balanced the little tyke on his chest as he also opened the front passenger's door.

Gil and I both sucked in a breath when Sunny stepped out onto the pavement, looking frail and unsteady. Darius was quick to close the door and wrap an arm around her waist to steady her, before the two of them moved slowly along the drive to the walkway, then up the steps and into the house.

"She's home," Gilley said softly. "She's finally home."

I nodded, wondering if Shepherd knew. I wanted to call him, but I was still working up the nerve to have a fight with him later and didn't want to jinx it.

"I wonder when we can go visit her," I said.

"Let's bring them some lasagna in the next couple of days," Gilley suggested.

Gilley made the best lasagna I'd ever tasted. "That's a great idea," I said, putting the car into drive and heading for town, with thoughts of Sunny heavy on my mind.

"Did Shepherd get his tux cleaned?" Gilley asked me after a while.

Our party was black tie and formal wear, because a party featuring the reappearance of Julia Entwistle after a decade of withdrawal from public life would demand nothing less.

"I haven't told him about the party yet," I said.

"You *what*?" Gilley said. "Cat, the party is *tomorrow*! You can't have that man showing up in a wrinkled tuxedo. Wait, *does he even own a tuxedo*? Ohmigod, what if he shows up in a plaid shirt and Dockers?"

I looked at Gilley incredulously. "What has gotten into you?" He was breathing heavily and gripping the seat belt tightly.

Gilley merely shook his head, and I thought maybe he was having a panic attack.

"Gil," I said, thinking about pulling over to tend to him and unable to see a space anywhere to do that in the crowded downtown streets. "Remember? Shepherd isn't going to come. I'm going to pick that fight with him, and he'll stomp off and not show up."

Gilley's breathing slowed almost immediately. "Ohmigod," he said, fanning himself. "I forgot that particular detail."

"Yeah, I know," I said, eyeing him again. "This will all be fine by the end of the day, okay? And then we'll have all of tomorrow to pamper ourselves and get ready. Which reminds me, I have to pick my dress up from the dry cleaner's on North Main. We can hit that after we're done picking up the extra bottles of champagne."

"There, Cat!" Gilley suddenly yelled.

I hit the brakes, thinking he was pointing to something I was about to hit. "What? What!" I looked all around and didn't see anything.

Gilley continued to point. "That spot right there!"

I realized he was pointing to an open parking space in front of a high-end boutique. "That's two blocks from our next stop," I said testily. Man, he was getting on my last nerve.

"No, pull in there!" Gilley insisted.

Frustrated that he was being so irrational, I pulled into the spot and put the car in park. I was getting ready to lecture him about toning it down a notch when Gilley jumped out of the car, looked back at me, and said, "I'll be right back."

With that, he slammed the door and ran into the boutique, for what I couldn't imagine. He already had his tuxedo pressed and hanging on the door to his bedroom.

I waited for several minutes and was about to head in to look for him when he popped back into sight, holding a garment bag. "What in the . . . ?" I muttered.

Gilley came around to my side and opened up the rear door, where he hung the garment bag on the hook behind my seat. Then he grinned at me like he had a secret and came bounding back to the front passenger side.

"What's in the bag, Gilley?"

"Your gown, Cinderella," he said.

I furrowed my brow. "My gown? What're you talking about? Did you pick it up at the dry cleaner's and bring it down here? I hope you didn't alter it. You know it fits me like a glove."

"Yes, I know that gown, which you've worn three times since you bought it and have been seen everywhere in, fits you like a glove."

"What's that supposed to mean?"

"Sugar, you're the host of *the* best party in town this weekend. No *way* should you show up in last year's fashion."

I glanced over my shoulder suspiciously. "How much is that setting me back?"

Gilley's grin widened. "Zero dollars and zero cents."

"Come on, stop playing," I said with a sigh.

"I'm not playing. I told Willem about it, and he said that he definitely wanted to pick up the tab for the gown."

I had been about to pull out of the space with the car in reverse, but the minute Gilley said that, I put the car back into park and pointed to the boutique. "Take it back," I said firmly.

"What? Why?"

"Because I doubt it'll fit—"

"Oh, please! Like I don't have your exact measurements by now," Gilley said, with a roll of his eyes.

"*And* because you're taking advantage of Willem, and I'm not having it! We're already over budget as it is."

"By five hundred dollars," he said, crossing his arms and offering me a petulant pout.

"That's still fifty thousand five hundred dollars you've spent so far, Gil! That's outrageous!"

"Oh, please, Catherine. That's the price of a modest wedding. Willem gets it."

I glared at him. "Take the gown back."

"No."

"Fine. Then *I'll* take it back. Is the receipt in the bag?" I unbuckled myself and was on my way out of the car when Gilley stopped me by grabbing my arm.

"Cat, it's one of a kind. There are *no* returns."

My eyes widened. "How much did you spend on this one-of-a-kind creation?"

"I'm not telling," he said stubbornly.

"Then I'm not wearing it," I replied angrily, moving out of the parking spot to carry on down the street. I was furious with him for taking advantage of Willem's generosity. The gown I had waiting at the dry cleaner's was perfectly acceptable for tomorrow's festivities.

"Okay, fine. Don't wear it," Gilley said and began to whistle.

I had a bad feeling, and it was made worse by the fact that when I pulled into the lot of the dry cleaner's, Gilley began to inspect his nails. I pulled down the shade and flipped up the lid on the vanity mirror, expecting to see the ticket for my dress, but it wasn't there. "Where's my ticket?"

"Probably in a stack of other tickets in there," Gilley said, waving his hand casually toward the dry cleaners.

And then I knew. "*What* did you do with my gown, Gilley?"

"I put it someplace safe."

I let my head fall forward onto the steering wheel. "I will kill you before this day is through, you realize that, right?"

Gilley grinned wickedly at me. "Don't do that. Then you'll have to throw another party."

We didn't speak for the rest of the afternoon. Gilley tried to make small talk, but I would only glare at him. Finally, we got home, and I left the gown in the car, determined to find something else in my closet that I could wear.

A half hour later Gilley found me in my closet, sorting frantically through my formal wear for a dress or a gown even half as good as the one that he had hidden. "I'm not wearing it," I said when he entered with the garment bag dangling from his arm.

"Come on, Cat. Just look at it, will you?"

I pressed my lips together in frustration. I did in fact want to see the gown, and I hated my curiosity. But I couldn't let Gilley know that, so I simply crossed my arms and glared at him.

He dropped the lower half of the garment bag and unzipped the gown.

My breath caught at the sight of it. The garment was made almost entirely of black velvet. It had a full, floor-length skirt, a cinched waist, and a sleeveless halter top. The neckline was a deep V, and it flared wide at the top, with a collar that turned up and was made of white silk sewn onto a black silk background, and that ensemble lined the entire length of the V, with small black buttons completing the vertical trim. There were also two cuffs made of white silk that were made to be worn like bracelets.

"Oh, my," I said, breathless at the sight of such a spectacular gown.

"See?" Gilley said, moving forward to drape the gown in front of me and pivot me toward the full-length mirror. Even still on the hanger, the thing looked gorgeous next to my skin.

"Damn you, Gilley," I said, shaking my head.

"What? Cat, you'll be magnificent in this!"

"Exactly," I said, reaching up to touch the soft fabric. "There's no way I can take it back now that I've seen it."

Gilley's smile was a mile wide. "Told you so."

"But *I'm* paying for it," I said next.

"You won't like the price."

"Of course I won't like the price. How much?"

"Willem told me not to tell you."

"For God's sake, Gilley! Just tell me!"

"Take it up with Willem, Cat."

And with that, Gilley placed the hanger in my hand and began to walk out.

Quickly, I raised the collar to eye level and looked for any sign of a price tag, and of course there was none, but the small tag at the back of the collar read VIVACE.

"Gilley!" I yelled, to stop him.

Gilley looked over his shoulder and said, "How else were we going to get Antonio here? He turned down our RSVP, remember?"

He'd been the only suspect we'd identified to turn down our invite.

"You got him to come?"

"Maybe. I had a long talk with his personal assistant and made sure to tell her that Antonio would do well to attend the party, where his most gorgeous creation was about to be paraded around in front of the wealthiest woman on Long Island and all her close friends. What a shame it would be if he couldn't attend and bask in the glory of all the envious whispers his gown was about to inspire."

I shook my head and gave in to a smile. "You are one sneaky devil."

Gilley curtsied, then moseyed out the door.

I was left standing with the gown in front of the mirror, and I wanted to cry over the fact that Shepherd would miss seeing me in it.

After hanging the garment on a hook near the mirror, I looked through my shoe collection for a suitable pair of pumps, and when I'd selected those, I moved on to jewels.

"Pearls," I said to myself. "But should I wear a choker or opera length?"

"Opera length," I heard behind me, and I whirled around to see Shepherd standing there, wearing a grin on his face. "Especially if you're going to an opera."

"Hey there," I said.

"Hey, yourself. What're you picking out, and where do you want to drag me?"

I took a deep breath. It was now or never. "Actually, I've been meaning to tell you. Gilley and I are throwing a party here tomorrow night and—"

"A party? What party?"

"It's Julia Entwistle's birthday," I said.

"Julia Entwistle?" Shepherd said, scratching at his five o'clock shadow. I suddenly realized that he looked exhausted. "Sounds familiar . . ." Shepherd paused to think; then he had it and snapped his fingers. "She's Willem's mother, right?"

"Grandmother."

"Oh, yeah. That's right. She's having a birthday party here?"

"She is."

"I didn't realize you guys were that close."

I cleared my throat. "Well, Willem called with some news."

"What news?"

"He and Chanel eloped, and now they're in Thailand on their honeymoon."

I watched Shepherd's expression carefully. There was history there, which I knew was best left untouched, but I couldn't help looking for any signs that what I'd just told him bothered him.

If it did, he was careful not to show it. "Good for them," he said. "What does that have to do with Julia?"

"Willem felt bad that he won't be home in time for his grandmother's birthday, and he asked if I might throw a party in her honor."

"Oh," Shepherd said. "And you want me to come."

"Yes." I didn't elaborate, lest Shepherd ferret out the lie I was about to tell.

"Okay," he said agreeably. "Should I bring beer?"

I blinked once, very slowly. "No," I said. "Shep, this is a black-tie affair."

"Black tie? Oh, come on, Cat, you know I hate those kinds of parties."

"Yes, yes, I do," I said.

"Do you really need me to attend?" he asked carefully.

And that was my cue to blow up, and blow up I did. With very little effort, I started a fight where we were both yelling at each other, and it ended with Shepherd leaving in a huff and vowing to skip the party.

After he'd gone, I knew I should've felt relieved, but I didn't. Instead, I sank to the floor and cried.

Chapter 14

"This is quite the turnout," Gilley said as we stood in the doorway of the patio at Chez Cat, surveying the crowd. All the guests were friends of Julia, save for our suspects, of course.

"It is," I said, smiling at the excellent job we'd done putting this little soiree together in only a week.

The orchestra began to play a foot-tapping tune, and I was happy to see some of the couples taking to the dance floor. Our *Dancing with the Stars* theme seemed to be going off without a hitch, and it was a nice way for me to corner a few of our suspects and make casual conversation, which was really about sussing out any lingering anger they might still hold for Yelena, and perhaps an alibi—or lack of one—for the night of her murder.

What we needed were some viable prospects to present to Marcus. Those would be the men he'd subpoena and put on the stand—specifically targeting the question of any extortion attempts made by Yelena.

If they were caught in a lie, Marcus could subpoena their financial records and trace any unexplained large withdrawals back to similar deposits made to Yelena's bank account.

And Marcus had already had some success in obtaining a partial printout of her most recent transactions, and she had made at least three large deposits of fifty thousand dollars or more.

We suspected that one of those deposits might have come from Aaron, because the timing fit the waning days of their relationship, but there were two others that were questionable. One for the period right before Aaron and Yelena began dating, and the other for immediately after. That last deposit was for two hundred thousand, which we knew was the same amount carried but not delivered by Mark Purdy.

Since we couldn't be sure if Yelena was extorting the men she named only in her show or others from her past, it'd be necessary to question all the lovers we could identify.

"Who are you focused on?" Gilley asked me.

"I'll take Vivace, Bosch, and Chipperfield."

"Perfect. I'll take McAllen, Goldberg, and Leahy."

"Wonderful," I said. Then I scanned the crowd. "Is June here?" I asked, speaking of Lover Number Eight's sister. "I don't think I see her."

"Not yet," Gilley said. "But I'm hopeful."

"What time did Julia say she'd be arriving?"

Gilley lifted his wrist to note the time. "She should be here in the next twenty minutes. She wanted to be the last to arrive and make her entrance."

"And Marcus is bringing her, correct?"

"He is. He's going to act as her bodyguard, which means that he'll be able to overhear any conversations had by Julia and one of our suspects."

Julia was our backup plan in case we couldn't convince any of our suspects to talk, and Marcus would make sure she stayed safe in their presence.

"Okay then," I said, feeling both nervous and anxious. "Let's rock and roll."

Gilley offered his fist for a fist bump, and I obliged. I had begun to turn away when he stopped me and said, "By the way, Cat, can I just say that you are a *vision* in that gown?"

I smiled and gave him a spontaneous hug. I was still smarting from the fight that Shepherd and I had had, and it hurt that he wasn't here to appreciate how gorgeous I looked tonight. The gown fit me like a second skin, and the black velvet against my very pale white complexion was a delicious contrast. I couldn't imagine a more flattering look than the one I had on, and it was nice to hear it said out loud by someone I trusted.

"Love you," I whispered in Gilley's ear.

"Back at you," he said, squeezing me tight before letting me go.

With a deep breath, I turned to the crowd and selected my target.

I weaved my way through the cluster, stopped in front of Antonio Vivace, and smiled up at him gamely. "I've been dying to talk to you since you arrived," I said to him.

He grinned approvingly and said, "You are exactly the woman I would want to wear that gown."

I bowed my head and extended my hand. "Catherine Cooper," I said.

He took my hand and brought it to his lips. After kissing my knuckles, he said, "Antonio Vivace."

Glancing over my shoulder toward the dance floor, I said, "Antonio, may I have this dance?"

His grin widened. "Of course."

We stepped onto the dance floor, and I quickly discovered that he was a fabulous dancer. I was just okay, but with Vivace leading, I felt like a pro.

I spoke about how much I admired his creations, then segued into a casual mention of Yelena. "I discovered you through a friend of mine," I said.

"Oh?"

"Yes. She wore your creations almost exclusively, and she always looked so radiant." I then sighed sadly.

Vivace's smile faded, and his perfectly timed steps faltered for a moment. "You must be speaking of Yelena Galanis."

"I am," I said. "I didn't know her for very long, but I adored her."

The designer's gaze traveled to a spot above my head, and it was clear he was avoiding meeting my eyes. He said nothing, so I continued.

"What a terrible tragedy it is that she's no longer with us," I said.

"Mmm," he said, not quite a confirmation or a necessarily suspicious indicator.

"You knew her well, though, correct?"

"I did," he said.

"That's right," I said. "She dated you briefly, didn't she?"

Vivace's eyes met mine, and the look on his face was piercing. Suspicious. "She told you that?"

"In a roundabout way," I said. "Actually, I guessed it

based on how many compliments she paid you both as a designer and a person."

"Pffft," he said. "I doubt that."

"No, it's true!" I insisted. "She only spoke highly of you, and it was in a way that made me think she had some romantic feelings and that perhaps they were returned."

Vivace offered me the tightest of smiles. "Yelena was the least romantic woman I've ever met. She wasn't who you think she was, Catherine, and if she treated you well, it was only because you hadn't known her very long."

I widened my eyes in surprise, even though I was definitely not surprised. "My goodness," I said. "What did she do to you, Antonio?"

The song we'd been dancing to ended, and he abruptly stopped moving me around the dance floor. After letting go of my hand, he offered me a deep bow, then stood straight and said, "It was a pleasure, madame."

With that, he walked away.

"Hmm," I muttered. That was interesting.

Moving off the dance floor, I next approached Brad Bosch, who was incredibly handsome and well built. "Hello," I said gamely. He was standing by himself, so my overture seemed natural.

"Hi," he said, looking relieved that someone had approached him. Then he stuck out his hand. "Brad Bosch."

"I thought you looked familiar," I said. "I'm Catherine Cooper."

"Our host," he said.

I nodded. "Are you here alone?" I asked next.

He grimaced. "Yeah. I got my invitation on short notice, and the girl I've been seeing is in the City this weekend."

"Well, it was so nice of you to come."

He shrugged. "It's not every day that you get to meet a legend," he said. "Which is why I was a little curious how I ended up on the guest list."

"Julia's idea," I said. "She gave me a list of dear friends and a list of people she'd heard of and wanted to meet, and your name was at the top."

He eyed me with renewed interest. "Did she hear about my campaign?"

"Your campaign?"

"I'm running for New York's First District next year."

I blinked in surprise. "You are?"

"Yeah," he said. "And if I got Julia Entwistle's endorsement, it could be a game changer."

"Definitely," I said. "That must be why she invited you."

Bosch's smile was radiant. "Can you get me a private audience with her?" he asked next. "I've been working on my pitch ever since I got the invite."

I returned his smile. "Of course, I can," I said, deciding there and then to allow Julia to gently interrogate Bosch. He'd probably be willing to tell her anything to gain her endorsement. She could tell him that she heard he'd suffered a recent loss with the death of Yelena Galanis, and see what reaction and information he offered in return.

Looking over Bosch's shoulder, I pretended to spot an old friend and said, "Brad, would you excuse me? I see my dear friend Ike Chipperfield is here."

Bosch's reaction startled me. He stiffened, and his expression turned to barely hidden anger. "You know Chipperfield?"

"I do," I said. "He used to date a friend of mine. She died recently, and I want to express my condolences."

Bosch nodded curtly. "Sure," he said. "I heard about that too."

I wasn't sure if he meant that he'd heard about Yelena's death or about the fact that Ike Chipperfield had dated Yelena behind Bosch's back. His quick switch to a simmering anger was pretty telling, however.

I pretended not to notice and squeezed his arm. "Thank you. I'll swing back around to take you to Julia as soon as she gets here."

"Great," he said stiffly.

With a parting smile, I left his side and moved over to Ike Chipperfield. He was standing with a couple, making small talk, but I noticed as I left Bosch that Chipperfield was glaring in our direction. Clearly, there was no love lost between these two.

Stopping in front of the threesome, I nodded to the couple and focused on Chipperfield. "So sorry to interrupt," I said. "But, Mr. Chipperfield, I have to tell you I'm such a huge fan of yours."

Chipperfield looked me up and down, and I thought I met his approval, because without even taking his leave of the couple, he offered me his arm and said, "May I have this dance?"

"Of course!" I said, taking his arm.

He moved us out to the dance floor, and we began to tango. Chipperfield was also a good dancer, not as smooth as Vivace, but still very good.

"You're a wonderful dancer," I said to him.

He beamed at me. "You're not so bad yourself, kid."

I smiled in return, even though being called "kid" got under my skin a little.

"How long have you been a fan of mine?" he asked me.

"Ever since I moved to the Hamptons," I said. "You

were the first newscaster I watched in my new house, and you made me feel like I could fit in here."

"Oh, yeah?" he said.

"Yeah. You're so warm, Ike. It's like you're our friend rather than some robotic anchorperson."

"I practice my delivery to make sure I come across that way."

"Well, it's paying off. When I first offered to throw Julia a birthday party, I mentioned to her that I very much wanted to invite you, because I'd heard such good things about you, from a personal perspective."

He cocked his head a little. "From who?"

"From my friend," I said. "She just passed away, in fact. She spoke so highly of you, and inviting you here was my little way of honoring her memory."

Chipperfield's grip on my hand tightened. "Yelena Galanis?"

"Yes," I said, trying to look surprised. "I know you two knew each other, but I didn't realize you'd be aware of her death."

"I'm a newscaster," he said. "I'm aware of everything."

"Ah," I said. "Well, you should know that she adored you."

Chipperfield's mouth twitched a little. He, like Vivace, didn't believe me, either. "Is that why you invited Bosch?" he asked me.

I glanced over my shoulder in Bosch's direction. He was staring at us with daggers in his eyes. "It is," I said. "But how did you know that they used to date?"

He didn't answer me directly, but he did say something telling. "Those two deserved each other."

Again, I widened my eyes in mock surprise. "You say that like you didn't care much for Yelena."

He shrugged. "People change," he said. "She certainly did."

"Oh," I said. "I'm sorry you had that experience with her. She was nothing but kind to me."

"You must not have known her very long."

It was striking how similar that sentiment was between him and Vivace. They both clearly held the same disparaging view of Yelena. Either of them could have taken that anger and bitterness to the next level by murdering her.

Out of the corner of my eye, I saw someone waving toward me. Turning to look, I realized that it was Marcus. He stood in the doorway, with Julia out of view.

"Ike, would you please excuse me? I see that our guest of honor has arrived."

"Sure," he said. But before I could leave him, he squeezed my hand and said, "Could you arrange for a quick audience with me? Julia Entwistle is a legend, and I've always wanted to interview her. I've reached out before, but I could never get a return phone call. I figure it'll be harder to turn me down face-to-face."

"I'm sure she'd love that," I said, pulling my hand gently out of his. "I'll talk to her right away about it."

"Great," he said. "Nice meeting you."

"You as well."

I took my leave and hurried over to Marcus.

"Hi!" I said, so relieved to see him.

"Catherine," he said dipping his chin in greeting. Looking me up and down, he added, "You look beautiful."

I blushed and was quick to return the compliment. "As do you, Counselor."

Marcus was wearing a tux with Swarovski crystal buttons that had to be a custom fit, a black silk shirt, no tie, a white diamond-pattern pocket square, and gold-rimmed diamond cuff links. He bowed slightly to let me know he appreciated the compliment, then thumbed over his shoulder. "Julia is in the family room. She'd like it if you'd escort her out here."

"Perfect," I said, then turned to point to a small tent at the far end of the party area. "I've got a table and chairs set up over there so that she can receive her guests in comfort."

"Nice," he said. "You walk her out and I'll fix a plate for her."

I nodded and headed to the family room to fetch Julia.

I came up short when I saw how radiant she looked, dressed in a sheer persimmon blouse—which made her skin and eyes pop—with a black camisole and a black, shimmery full skirt that fell to her feet. Draped around her neck was an absolutely giant round black gemstone nested in a ring of diamonds and gold.

"Oh, my God," I said breathlessly. "Julia! You are *resplendent*!"

Julia batted her eyes at me. "Thank you, dear. As are you!"

"Thank you," I said, feeling that familiar blush touch my cheeks.

"Come over here and take a picture with me," she said, holding out her phone. I took it and shouldered up next to her to take a selfie of the two of us.

"Would you text that to Willem and Chanel for me, Catherine? I seem to have forgotten my glasses."

"Of course," I said, then sent the photo to Willem and then sneaked in an extra text of the photo to myself.

"How is it out there?" she asked when I handed her phone back to her.

"It's perfect, Julia. All the guests on your wish list are here."

"And the suspect pool?"

I grinned. "Nearly all of them showed."

"Good," she said, an eagerness in her eyes.

Pointing to the crowd outside I said, "Two of the suspects I've questioned so far would like a private audience with you."

"Which two?"

"Brad Bosch and Ike Chipperfield."

"The news anchor?"

"Yes."

"I never did care for his style," she said. "He's so fake."

I nodded in agreement.

Julia sighed. "I can feign interest for the evening, though, not to worry. Who's the other one?"

"Brad Bosch. He used to play for the Giants, and he's just confessed to me that he plans to run for the First District's House seat."

Julia puffed out a laugh. "Good luck in that race," she said. "Our congressman is very popular around here."

"Bosch believes that your endorsement could make the difference, and if you feign interest, I'm pretty sure you can get him to talk about his relationship with Yelena. She wasn't well liked by any of the men I spoke to."

"I don't doubt it," Julia agreed. "Anyone else I should hold a private audience with?"

"Gilley took Tucker McAllen, Liam Leahy, and Joel Goldberg. I'm not sure where he ended up with them. We haven't had a chance to talk."

"I definitely want to have a go at Goldberg," she said, fingering the gem at her neck.

I pointed to it. "His creation?"

"Yes," she said. "And he made it on short notice too. I told him I wanted the darkest sapphire he had, and he came through."

"That's a sapphire?" I asked. It had to be ten carats.

"It is," she said, smiling proudly. "I love it, so I hope he doesn't end up the killer."

I laughed. "Fingers crossed," I said. Then I offered her my arm. "Shall we?"

She took it and said, "We shall, but walk slowly, dear. I'm not as nimble as I appear."

I laughed again, and we made our way to the patio door. Julia paused to look out at the crowd of people, a few of whom had noticed her in the doorway and were looking very excited to see her.

"What a lovely setting, Catherine," she said in approval.

"Thank you," I replied. "Gilley and I worked very hard to make it special for you."

"And it shows," she said. Then she handed me the phone again. "Take another picture and send it to Willem. I want him to see the magic you've rendered."

I did as she asked, and then we proceeded forward. The crowd parted as we moved along, all eyes on Julia, and I felt so proud to be the chosen one to escort her to her table and chair.

After seating her, I realized that a couple had already sat down in the chairs opposite her. "Margot! Daniel!" she said with delight. "I'm so happy you could make it!"

I backed away from the table to leave them to each other's company and bumped into a body. Turning, I saw Marcus, holding a plate and champagne glass above my head.

"That was close," he said, motioning to the plate.

"Oh, Marcus! I'm so sorry!"

"Not to worry," he told me. "Nothing spilled." He then moved around me to discreetly set down the plate and a set of silverware for Julia, along with the glass of bubbly.

He then turned to me and whispered, "Want to fill me in so far?"

"Yes," I said. "I've made some progress, and there are a few interesting details to tell you about."

"Great," he said, offering me his arm and nodding toward the dance floor. "Do you dance?"

"I do," I said, taking his arm.

He guided me to the floor and twirled me around twice before bringing me close for our dance.

"You are good," I said, moving with him and finding it effortless.

"At most things," he said, bouncing his eyebrows.

I giggled but then turned to the business at hand and filled him in on every conversation I'd had and my impressions from all three men.

"Interesting," Marcus said when I was done. We were into our second song by now, and I was enjoying myself, even though I was technically amateur sleuthing.

"How did Gilley make out?" he asked next.

"I don't know," I said, looking around for my bestie. I finally saw him with Liam Leahy, and it appeared the two were getting along well. "I haven't had a chance to talk to him since we went our separate ways tonight, but I think he's making some progress."

Marcus glanced in the direction I was also looking. "Who's he with?"

"Vice Admiral Leahy," I said. "He also took Goldberg and he was also kind enough to take McAllen, who's simply an insufferable cad!" I hadn't forgotten McAllen's treatment of the poor server at the restaurant.

Marcus grinned. "Goldberg's the jeweler and the cad is the real estate developer?"

"Yes," I said.

"It'll be interesting to see if Gilley has the same experience with his three suspects," Marcus said.

"I'm gonna go out on a limb and say that it's likely to be a similar vibe. Yelena ended every relationship on bad terms, as far as I can tell."

"Yes," Marcus said. "Including with me."

"Julia wants to interview Goldberg herself, and she's agreed to speak to both Bosch and Chipperfield."

"I'll make sure to be near her for those conversations. No one here knows me personally, so that's a—"

"Pardon me," someone behind me said. "May I have this dance?"

I froze. I knew that voice.

"You may, Detective," Marcus said, twirling me in a half circle before releasing my hand. He then walked quickly away.

"Shepherd!" I said breathlessly. "What're you doing here?" And then I looked him up and down and couldn't believe how gorgeous he looked. His tux fit and flattered him, and he also wasn't wearing a tie, but he'd paired the deep black jacket with a band-collar white shirt. His five-o'clock shadow gave him a ruggedly handsome, yet sophisticated look, and I was smitten at the sight of him.

"I was tasked with reconsidering my choice to abstain from the evening's festivities," he said, putting a bit of poshness in his voice.

"You were tasked? By whom?"

Shepherd took me in his arms and began to sway us back and forth. "Sunny," he said.

"You spoke to her?"

"I went to see her," he said. "I had planned to stay there tonight, but when Sunny asked me why I was avoiding spending the evening with you, I had to confess that we'd gotten in a huge fight. I kinda knew she'd take your side, but I didn't count on the stern lecture and her *insistence* that I show up here to make things right."

"Wow," I said. "She must be feeling better."

"She's feeling feisty. She even gave Darius a hard time, and I've never seen Sunny give him so much as a glare."

"How'd he take it?"

"Better than I thought. He offered to loan me his tux."

"He did?"

"He did." Shepherd tugged on the jacket's lapel. "Tom Ford," he said.

"It's gorgeous on you."

"Not nearly as gorgeous as that gown is on you, pretty lady."

I smiled and blushed fully this time. "Thank you," I said. "But back to Sunny. What was she giving Darius a hard time about? He's been doting on her ever since she was checked into Stony Brook, right?"

"He has, but according to my sister, he hasn't been keeping up with the housework, and when I left her to come here, she was busy scrubbing the kitchen and doing her fifth load of laundry."

I laughed. "That sounds about right. My ex never did laundry. It would've piled up to the ceiling if I hadn't stepped in to do it."

"I suspect that's just shy of where their laundry was piled up to," Shepherd said. And then he looked at me meaningfully and said, "You are the most gorgeous woman I've ever known. Do you know that?"

I smiled, and my heart filled with love for him. "I love that you think so."

"I do. Seriously, that dress is amazing, and you're amazing in it."

Another blush hit my cheeks, and I looked down bashfully. "Stop," I said, unable to take in fully the compliment.

Shepherd bent his head to my neck and kissed me sweetly. "Stop what?" he whispered. After kissing me again, he added, "This? You want me to stop this?"

A different kind of heat filled my flesh, and I sighed and bent my head to expose more of my neck to him. "No. That you can continue."

"Goody," he said, then continued to nibble up and down my neck.

I twined my hands around his neck and felt so close to him, even though we were in the middle of a crowded dance floor. The feelings he was igniting were delicious.

"Steve!" I heard behind me. The sound made me jump.

Shepherd picked his head up abruptly and looked over my shoulder. "Sunny?" he said. "What's wrong?"

I turned to look behind me and saw Sunny standing there, wearing a loose plaid shirt and sweatpants. The outfit made her stand out like a sore thumb. Her complexion was pale, and she'd obviously been crying, as her eyes were watery and her cheeks were wet.

"I need you to see something," she whispered.

At that moment, Darius appeared. He looked out of

breath, and Finley was asleep on his shoulder. "Sunny!" he began, reaching out with his free hand to grab her arm. "Don't!"

She tugged out of his grip and held up a paper bag toward Shepherd. "I need you to look in here," she said. "I can't live with a lie. I can't live with what I've done."

A stream of tears poured out and flowed down her cheeks. Shepherd let go of me and took the paper bag, but Darius attempted to grab it away from him. Shepherd blocked the move and glared at his brother-in-law. "Don't!" he growled.

Darius looked almost panicked. "Please," he said. "Steve, don't open that bag. If you love your sister, you'll give it to me and forget we were ever here."

Shepherd's gaze flickered from Darius to Sunny, who was shaking her head and mouthing, *Please*, while pointing to the bag.

Shepherd opened the bag and looked inside. The color drained from his face, and I noticed that all the people around us had stopped to stare at the odd scene.

"What is this?" he asked Sunny.

"You know what it is," she replied. "It was me, Steve. It was me."

Shepherd let the bag drop to his waist; he seemed so stunned. I reached out and tugged on the bag. He let it go easily.

After opening it up, I peered inside and gasped at what was inside. It was the outfit that I'd seen Sunny wearing the day she'd gotten the tickets to Yelena's show for me and Gilley. But the clothing was literally covered in dried blood. It was smeared on the blouse and the joggers she'd worn that day, and there was no mistaking whose blood it was.

In that moment, everything clicked: Sunny's mysterious disappearance from the house right before Tiffany was going to put Finley in the tub, her equally mysterious return to change clothes and probably stuff the bloody clothing at the bottom of the laundry basket. And even the overdose of Ambien made sense. She had murdered Yelena and had felt so guilty that she'd tried to take her own life.

Still, it was an incredible shock to think that sweet, spiritual, gentle Sunny had committed a violent murder. The only thing I could think was that the Ambien tablet she'd initially taken had put her out of her conscious mind. That had to be the explanation, because anything else was unfathomable.

Shepherd finally recovered himself enough to take the bag from my hands and grab Sunny by the arm. "Inside," he said stiffly.

Darius looked at him like he wanted to deck him, but he followed along behind his wife and brother-in-law.

"Darius!" I called.

He looked over his shoulder with a furrowed brow.

"You can tuck Finley into Mike's bed upstairs. It butts up against the wall and there are extra pillows to hem him in while he sleeps. Third door on the left."

He nodded, and his expression turned briefly grateful; then he hurried to catch up to Sunny and Shepherd.

Before they were even inside, Marcus appeared next to me. "What happened?"

"Sunny killed Yelena," I said. I'd meant to speak softly, but my adrenaline got the best of me and my statement was a lot louder than I'd intended. In the crowd around us, several people gasped.

Murmurs began to spread through the crowd like undulating humming in a hive of bees, and Marcus took my hand and led me toward the patio doors Once we were inside, he closed the French doors and said, "Give me the details."

I explained everything to him, and he listened without interruption.

"Catherine," he said when I'd finished.

"Yes?"

"Do you have a dollar?"

I blinked. "Um, yes."

"Can you give it to me?"

I couldn't figure out what he wanted with a dollar, but I pointed toward the kitchen and led the way to the loose change jar on the counter.

Digging in the coins, I pulled out four quarters and handed them to him. "Sorry. I don't have any small bills. Will that work?"

"It will," he said, jingling the change. "You have just retained me to represent Sunny D'Angelo. Now, if you'll excuse me, I need to go where they are and stop any confession she might be making to Detective Shepherd."

I pointed toward the stairs. "I believe they went that way."

Marcus hurried toward the stairs and nearly sprinted up them. I was immediately filled with relief that he was here to take action.

Gilley then came running into the kitchen. "What's going on?" he said breathlessly. "There's a rumor going around that someone just confessed to killing Yelena."

"You didn't see?" I asked.

"See what? The last thing I saw was you and Shepherd dancing cheek to cheek."

"Sunny showed up," I said. "She confessed to murdering Yelena."

Gilley sucked in a loud breath and put his hand over his heart. "She did not!"

"She did."

"But . . . how? I mean, she was spaced out on Ambien that night. She couldn't have murdered her."

"She came here tonight with the clothing she'd worn that day. It was covered in blood. Like *covered*."

Gilley's hand traveled to his mouth, and he simply stared at me with huge, wide eyes. "What did Shepherd say?" he finally asked.

I shook my head. "Nothing. He just took Sunny upstairs to have a talk."

"Does Darius know?"

"He does. He tried to stop Sunny from confessing."

Gilley looked around. "Where's Marcus?" he asked. "We have to get Marcus to represent her!"

"He's already on the case. He's upstairs, stopping her confession."

Gilley's shoulders sagged in relief. "Thank God!" Then he turned toward the French doors leading to the patio. "What do we do about that?"

"I'm not sure," I said.

Gilley waved for me to follow him. "Come on, sugar. Let's go talk to Julia and see what she wants to do."

Chapter 15

Julia already knew about Sunny's confession. The murmurs had reached even her table. "We'll end this here," she said, taking my hand between both of hers. "Sunny is your dear friend, is she not?"

"She is," I said as unbidden tears blurred my vision.

Julia patted my hand. "There, there, Catherine," she said. "Marcus tells me he's the best attorney in the Hamptons. Send him in to defend her, and I'm sure he'll be able to stave off the worst-case scenario."

I nodded but felt such dread in my heart. "I'm so sorry that your birthday celebration is getting cut short."

"Pffft," she said. "I've had eighty-three other birthdays. They were all special in their own way, as is this one. Sometimes it's not about the length of the celebration, but the effort that went into making it memorable."

I attempted to smile at her kindness, but I was sure it

was more a grimace. "May I be allowed to throw your next party, Julia?" I asked. "I'd like to make up for this one."

"Absolutely!" she said. "But we'll have it at my home next time. That way you won't be burdened with so much cleanup."

I held out my arm to her, and she took it; then we made our way out of the tent and headed toward the French doors. Julia paused to thank many of her guests and apologized for the party getting cut short.

"I'm a bit tired," she told them. "I hope you'll understand the early end to the celebration. Please help yourself to some of those marvelous hors d'oeuvres. To go, of course."

It took maybe twenty minutes to make the rounds of all the guests, and both Bosch and Chipperfield looked monstrously disappointed, but when I introduced her to them, she sharply suggested they set up a lunch date for them individually. "We'll dine at the club," she said. "Are you a member of the EHGC?"

The East Hampton Golf Club was a very exclusive club. It was rated one of the best golf courses in all the Northeast, and I wasn't surprised that Julia was a member.

"No, ma'am," Bosch replied. "But I've played there as a guest once or twice."

"Wonderful," she said.

"I'm a member," Chipperfield said, then added a sneer at Bosch. "I'm there every weekend. Name the date and time and I'll be there, Mrs. Entwistle."

Julia smiled and patted him on the shoulder. "Excellent. Have Catherine send me your contact information, and I'll be in touch."

Once I'd gotten Julia inside the house, I said, "That was very kind of you, Julia, but in light of what's happened here tonight, I don't think we need to continue to grill the men on their whereabouts the night of Yelena's murder."

"Of course we do!" she said. "Marcus should be able to use the same tactic for Sunny that he was prepared to use for Aaron."

"I doubt that will work once the jury sees her bloody clothes."

"I'm sure he'll figure out a very good defense for her, my dear," she said, patting my hand.

I walked Julia to her car—a Rolls-Royce no less, and Gilley offered to drive her home as Marcus had driven her here. She was happy to have him play chauffeur, and the two were the first to leave, but everyone else quickly followed.

Once all the guests had left, I directed the servers and bartender who'd been hired for the event to help me organize the food and bring it inside. Within short order most of the area outside had been cleared of anything edible and drinkable.

I sent the servers home with most of the food. Relatively little of it had been eaten and I certainly didn't want it to take up extra room in my fridge only to slowly spoil.

I paid everyone and saw them off then headed back inside intent on making some tea to calm my nerves.

Just as I got out my favorite porcelain teakettle, there was a loud knock at the front door.

Thinking one of the servers had left something behind, I hurried to the door and was surprised to see three uniformed police and one detective in a suit jacket and tie standing there.

"Ma'am," the detective said. "We're here to see Detective Shepherd."

I wondered who'd called the cops, but stepped back and pointed to the stairs. "He's up there," I said. "I'm not sure which room he's in, but just follow the sound of voices and you should find him easily enough."

The three unis tipped their hats at me as they filed past, and the detective gave me a nod. I didn't smile or nod back, because I had a sinking feeling about why they'd come here in force.

Busying myself in the kitchen again, I kept one eye toward the stairs, and sure enough, the four of them soon came marching down, carrying the paper bag with the bloody clothes, with Sunny in the midst of them, her hands handcuffed behind her back.

She kept her gaze firmly on the steps in front of her as she made her way down, and then she kept her gaze on the floor as the unis took her out the door and over to one of two waiting police cars.

I watched out the window as they put her carefully into the backseat, and I felt those same unbidden tears well up in my eyes and dribble down my cheeks.

The detective remained at the bottom of the stairs. He seemed to be waiting for someone. Sure enough, Shepherd came down the steps slowly, looking utterly defeated. He and the detective spoke in hushed tones for a few minutes, and then the detective tipped an imaginary hat at Shepherd and headed out to the waiting car with only one cop in it. The others had already left, taking Sunny with them.

I left the window and walked over to Shepherd. He

was staring at the floor. "Hey," I said, placing a hand on his back. "How're you doing, Shep?"

"Bad," he said, his voice hitching with emotion.

"What happened up there?" I asked next.

"Sunny confessed. She said that she remembered being angry with Yelena, because she was under the firm belief that Yelena was going to hurt Finley. She remembered struggling with Yelena, and then she remembered changing clothes, but nothing more."

"She wasn't in her right mind," I said.

"I know that," Shepherd said. "If it weren't for her bloodstained clothes, I'd never believe it, but that's evidence that's hard to fake."

"What happens now?"

"They book her, then try her for murder in the first."

I bit my lip. That sounded so bad. "Is there anything we can do for her?"

"Sending Marcus up to represent her was a start. He made her stop talking the second he entered the room, but she'd already told me most of what she remembered. I interviewed Darius, and he said that Sunny found the clothes at the bottom of the laundry basket. She freaked out, and he tried to get her to burn the clothing and never confess it to me or anyone else, but my sister isn't one to hide from her mistakes. She's always owned up to any mischief she caused, and even though this is a thousand times more serious than any prank she's ever pulled, she wasn't about to let an innocent man go to jail for something she'd done."

Marcus and Darius came down the stairs at that point. A sleeping Finley rested once again on Darius's shoulder.

Darius glared at Shepherd, and the look was so harsh that I winced. "You should've protected her," he said.

"Obstruction isn't something I'm capable of, D."

Darius turned away, clearly disgusted. Holding out his hand to Marcus, he said, "I'll get you that check right away. In fact, if you want to follow me to the house, I can write it tonight."

"You can't go to the house, D," Shepherd said.

Darius turned again to him. "Wanna bet?"

"I'm serious."

"And I'm not?"

"They'll be searching your home, Darius," Marcus said.

Darius's expression turned to shock. "What do you mean, they'll be searching my home?"

"They'll have gotten a search warrant before they came to collect Sunny. It's what took them so long to arrive," Marcus explained.

Darius glanced at Shepherd, and he nodded solemnly.

"What am I supposed to do with Finley?" Darius demanded.

"You both can stay here tonight," I said. "There's a guest bedroom at the end of the hall upstairs. It's a queen bed, so there'll be plenty of room for you and Finley. And it's an en suite, too, Darius, so you'll have total privacy."

Darius looked at me, his thoughts unreadable. At last, he said, "Thank you, Catherine. We'll be out of your way first thing in the morning. They should be done searching my place by then, right, *Detective*?"

Shepherd nodded. "They should."

Without another word, Darius went back up the stairs, stomping as he went, clearly furious with Shepherd for upending his whole life.

Once he was safely out of earshot, Marcus said, "Are you going to charge him with obstruction?"

Shepherd shook his head. "No. Trying to talk Sunny out of confessing to me had no effect on her course of action. And I don't want Finley to go one second without a parent nearby."

Marcus nodded. "And will you be releasing my client, Mr. Nassau?"

"I'll call the D.A. first thing in the morning, Counselor. He'll be released by noon."

Marcus nodded again, then turned to me. "Did Julia make it home?"

"Gilley drove her," I said.

"My car is still at her estate. We took her Rolls here."

"When Gilley gets back, he can take you over there, you can pick up your car, and he can leave Julia's car in her driveway, and then you can drop him off back here."

"Good," he said.

As if on cue, my own drive lit up as Gilley pulled in. Marcus nodded to both of us and headed outside to inform Gilley of the plan.

Shepherd stepped to me and put his arms around me. "What a night," he said.

"Indeed. Are you staying over?"

Shepherd loosened his hold and said, "No, sweetheart. I have to go to the station and fill out some paperwork. They'll take me off Yelena's case and probably assign it to Santana, while I take over his case."

"Mark Purdy," I said.

"Yep."

"Did Santana put a few leads together?"

"He did not," Shepherd said. "Not a single lead, in fact."

"I might have a direction for you to follow," I said.

Shepherd's brow rose. "Yeah?"

I nodded. "You might want to see if there's a connection to Gene Bosworth. Or his sister."

"Who's Gene Bosworth?"

"Lover Number Eight."

Shepherd blinked in surprise. "*Yelena's* Lover Number Eight?"

"Yes."

"How do you know that?"

"Gilley and I were curious about the identities of the other lovers, so we did a little sleuthing."

Shepherd closed his eyes and sighed. "I knew you were gonna stick your nose where it didn't belong," he said.

"Then it shouldn't surprise you that we sussed out the identities of nearly all her lovers."

"You got a list for me?" he asked.

"I can send you a photo of the whiteboard we used to keep track of them."

"Do that," he said, kissing me on the cheek. "I gotta get going."

"I know," I said, wrapping my arms around him for a final hug.

When he'd gone, I headed upstairs and took off the gorgeous gown I'd been wearing and slipped into my nicest silk pajamas. After grabbing a pillow and a blanket, I made my way back downstairs and over to Chez Kitty.

I didn't want to sleep alone tonight. Even though Darius was down the hall, I craved the comfort of having Gilley close by.

Spooks looked up when I came through the door, then came bounding over to me to wriggle against my legs and make little whines of happiness that I'd come to visit him. After making my way over to the couch, I arranged the pillow and blanket before crawling under the covers. Spooks jumped up on the couch and stretched himself out so that he could lie next to me.

It was exactly the companionship I needed tonight.

I fell asleep quickly and barely woke when Gilley came through the door. He put an afghan over my blanket, covering Spooks and me, told the dog to stay, then headed off to bed.

I was left to dreams of a beautiful yellow- and orange-colored parrot locked in a birdcage, crying out her innocence.

The memory of that dream would stay with me for a long time to come.

Chapter 16

The next morning, while Gilley and I were finishing up a breakfast of fruit and yogurt, my phone rang with an incoming call from Willem.

I grimaced when I saw his name pop up on my screen. I felt terrible that the party he'd paid a ridiculous amount of money for had been shut down several hours early because of Sunny's confession.

"Willem," I said, answering the call.

"Hi, Catherine. I hope it's not too early there?"

"No, you're fine. Gilley and I were just polishing off breakfast. You've probably heard about the party, huh?"

"I did. Is there anything I can do for Mrs. D'Angelo?"

His question surprised me. I thought he'd be far more concerned with the fact that his grandmother didn't get the celebration she deserved. "That's lovely of you to ask," I told him. "But I think she's in the most capable of hands. We got her the best defense attorney in the Hamptons."

"Marcus Brown," Willem said. "Grams told me all about him. She was very impressed by him."

"I've known Marcus for two years now, and I can agree with Julia. He's definitely impressive."

"And how are you?" Willem asked next.

I shook my head, awed by his compassion. "I'm fine, Willem, thank you so much for asking. I'm sorry Julia didn't get the celebration she deserved."

He chuckled. "She had a terrific time. She couldn't stop talking about how perfect the setting was, and how much the guests seemed to be enjoying themselves until the incident. I'm so grateful to you and Gilley for going to so much trouble on her behalf."

"We'd do it again in a heartbeat."

"Speaking of which," Willem said. "She was hoping to pick your brains for ideas for our reception. Would you and Gilley be up for lunch with her today?"

I blinked and caught Gilley's eye. He wore a confused and curious expression. "I'm certainly free for lunch with her but let me check with Gilley." After placing a hand over the microphone, I said, "Julia is inviting us to lunch to pick our brains for ideas for Willem and Chanel's reception. Are you free?"

"Definitely."

Upon uncovering the microphone, I said, "Gilley would also be delighted to attend."

"Great," Willem said. "If you can get to her estate by noon, she'd appreciate it."

"We'll be there. Oh, and, Willem, one more thing. Would you send me the receipt for the Vivace gown you got swindled by my partner to purchase on my behalf?"

"Um, no, Catherine. It's my way of saying thank you for hosting the party and for now agreeing to help Grams plan the reception."

"Willem, it's too much," I insisted.

"Not in my book," he replied. "Besides, Chanel and I were blown away with how gorgeous you were in that gown."

I smiled. He was such a sweet man. "Thank you," I said. "Truly."

"Of course," he said. "It was the least I could do."

After I hung up with him, I turned to Gilley. "He's so lovely, you know?"

"I do know," Gilley said. "And I told you he wasn't going to let you pay for that gown."

"I still feel guilty about it."

Gilley shrugged. "Don't. Or if you do, maybe donate what you think the gown cost to a charitable organization."

I poked him with my finger. "That is *exactly* what I'll do!"

"See? There's a solution for every problem."

"We can drop the check off on our way to Julia's."

"Perfect!"

"Just tell me what the gown cost and I'll go fill that check out."

Gilley laughed. "Nice try," he said. "I've been sworn to secrecy, so no, I'm not going to tell you."

I pouted for a moment and then asked, "If I name a range, would you at least tell me that I'm in the ballpark?"

Gilley thought that over and said, "I think that'd be okay."

"Good. Was the gown in the range of between six and eight thousand?"

"You're in the stadium, but not yet on the field."

My jaw dropped. "Ten?" I said.

"You're in the outfield."

My eyes widened. The gift was far too generous. "Twelve?"

"You're on home base, Cat. And that's all I'll say about it."

Twelve thousand dollars was more than I'd ever paid for a gown. Even my couture wedding dress hadn't cost that much. I felt immensely guilty, even though I hadn't had a hand in the purchase.

And I also knew there was no taking it back. The only thing I could do was donate generously to my charity of choice.

After getting up from the table, I carried my dishes to the sink, gave them a quick rinse, and put them in the dishwasher. Then I moved to the door.

"You headed back to Chez Cat?"

"Yes. I want to make out that check while I still have the courage."

"You know, you don't have to donate the full twelve Gs."

I looked down at Spooks, who'd come over to lean against my legs and do his snorting routine in an effort to get me to stay. "I do, Gilley," I said, stroking Spooks's velvety head.

"I shouldn't have let you guess the price," he said.

I smiled at him. "I'm so glad you did."

After opening the door, I peered out at the beautiful day. In the driveway was Sunny's Range Rover, its rear window repaired. Darius's car was missing, though.

"Huh," I said.

"What?" Gilley said, getting up to come over to the door and peer out.

"Darius left already."

"What do you mean, he left already?"

I realized I hadn't told Gilley that I'd invited Darius and Finley to stay over. "The police obtained a search warrant for the D'Angelos' house, and he couldn't very well take Finley there while a team of strangers was turning the place upside down, so I offered to let him stay at Chez Cat for the night. He and Sunny drove separately to the party. His car was here when I came over last night, and now it's gone."

"Is that why you came here? You didn't want to be in the same space with him?"

I gave Gilley a disapproving look. "Of course not. I was unsettled by Sunny's confession and the early end to the party, and being here with you always makes me feel comforted."

Gilley nodded. "Sorry," he said. "Didn't mean to assume that Darius was a bad dude or anything."

"I don't think I would've minded the implication before Sunny tried to take her life, but after watching the way he cares for her and Finley, I've come to a different conclusion about him."

Gilley nodded. "Do you think he'll come back for Sunny's car?"

"I'm sure he'll want to, but he's probably got his hands full trying to put the house back in order after the police cleared out. If the keys are in it, and it's still here, then I think we should take it over to his house when we get back from Julia's."

"I like that plan," Gilley said. "He might know more about Sunny's case by then too."

"Yes," I said. "I'll be back here to collect you for lunch with Julia in a few hours, okay?"

Gilley saluted me smartly, clicking his heels, while I rolled my eyes and shut the door.

Three hours later we were on our way to Amagansett, but I took a slight detour south to the charity I planned to make a very large donation to.

Gilley was busy playing a game on his phone and didn't look up to see where we were headed until I pulled into the parking lot.

He gasped when he saw the building. "You're making a donation here?"

"I am," I said. "It's the least I can do to help support the place responsible for bringing Spooks into our lives."

Gilley's eyes welled up. "Oh, Cat. Thank you."

I squeezed his arm and pulled the check out of my purse. "Be right back," I sang.

"I'm coming with you!" Gilley said, and he scrambled out of the car.

We went inside and inquired about where to drop off a donation. The manager of the shelter came out of her office, and when I handed her the check, she, too, began to cry. Then she hugged me fiercely and thanked me over and over.

I was so moved by her reaction that I vowed to make a similar donation every year.

Once we were back in the car, Gilley said, "You are a *good* person, Catherine Cooper."

I grinned. "I try," I said. "It's such a deserving charity. Spooks is such a lovely boy, and all the dogs we looked at were obviously well fed and well taken care of."

We chatted a bit on our way to Julia's, mostly about mundane things, but then I realized that I'd never gotten the lowdown on any of the suspects that Gilley had questioned.

When I asked him about it, he said, "Ugh. They were a merry bunch."

"I detect a hint of sarcasm."

He nodded. "And none of them had any love lost for Yelena."

I looked at him sharply. "The same with my three," I said. "Especially Vivace. He scowled from the time I mentioned her name to the end of our dance together. He didn't reveal a lot verbally, but his body language and expression spoke for his true feelings. He didn't seem to be sorry at all that she was dead."

"But why does any of it matter now?" Gilley asked. "Sunny already confessed to the crime."

"I'm not sure I trust her memory, Gil. She was in a semiconscious state at the time she confronted Yelena, and for all we know, she could've walked in on the murderer, and a struggle ensued, where somehow Sunny got away, or she could've come in right after Yelena was stabbed to death, and tried to bring her friend back to life. In both of those scenarios her clothing would've gotten stained with Yelena's blood."

"Then our suspects are still suspects?"

I nodded. "The thing that keeps sticking out to me is Mark Purdy's murder. I just know there's a connection, but I can't figure out how."

"Have you talked to Shepherd about any of this?"

"A bit. He's certain he'll have to swap out Yelena's case for Purdy's."

"The whole situation must be impossible for him," Gilley said.

"Yeah. I'd say that it is."

At that moment we arrived at Julia's grand estate. I pulled into a spot next to the Rolls-Royce she and Marcus had ridden in the night before, and we approached the door.

After climbing the steps, Gilley rang the bell, which gonged like a church bell, and the door was opened by Julia's dour-faced personal assistant, Nancy.

"Ms. Cooper," she said, with the slightest nod to me. "Mr. Gillespie," she added, acknowledging Gilley.

I offered her a grimacing smile, but Gilley took her cold greeting as a personal challenge. "Nancy!" he exclaimed, placing both hands on her shoulders and adopting a look of pure joy. "You look marvelous! Have you done something with your hair? It's stunning! And look at this figure, woman! I can see that you've trimmed down a bit since last time, hmm? Try not to lose too much weight, or you'll blow away at the slightest breeze!"

Nancy blinked rapidly, and I suspected she badly wanted to take a step backward, but with Gilley firmly gripping her shoulders, what could she do?

"Ahh, it's been too long," Gilley said when she continued to blink in alarm. "We really should catch up soon, m'kay?"

Nancy's head began to bobble a bit. I had to press my lips together to avoid bursting into laughter at her shock at being accosted by Gilley's enthusiasm and joie de vivre.

"Is Julia in?" I asked, stepping up to the threshold so

that Gilley was forced to let go of Nancy's shoulders. "She invited us for lunch."

Once free of Gilley's grip, Nancy did take a step back. And then another. And a final third, just to be sure she had enough of a head start should Gilley come at her again. "She's seated on the back terrace. This way, please."

She then swiveled on her heel and began to walk quickly away. We closed the door and hustled after her.

The walk was long. And it made me appreciate just how enormous the estate house was. I guessed it was anywhere from twenty to thirty thousand square feet, as evidenced by the sheer depth of the place and the number of massive rooms—each exquisitely decorated—that we passed on the way to the back terrace.

At last, we came through a set of French doors, to appear in front of a covered terrace, with a pool to the far right and a small lake with a fountain spraying water into the air on the left.

A gorgeous teakwood table was also off to the left, and at its head was seated our favorite octogenarian, Julia herself, looking resplendent in a thick burgundy angora sweater with an overly large cowl-neck, which gave a bit more girth to her small frame.

She pressed her palms to the table at the sight of us and, with shaking arms, pushed herself out of her chair to welcome us to the table. "Hello, my darlings!"

We quickened our step, moving around Nancy, to take turns gently hugging Julia. Gilley allowed me the first hug, and Julia held Gilley's hand after he'd bent to hug her, too, and pulled on his arm to bring him around to the other side of the table, next to her on the left. I took up the chair on her right, which also had a place setting, and we all sat down, smiling broadly like old friends who hadn't seen each other in a long while, rather than friends who'd been together the night before.

"Julia," I began, "can I first simply say that I'm so sorry your birthday celebration turned into such a fiasco?"

"My dear, Catherine," Julia replied, "please do not feel sorry for an old woman who's had more than her fair share of birthday celebrations. Besides, last night's party was one for the ages! I mean, a parade of suspects all in view was stupendously thrilling. Although, poor Sunny, I feel so terrible for her."

"We do too. She's a dear friend," Gilley said.

"She's the sister to Detective Shepherd," I added.

"His sister? Oh, my, Catherine, I'm so sorry! That would make her practically family."

I was surprised that Julia seemed to remember that Shepherd and I were a couple.

"Sunny is such a gentle, loving, kind person," Gilley said, and I was surprised to see his eyes misting. "I can't imagine that she, of all people, could take the life of a friend. Especially one as close to her as Yelena."

"Oh?" Julia said, just as plates of Caesar salad and fresh, steaming-hot sourdough baguettes with pads of butter arrived and were served silently by a woman in a gray uniform with a white apron.

"She is truly a gentle person," I said. "Neither Gilley nor I think that she actually murdered Yelena."

"But she confessed, no?" Julia said.

"She did," I said with a sigh. "Which is the problem. She took an Ambien earlier in the day, and it has a history of putting her in an apparent wakeful state, but she's actually asleep and doesn't remember what she did during that time."

"Oh, dear," Julia said. "It's all so tragic."

I nodded in agreement. "Still, my gut says she didn't do it. Gil and I think either she walked in while Yelena was being attacked, and tried to stop it, or she walked into her dressing room right after and tried to do CPR or something."

Julia tsked a few times and shook her head. "If she didn't kill Yelena, who did?"

"That's what we'd like to know," I said.

"I take it you two are still investigating, then?"

"We are," I confirmed.

"Good," she said. "I'll help."

"How?" Gilley asked.

"I've set up two lunch dates with Mr. Football and Mr. Full of Himself."

Gilley's brow furrowed.

"Brad Bosch and Ike Chipperfield," I said.

"Ahhh," Gilley said. "Well done, Julia."

"I don't want you to probe them for clues alone, though," I said. "Is it all right with you if I ask Marcus to tag along?"

"Of course!" she said. "I so enjoyed his company last night."

"Great. And, on that note, Julia, do you think you could arrange a meeting with another suspect?"

"Who?"

"A woman named June Murdock. She didn't show up last night even though she sent an RSVP."

Julia pursed her lips distastefully. "June," she said.

"Do you know her?" Gilley asked.

"We're acquainted," she told him in a clipped tone.

Gilley and I exchanged a look, and I could tell we were both trying to decide whether or not to press the issue. "It doesn't sound like you think much of her," Gilley finally said, much to my relief.

"True," Julia said, and she began to poke at her salad like she was spearing fish.

Gilley and I again exchanged a look. He shrugged subtly, like he didn't know what else to say to get her to open up.

I was just about to try to prod Julia gently when she set down her fork, sighed heavily, and said, "June had an affair with my husband."

I gasped, and Gilley dropped his fork. It clattered against his china lunch plate. "Sorry," he said, wincing.

Julia's mouth worked from angry pursed lips to a sad frown and back again. At last, she said, "Richard was a good husband for over fifty years. He had one slip the whole time we were married. I knew immediately when it happened. I also knew that June had targeted my husband specifically, because of his friendship with her brother, Gene."

My eyes widened as Gilley asked, "Why would your husband's friendship with Gene Bosworth provoke June to target your husband?"

Julia snorted derisively. "To make Gene jealous, of course."

I bit my lip to prevent a bubble of excitement from leaking out of me. "So, it's true," I said. "Gene and his sister were . . ." I didn't think I could even finish the sentence, their illicit relationship so disgusted me.

"Involved in an incestuous relationship?" Julia said. "Yes. Yes, they were."

Again, Gilley and I traded looks of eager excitement. "Julia," I said, treading as carefully as I could. "We believe that Gene was Lover Number Eight in Yelena's show, and that June was paying off Yelena to keep her quiet about her true relationship with her brother."

"Doesn't surprise me," Julia said. "After June got married and began to refuse her brother, he tried to get even with her by courting the most glamorous loose young women who would have him. Yelena would've fit that profile perfectly.

"Tell me," she said, placing her elbows on the table and leaning in toward me. "What does June's payoff to Yelena have to do with her murder?"

"We're not sure," I said. "But a man named Mark Purdy was wearing a ladies' size-ten raincoat—Yelena's size—lined with two hundred thousand dollars when he was found dead in the alley behind the coffee shop down the street from the theater. We suspect there was a professional relationship between Purdy and June, and we also believe that the money lining Purdy's raincoat came from her."

"And this Mr. Purdy was murdered the same night as Yelena?"

"Yes," I said.

Julia sat back in her seat and subtly shook her head. "My, my," she said. "What a tangled web."

"Agreed," I said.

"Was the weapon used to kill Yelena also used to murder Mr. Purdy?"

"No," I said. "The method of death for him was exsanguination. From a piano wire across Mr. Purdy's neck."

Julia's eyes again widened, and Gilley made a slashing motion across his neck. A bit macabre for the moment, but that was Gilley.

"That's horrible," Julia whispered.

"It is. And it's the second reason that we don't believe that Sunny murdered Yelena. It's unfathomable to us that she'd be able to commit not one, but two murders back-to-back. And one by way of piano wire?" I shook my head. "I'm not buying it."

"You're right," Julia said. "Sunny appeared far too fragile to have overpowered a man."

"So, you see why we're trying so hard to find an alternative theory," Gilley said. "One that checks all the boxes."

"Indeed," Julia said, and I could tell she was trying to put the pieces together herself by the faraway gaze she held while looking down the length of the table. And then her eyes came back into focus, and she said, "It's a mystery within a mystery. Sunny D'Angelo's confession and the bloody clothes really throw a monkey wrench into things, don't they?"

"In a huge way," Gilley said.

"Gilley," Julia said. "Tell me again which of Yelena's lovers you questioned last night?"

"One, Four, and Five," he said.

"Tucker McAllen, the real estate developer; Joel Goldberg, whom you've met; and Vice Admiral Liam Leahy," I reminded her.

"What did you learn from them?" she asked Gilley.

"Not much, other than they seemed to feel no remorse for Yelena's passing."

"That's curious," Julia said, tapping her chin.

"None of the men on my list cared much about her, either," I said.

Julia sighed. "Which means that any one of them could've been her murderer."

"It does," I agreed.

"Is there anyone on the list you haven't identified?"

"Lover Number Two, Lover Number Ten, and Lover Number Twelve," Gilley said.

"Are you completely stumped on their identities, or do you suspect who they might be?"

"We suspect a few things about them," I said. "Lover Number Two, we believe, is a congressman. Lover Number Ten, we think, is a race-car driver, and Lover Number Twelve is the son of a queen, a lazy playboy, a commitment-phobe."

"That's an interesting crowd," she said. "Twelve sounds like someone connected to royalty."

"It's not Aaron Nassau," I said quickly. "He's Lover Number Eleven."

"Could she have repeated herself?"

"You mean, could she have used the same man twice in the script?" I asked.

"Yes."

I looked at Gilley. He shrugged. He didn't know. "I suppose anything is possible," I said.

"But you don't think she did, correct?"

"No," I said. "Aaron is neither a playboy nor a commitment-phobe. He is wealthy, but he's not the son of a queen. I mean, you know him, Julia. He's what, sixteenth in line to the Danish crown?"

Julia nodded. "Something like that. But to your point, yes, that description does sound significantly different than who I know Aaron to be."

"Until we can identify the three remaining suspects, we're stuck with only probing the other eight," I said.

"Not Aaron?" she asked, and I could tell she was playing devil's advocate in asking me that.

I shook my head. "Of everyone we've talked to so far,

he's the only one who showed remorse upon hearing about her passing. What's more, he wouldn't admit that Yelena tried to extort him, and he said that the reason his letter opener was discovered in her dressing room and used as the method to kill her was that he allowed her to take it."

"And you don't believe that he allowed her to take it?"

I shook my head. "The letter opener is worth at least fifty thousand dollars. It's inlaid with precious gemstones and made of fourteen-karat gold."

Julia sat back in her chair as if she was satisfied. "All right," she said. "I trust your judgment and my own regarding Aaron. I'll do my best to ferret out any information from Mr. Bosch and Mr. Chipperfield, and perhaps I'll even pay Mr. Goldberg a visit. Now that I've purchased something rare and expensive from him, he might be inclined toward some small talk."

"Gilley?" I said. He looked at me expectantly. "Are the other two on your list worth investigating any further?"

Again, Gilley shrugged. "I don't know, Cat. They clearly weren't sad that Yelena was dead, but I didn't really get a murder vibe off of them. Especially the vice admiral. He struck me as a very by-the-book kind of guy. You know, like Shepherd."

"Huh," I said. "If he's like Shepherd, no way is he the killer."

"McAllen would have far too much to lose," Julia said. "He's an absolute pig of a man, but I don't see him doing something so irrational that could jeopardize his future. Not when he's at the peak of his power."

"Good point," I said. "So, really that just leaves Bosch, Chipperfield, and Goldberg to focus on."

Julia reached out to pat my hand. "You let me worry about them. The two of you should focus on discovering the identities of Two, Ten, and Twelve."

Gilley and I both nodded, and Julia took the napkin from her lap and stood up carefully.

"Now, shall we walk the grounds and plan my grandson's wedding reception?"

"We shall," I said, getting up along with Gilley.

"This will be fun!" he said, clearly excited.

And we set off on an afternoon of party planning.

Chapter 17

Pulling into my driveway after a wonderful afternoon spent with Julia, Gilley and I both saw that Darius hadn't yet come to retrieve his wife's car.

"Fingers crossed the keys are inside the Range Rover," Gilley said.

"Hopefully, they're not still with Sunny," I agreed, thinking that could be why Darius hadn't come back for the car. If he didn't have a spare key fob, then Sunny's car could be sitting in my drive for quite a while.

Gilley hopped out and went over to the Rover to have a look. He pulled up on the door handle and discovered that the car was unlocked. Looking back at me he bounced his eyebrows.

I rolled down my window and said, "That's a good sign."

He then got in, looked around, looked at me, and

shrugged. Then he leaned forward to press the START button, and the Range Rover came to life.

"It's about time that worked," I said.

Gilley closed the door and buckled up, and I let him take the lead over to Sunny's house while I followed behind. He pulled the SUV over to the garage, and to my surprise, the garage door began to lift. Gilley pulled forward, parked the Range Rover, sat there for a moment then got out of the car and exited the garage, hurrying over to my car, but he didn't get in.

"The garage door won't go down," he said.

"Yeah. It sticks apparently. It did that when I came over to get the tickets to Yelena's show."

Gilley pointed to Darius's car parked in the drive near the door. "He's home. Let's go tell him we dropped off Sunny's car and parked it in the garage," he said.

"Good idea," I said, getting out of the car.

Together we approached the front steps, but as we got close, we could hear music coming from the backyard.

Gilley and I exchanged curious looks, and I pointed to the back gate, which was open. As we neared the source of the music, it became clear that Darius was playing one of his acoustic guitars and singing a lullaby.

"Oh, wow," Gilley whispered. "He's good!"

He was good. His voice was husky and deeper than his speaking voice. He had perfect pitch, and it was such a pleasure to hear him sing that both Gilley and I stopped to listen to the whole song.

Every few chords, we'd hear Finley cackle with laughter and clap his hands. Now we knew who Darius was singing to.

When he finished the song, Gilley and I finally stepped

around the corner and called out to him. "Hi, Darius!" Gilley yelled.

Darius jumped but quickly recovered himself. "Hey, guys," he said. "Sorry! Did you knock, and I didn't hear you?"

I shook my head. "No, we brought Sunny's car back and parked it in the garage but we can't get the door to close so we came looking for you and heard that gorgeous singing voice of yours and had to investigate."

Darius broke out into a bashful grin. "I have always loved to sing," he said. "Just not in front of an audience."

"Such a shame. Because you are good!" I said, sitting down in one of the patio chairs next to Darius.

Gilley walked toward Finley when he saw the little tyke make eye contact with him, and he stuck out his arms, like he was coming in for a hug.

Finley, who was seated in his toy car, let out a squeal of delight and held his own arms out too.

Darius and I watched them in silence as Gilley picked Finley up and began to dance with him.

I chuckled, and so did his dad. Gilley whirled in a series of spins that took him off the patio and onto the beach. It was clear that Gil wanted to play with Finley for a minute, so I took the time to ask Darius about Sunny.

"How's our girl holding up?"

Darius shook his head and stared at the ground. "It's like a nightmare," he said. "I keep thinking she's gonna come home and walk right out here to tell me that it was all one big mistake."

I bit my lip. I couldn't imagine how hard this might be for him. If Sunny was convicted, he'd have to raise Finley alone.

"Has Marcus said anything about her defense?" I asked.

"Not much. He asked me to put him in touch with her doctor, to get a history of her Ambien-induced amnesia. And he said he might be going with an insanity defense— which, ha, I can't *even* wrap my mind around."

"If it keeps Sunny out of jail . . ."

"That's just the thing, though, Catherine. She'd be out of prison, but she'd be imprisoned in a mental health hospital. Probably for life."

I felt like Darius had just gut punched me. Sunny's options weren't really options. "Gilley and I have been looking into other suspects," I said.

Darius looked at me in surprise. "Other suspects?"

I nodded. "We found a copy of Yelena's script, and we've been able to identify nine out of twelve of her lovers."

"You think one of them did it?"

"I do. I think that Sunny might've walked in on Yelena when she was being murdered, and Sunny probably rushed in to help, which is how she got the blood on her clothes, and then she ran out of there, and whoever committed the murder tossed the letter opener aside and ran after her, but she got away. She then went home, changed, got back in her car, and drove to the park. The guilt of not being able to save Yelena caught up with her, and she swallowed your entire prescription."

The expression on Darius's face told me he doubted my explanation. "You think a jury's going to believe that?"

"If we can catch one of the lovers in a lie, I think they just might."

"Who've you identified so far?" he asked.

I reached into my purse and pulled out the script and also pulled up the photo I'd taken of the whiteboard. Showing them both to Darius, I said, "This is who we've got so far."

Darius read sections of the script and eyed the list of names. "I know she dated some of these guys," he said. "I'm a Giants fan, and Yelena bragged that she was dating the quarterback. I knew she wasn't dating Jones or McCoy. They're too young and too successful to have gotten involved with her, so Bosch makes sense."

I squinted at him. "Is there anything you might know about the three missing names?"

Darius studied the opening lines for each of those lovers for a moment. "Okay, so Lover Number Ten is gonna be Killington Cavill."

"Who's that?"

"He's a Scottish race-car driver. He's really good. He came to the States to drive a car for Team Penske. Sunny and I saw Yelena and Cavill dining outside at the end of the summer about a year ago. Sunny said that Yelena was really into Cavill, but she was worried that the relationship was starting to go downhill, because Cavill was talking about going back to Scotland."

"Did he go back to Scotland?" I asked.

"I think so," Darius said. And then he squinted at something in the text of the script, and I heard him take in a sharp breath.

"What is it?" I asked.

He tapped the script. "I know who Number Two was."

"Was? Or is?"

"Was," he said, and he looked sad.

"Who?"

"My uncle Roy."

It was my turn to sound surprised. "*Your* uncle?"

"Yeah. 'Fraid so."

"Yelena dated your uncle?"

"For about four months. She came over one Sunday for barbecue, and Uncle Roy stopped in to say hi. They met and hit it off, and I tried to warn him about Yelena, how she went through men, but he was diggin' the fact that this pretty, much younger woman was attracted to him, so he didn't listen. He got his heart broken when she called it off with him. He died of a stroke about two months later."

"Oh, Darius, I'm so sorry."

"It's okay. He had a good life. He made a bundle, retired, and moved out here to be closer to me and Sunny. He was more my dad than my own dad, actually."

"Was he a congressman?" I asked.

"A congressman? No. What made you think that?"

I pointed to the line in the script. "'He spent his days at the house on the hill.'"

Darius let out a short laugh. "No, Uncle Roy was a stockbroker for thirty years. He moved into a house up there." Darius pointed to a bluff overlooking the ocean. "It's up a steep hill," he said.

"Ahhh," I said. "Okay, I get it." Then I pointed to the script again. "Any guesses about Lover Number Twelve?"

Darius read the lines and shook his head. "No clue," he said. "Ever since COVID ended, I've been working a lot in L.A., so I haven't been around. I could ask Sunny if she knows."

"Would you?"

"Sure," he said. "If this will help her case, then I'll definitely try to get the name from her."

"You are a gem," I said happily. Darius had solved two

riddles in about five minutes, and I felt such a wave of relief knowing that the two men he identified had been out of the picture at the time of Yelena's murder—although I'd have to have Gilley look up Cavill and make sure he was still in Scotland.

Next to me, on the table, something buzzed. I looked down and saw that it was Darius's phone.

"Andrew is calling," I said, picking up the phone and offering it to him.

"Great!" he said, handing me the script and my phone, then taking up his own. "He's my real estate guy. Excuse me." Darius moved off toward the house to speak privately, and I sat in one of the Adirondack chairs and watched Gilley run around Finley as the toddler stood still and laughed and laughed at Gilley.

It was good to see Finley so unaffected by his mother's absence. I knew that was unlikely to last, but the boy was young enough that it might not be as awful as you'd expect.

After another few minutes, Darius came back over to me and sat down again. "Sorry about that," he said. "I'm selling my place in L.A."

"The condo?"

He pulled his chin back in surprise. "You know about the condo?"

"I do. Sunny told me. Why're you selling it?"

Darius's gaze traveled to the ground again. He was clearly embarrassed. "I'm trying to raise money for Sunny's defense. Marcus told me it could be as much as a half a million."

"Yikes," I said.

"Yep," Darius said, looking sadly at Finley and Gilley playing together. "I'd pay anything to get Sunny off the hook. She's the love of my life." His voice hitched as he said the last part.

"We'll do whatever we can, Darius," I said softly. I really felt for him.

"Thanks," he said, then offered a grateful smile.

A moment of awkward silence followed, and I asked, "Do you and Finley have enough to eat?"

"You mean for dinner and stuff?"

I nodded.

"Yeah. I guess. He's got plenty of food, but I haven't been very hungry."

"We'd like to make you a lasagna. Would that be okay?"

"You kidding? Lasagna is my favorite. That'd be great, Catherine. Thank you."

Gilley came up to us, holding Finley on his hip. "Whew!" he said. "This tyke has got some energy!" Gilley poked Finley's belly button, and the boy squealed in delight.

Darius stood and held his arms out. "It's almost dinner-time for him," he said.

I got up too. "We'll leave you to your daddy duties, but we'll see you soon, okay?"

"Great. And, Catherine?"

"Yes?"

"Thank you. And I mean that."

I grinned. "Of course, Darius. Of course."

When we were once again on the road, I said, "Is it okay with you if we stop at the grocery store?"

"I've got all the supplies I need for dinner, sugar."

"What're we having?"

"Chicken Veronique."

"Ooh," I said. "I love your chicken Veronique. But I

was hoping we could pick up all the ingredients to make your famous lasagna tomorrow."

"You know that takes me all day, right?"

"I'll be there to help," I said. "I want to make it for Darius and Finley."

Gilley's brow shot up. "Oh yeah," he said. "I totally forgot about bringing them over something easy to heat up so they wouldn't have to worry about dinner. Thanks for reminding me. And yes, we will absolutely make that tomorrow."

"Yay!" I said, happy that he was willing to put in the time to make his famous dish.

We arrived at the grocery store, and just as I slid into a spot, my phone rang. "It's Marcus," I said.

"You talk. I'll shop," Gilley said.

I nodded, and Gilley hustled out of the car.

"Marcus," I said happily. I always enjoyed talking to him.

"Catherine," he said. "Got a minute?"

"I do. What's up?"

"A couple of things."

"Tell me."

"For starters, the D.A. just sent over some exculpatory evidence that the new detective—"

"Santana?"

"Yeah, that sounds right. That Detective Santana found when he subpoenaed Yelena's phone records."

"What did he find?" I asked, knowing it was bad.

"A series of phone calls between Yelena and two numbers, both registered to Sunny D'Angelo, placed approximately twenty, ten, and five minutes before the start of her show."

"Sunny had *two* phones?"

"It looks that way."

"I've only ever called her on the two-four-two-four number," I said, remembering the last four digits of Sunny's number because my birthday was on the twenty-fourth of the month.

"She had another number listed with a three-eight-three-eight subscriber number."

"What's a subscriber number?"

"The last four digits of a telephone number."

"Ah," I said but then got back to the topic at hand. "So Sunny was calling her from both her phones?"

"And Yelena was calling her back at both numbers."

"How long did the conversations last?"

"A minute or two for the first two calls, placed by Yelena to the three-eight number, then another call out to Sunny at the two-four-two-four number, and that one lasted ten minutes, but the last call was from Sunny's phone to Yelena, and that lasted thirty seconds."

"Could Sunny have left a message?"

"It's possible. Still, it doesn't bode well for Sunny's case that she and Yelena were having phone calls back and forth with each other in the hours before Yelena's murder. And it bodes even less well that the three-eight-three-eight number has been disconnected."

I blinked. "It was disconnected?"

"Yes. The morning of the day Sunny confessed to murdering Yelena."

"Whoa," I said.

"Agreed," Marcus said.

"Did you ask Sunny about it?"

Marcus sighed, and I could tell he was tired. "I did."

"And?"

"And she's all but catatonic, Catherine. She won't respond to any of my questions. She just sits there, staring at nothing, and cries."

I closed my eyes and felt tears sting the back of my lids. I couldn't imagine what Sunny's mental state was right now. I felt so bad for her.

"So, what are you going to do?" I asked.

"I'm going to call Darius and see if he can meet me at the county lockup and try to coax her out of her despondency. I'm hoping he can get her to answer my questions at least."

"That's a good plan," I said. "He's really worried about her. When are you going to go back for another talk with her?"

"Tomorrow, after we finish up at the EHCP and I drop Julia off at her home."

"You're accompanying her to the club," I said.

"Yes. She works quick and dirty, and I like her style."

"Good, Marcus. That's good. Make sure she stays safe, okay?"

"Definitely. Now, tell me about any progress you've made."

"Well! Darius has actually shed some light for us on that front. He's helped me identify two of the remaining three mystery men."

"Which ones?"

"Two and Ten."

"The man you think is a member of Congress and the race-car driver?"

"Yes. Good memory."

"It comes in handy," he said. "So, who are they?"

"Two was Darius's uncle Roy."

"Darius's *uncle* dated Yelena?"

"He did. Roy was loaded, and that was all that mattered to Yelena, apparently."

"Was he a congressman?"

"No. Turns out he actually lived on a hill. It's not far from their home, in fact."

"Where is he now?"

"Dead. Darius said he died a year ago."

"Natural causes?"

"Stroke," I said. "Anyway, Lover Number Ten is a guy named Killington Cavill."

Marcus grunted. "I'm familiar with that name. He drove for an oil company."

"Tire," I said. "Penske."

"Okay, so where is he now?"

"We think he's back in Scotland. I'm going to have Gilley look into it tonight, see if he can't pinpoint if that's true and for how long Cavill has been back in his homeland."

"Good," Marcus said. "No luck with Number Twelve?"

"No," I said. "Darius couldn't fit the description to anyone he knew that Yelena had dated."

"It would be nice to have all the names locked down," Marcus said.

"It would. Gilley and I won't give up, but for the moment, that guy remains a mystery."

"All right, Catherine. Really good work so far. I'll be in touch."

With that, Marcus was gone. A moment later, Gilley appeared with a grocery cart brimming with paper bags. I got out and helped him load up the car.

"We really need all this just to make lasagna?"

"The best ingredients make the most delicious meals, sugar."

"Good point."

On the way home, I filled him in on my conversation with Marcus.

"I hope they can coax Sunny out of her despondency," Gil said. He looked as worried as I felt.

"If anyone can do it, it'll be Darius."

"Not Shepherd?"

"No," I said. "I doubt Marcus would allow Shep anywhere near Sunny right now."

"Why do you say that?"

"He's the cop that turned her in. If she confesses even one detail that helps the murder charges against her, he'll report it to Santana."

"He'd do that to his own *sister*?"

"He's already done it to her," I said.

Gilley sat with his arms crossed as he fell silent and stared out the window. I could tell he wanted to say something judgmental and was holding it back.

"What?" I asked.

"Nothing."

"Gil," I pressed. "Say what you're going to say."

"Fine. Do you think dating someone who's capable of throwing his twin sister in jail is a good idea?"

"What was he supposed to do?" I asked him. "She confessed to murder in front of him and fifty other people standing close by. It's not like he could've pretended that she hadn't said what she'd said *and* hadn't backed that up with a paper bag full of bloody clothes."

Gilley scowled and went back to staring out the window. "Well, *I* could never date someone like that."

"Come on, Gil," I begged. "Shepherd's a good guy caught in an impossible situation."

"I still don't like it," he insisted.

"I don't, either, but I'd rather date a principled, honest, decent man than a liar and someone unprincipled. I had that in my last relationship. I don't need it in this one."

"Maks?" Gilley asked in surprise, referring to a man I'd briefly dated before Shepherd.

"No, not Maks," I said. "Tom."

"Oh, your ex."

"Yes."

Gilley sighed. "Okay, Cat, it's your life. Live it however you want."

We arrived at Chez Kitty a few minutes later, and Spooks greeted us warmly at the door, with lots of tail wagging and wiggling against our legs.

"Poor guy," I said, setting down the groceries and then bending to give Spooks a hug. "He's been home alone all day."

"I gotta get a walk in for him," Gilley said, looking through the window at the darkening sky.

I pointed to the door. "Go," I said. "I'll put the groceries away and start the pasta and cut the grapes for the chicken Veronique."

Gilley grabbed Spooks's leash and kissed me on the cheek. "You're a lifesaver," he said. "I'll be back in twenty minutes."

I spent the next five minutes just hauling in all the bags from the car and unpacking them. Then I put hot water from the hot water spigot into a pot, set it on a burner, and turned the flame to high. I then got out a knife, a cutting board, and the green grapes in the fruit bowl on the counter. Checking on the water for the pasta, I was happy to see it beginning to boil. I got some penne pasta out of the cupboard and dumped the whole box in. After setting the timer on my watch, I picked up the knife. I had cut exactly two grapes when I heard the front door open.

"That was fast," I called out to Gilley.

"What was fast?" Shepherd replied.

I whirled around. "Oh!" I exclaimed. "I wasn't expecting you tonight."

Shepherd rubbed his eyes and blinked several times. "I know. I should've called, but I really wanted to see you and couldn't handle it if you'd said no."

I set down the knife and hurried over to him, then hugged him fiercely. "I'll always have room for you here, Shep."

He hugged me back just as tightly, swaying the two of us back and forth. "Thank you," he said softly. Then, with a big inhale, he said, "Hey, good lookin'. Whatcha got cookin'?"

"Chicken Veronique. Would you like some?"

"Depends on what *Veronique* means."

I laughed. "It's a dish made with chicken, pasta, green grapes, white wine, and lots of cream."

"That sounds good," Shepherd said, and he looked surprised.

"Gilley's recipe," I admitted, pointing to a seat at the table before I returned to the grapes. "Sit," I told him. "And tell me how your day was."

"Exhausting," he said.

"Did you work on the Purdy case?"

"I did. All damn day. Went in circles on it. There's technically no phone record on Purdy's phone or in his records that matches up with any of the guys on your suspect list."

"Oh! I have another name for you."

"Who?"

"Killington Cavill."

"The race-car driver?"

"Everybody knows this guy but me," I said.

"He's a really good driver," Shepherd said, getting up to go to the fridge and peer inside it hopefully.

"Bottom of the door," I said. "On the left."

"Ahhh," he said, bringing up a bottle of pale ale. "You two really know how to spoil a guy."

"Back to Cavill," I said. "We think he went back to Scotland a year ago."

"You haven't checked?"

"Not yet."

"I'll look into it," Shepherd said. "How'd you pinpoint the name?"

"Darius. I showed him the script, and he told me that Yelena had dated his uncle, and he remembered seeing her with Cavill during the pandemic."

"Hold on," Shepherd said. "Yelena dated Darius's uncle Roy?"

"You knew him?"

"I did," he said. "Sweet old guy. Had a ton of money."

"Which is probably why Yelena found him attractive."

Shepherd grunted. "Yeah. That seems to have been her pattern. How's D doing, anyway?"

"He seems to be holding up," I said. "Or as well as can be expected. When we saw him today, he was singing a lullaby to Finley."

"He was?"

"You sound surprised."

"That just sounds really nurturing, and I never took Darius for the nurturing type."

"Why not?" I asked.

He shrugged. "Darius didn't have much of a home life growing up. His parents split when he was four, and his mother moved through husbands like a beaver through wood."

"Really?" I said. "That's sad. Does she live around here too?"

"Nah," he said. "She's in Singapore, on husband number six. Or maybe seven. Each one of them she takes to the cleaners when she files for divorce, but this latest husband made her sign a prenup."

"A gold digger like her signed a prenup?" I said.

Shepherd tipped his beer at me. "I found that curious, too, until Darius told me that they actually worked out a compromise. If his mom stays with this husband for the next ten years, she'll get half his money."

"Wow," I said. "Why do kind men always end up with the worst women?"

"Don't know," he said. "Still, Darius's mom isn't *all* bad. She's made Finley the heir to her fortune."

"Well, that's comforting," I said. "Finley will never want for anything."

"Except his mother," Shepherd said. I stopped slicing the grapes and went to him, hugged him around the shoulders and kissed the top of his head. "I love you," I said. "And I'm so sorry you and your family are going through this."

"My hope is that Santana bungles the investigation. I'm counting on Marcus to seed some doubt into the jury."

"He will," I said. "He will."

Shepherd patted my arm and said, "Back to the Purdy case. It turns out the counselor wasn't as retired as he let on."

"He was still seeing clients?"

Shepherd held up three fingers while he took a long pull from the bottle.

"Only three?" I asked.

"Yeah. Two are elderly women with too much money and too many squabbling family members. I talked to both of them. They know each other, and the one recommended the other. They were really upset to hear that Purdy died."

"I bet," I said.

"He was well liked by his clients," Shepherd continued. "I called a few from the last couple of years. They all raved about him."

"Who was the third client?" I asked.

"That's some shell company, which I'm having a heck of a time tracking down. It's gonna take me a week of red tape to come up with a name connected to it."

I looked up from the cutting board, having cut a nice pile of grapes. "I have faith," I told him, moving to the stove to stir the pasta.

"Where's Gilley?" Shepherd asked. "And Spooks?"

"They're on a walk. They should be back any minute."

"Aw, man," Shepherd moaned. "I am starving. I was hoping you guys would already have dinner made."

"We're not the only ones who can cook, you know."

"Are you looking at me?"

"Yep."

"Cat, you *know* I can't cook."

"Anyone can cook, lovey. You just need to commit to learning how."

Shepherd got up and came over to me. "Okay, Obi-Wan. Teach me."

I got out all the ingredients from the fridge, including

the chicken tenders, and began to heat them in a frying pan. I showed Shepherd how to tell when the chicken was done by pressing on his palm, then on the chicken, so that he could compare the two pressures.

When the chicken was done, I had Shepherd slice the tenders up into bite-sized pieces while I stirred a quarter cup of white wine into the still hot pan. It bubbled almost immediately.

"Would you hand me that?" I asked, pointing to the flour jar on the counter closer to him.

Shepherd slid it over to me. "Whatcha gonna do with that?"

"Make a roux."

"What's a roux?"

"It's when you add a little bit of melted butter to a little bit of flour, stir until the butter is absorbed, then add a little more melted butter, and a little more and more, until the roux is the consistency of cream soup."

"Okay. My next question is, why?"

"It's what we're going to use to thicken the sauce," I said before showing him how I did it. I put some butter in a small dish, placed the butter in the microwave, and melted it. Then I filled another small dish with a generous teaspoon of flour, pulled the butter from the microwave, swirled it around to melt the last bit of it, then added a little to the flour and stirred that until it was absorbed. I continued adding butter until the roux was the consistency of soup.

Shepherd then watched while I poured a whole cup of cream into the pan with the bubbling wine and stirred it to keep it from overheating. Then I folded in the roux and stirred until it thickened the sauce right before tossing in the grapes, and waited for them to heat up a bit. Once they were just starting to soften, I tossed in the chicken tender pieces, finishing it all off with a bit of salt and pepper.

Shepherd stuck his finger into the sauce to taste it. "Mmm," he said. "That's good!"

I smiled and removed the sauce from the heat, drained the pasta, and had Shepherd set out three place settings while I loaded up three plates with pasta then sauce.

"I'm sorry!" Gilley called out as he burst through the door. "Spooks saw a cat and pulled the leash right out of my hand! I had to chase him for, like, a mile before I got him to come back."

Shepherd and I turned to look at Gilley, then Spooks, then Gilley again.

Spooks was panting and looking rather proud of himself.

Gilley was panting and looking rather frazzled.

"Come," I said to him, picking up two of the plates and bringing them to the table. "Sit. We'll eat, and you'll feel better."

"Thank God you made dinner," Gilley said. "I'm starved!"

"Feed Spooks first, though," I said.

Gilley snapped his fingers and got out Spooks's new bowl, poured a half a cup of kibble into it, and set it on the floor. The pup went right to it, and he would've gulped it down, but the new bowl was a maze of curved ridges, which allowed him to eat only one bit of kibble at a time.

At last, we all sat down and ate together, and I didn't remember ever feeling more comforted by the presence of these two men.

Just as we were finishing up, Shepherd's phone buzzed. He took it out of his pocket and looked at the display, his brow knitting when he read the caller ID.

After getting up, he walked a few steps away and took the call. "Lieutenant," he said.

"Oh, God," I whispered to Gilley. "I hope he's not in trouble again."

"Why would you think that?"

"Why else would Shep's lieutenant be calling if not to bawl him out for some petty thing?"

We both watched Shepherd intently as he ran a hand through his hair and was obviously rattled by whatever his boss was telling him. "When?" he asked sharply.

Gilley and I exchanged a nervous look.

"Where's he now?"

There was a set to Shepherd's shoulders that told us the news was bad. Just how bad, I thought, we'd soon find out.

"All right. I'll head there now."

Clicking off the call, he turned to look at us, and something in his eyes made my own eyes well up. The news wasn't just bad. It was personal to us.

"What?" I said, my voice cracking.

Shepherd came back to the table and sat down. Taking up my hand, he said, "There's been a car accident."

My first thought was that it had to do with my sons, and the tears overflowed and slid down my cheeks. "Wh-wh-who?" I said.

"Marcus," he said.

I blinked and shook my head a little, unable to take in fully what Shepherd was telling me. "Who?" I repeated.

"Marcus Brown," Shepherd said.

I put a hand to my mouth, and Gilley stared at Shepherd in stunned silence. "But I just talked to him," I squeaked.

"When?" Shep asked.

"Like, an hour and a half ago."

Shepherd nodded. "I'm going to the hospital," he said.

"He's in the hospital?" Gilley said, his own eyes watering.

"Yeah, Gilley. It's bad. They had to use the Jaws of Life to get him out of his car."

"Did he lose control?" Gilley asked and I was surprised to see he, too, was crying.

Shepherd shook his head. "It was a hit-and-run. We think Marcus may have been targeted."

I was also shaking my head. This couldn't be happening. I adored Marcus, and I didn't want him hurt. I didn't even want him scratched.

"We'll go with you," Gilley said, jumping to his feet.

Shepherd nodded. "We need to go now, though."

I got up and grabbed all three plates, hustled them to the sink, then hurried to get my coat and purse. "I'm ready," I said while Shepherd was slipping into his.

Gilley didn't even bother with a coat. He just headed to the door and hurried outside.

"Are you okay to drive?" Shepherd asked me.

"Why? You're not taking us there?"

"I'll be working the case all night, Cat. You'll need your car."

I was panting with worry. "I'll be okay," I said.

Shepherd kissed the top of my head, and we moved on out the door.

Chapter 18

We arrived at the hospital and followed Shepherd inside. Gilley and I were both silent and numb. I'd prayed all the way over, and while I walked behind Shepherd, I continued to pray.

Shepherd came to a stop at the information desk. He spoke softly, but I still heard him and saw him flash his badge as he asked about Marcus.

The information desk clerk pointed to his left and said, "That way, past the elevators to the end of the hall. Then turn right and follow that hallway to the end. The trauma unit is through the double doors, and you can ask the nurse on duty for more information about Mr. Brown, Detective."

"Thanks," Shepherd said, then thumped the counter between them two times before turning away, back to us. Pointing ahead, he said, "This way, you two."

Again, we trailed behind Shepherd, who was following the clerk's directions. At last, we came through a set
of doors, and immediately, I felt the energy shift to one of
urgency. Doctors and nurses were rushing around in a no-
time-to-waste kind of way.

Gilley inched closer to me and took up my hand. I
squeezed it to reassure him, but I felt so vulnerable and
scared in that moment, so I stopped several feet behind
Shepherd, who approached the nurses' desk with his badge
out.

He and the nurse spoke; then he nodded and came
back to us.

"He's in surgery," Shepherd said. "He's got a collapsed lung and some internal bleeding. The nurse will
have the surgeon come out and speak to us as soon as
they're done operating."

I swallowed hard, barely managing to hold down a
sob.

Shepherd stood across from me and Gilley, and then
he opened his arms wide and said, "Get in here, you
two."

We both rushed forward and wrapped our arms around
him and each other, and that hug did me a world of good.

Afterward, we sat quietly in the waiting area, where a
TV with the sound off but closed-captioning on played a
sitcom.

As the time closed in on 9:00 p.m., a woman in scrubs,
booties, and a surgical cap walked in and said, "Detective?"

Shepherd got up, and Gilley and I did too. He moved
forward to walk a few feet away with the surgeon; we
held back but took up holding each other's hands again.

Shepherd spoke to the surgeon at length, and I saw him taking down the details on the small pad of paper he always kept on him.

At last, they nodded to each other, and she walked away, while he turned back to us.

"He's stable," he said.

Gilley and I both let out a huge whoosh of air. "Oh, my God," I said, putting my free hand to my chest, where my heart was thumping wildly inside. "Thank God!"

Gilley put both his hands together in prayer and looked skyward, then shook his praying hands at the ceiling. "Thank you, thank you, thank you!" he said.

Shepherd also looked relieved. "He's in the ICU right now, and they'll keep him sedated for at least the next twenty-four hours, but the surgeon said she was able to stop the bleed and repair and expand his lung again. She also needed to put a few pins into three of his ribs to support the rib cage and keep it from collapsing again. He's also got a pretty good head wound, but the CT scan didn't look too bad, she said. He's probably got a solid concussion but no brain bleed."

"That all sounds so horrible!" I said.

"It couldn't have been fun," Shep agreed. Then he sighed and said, "Now that you know he's okay, why don't you two head home? I've got to get to the scene and take a look at the car and get an estimate for how fast the other car was going, and from which direction."

"There were no witnesses?" I said.

"I don't know that yet, Cat. That's why I've got to go."

I nodded. "Understood. But will you monitor his condition and let us know if anything changes?"

"I will," he said. "Do you guys know who to contact about getting a number for his next of kin?"

"His paralegal is named Jasmine, but I don't know her last name," Gilley said.

"Taylor," I said, recalling her introduction to us.

"Terrific," Shepherd said, jotting that down before closing his little notebook and putting it back in his blazer pocket. "I'll call her next, tell her what's happened, and be in touch."

"Oh!" I said, remembering Julia's get-together with Marcus the next day. "Can you tell her to make sure Julia knows that Marcus won't be available to accompany her to the club?"

"What club?" Shepherd asked.

"The EHGC. They were going to have lunch tomorrow."

"They know each other?"

"They do," I said.

"Yeah, okay. I'll pass along the message. You guys drive safe, and I'll be in touch."

With that, we went our separate ways.

When we got back home, Gilley and I got out of the car and he said over the hood, "Would you like to stay over again?"

"I would," I said.

"Good. But this time, sleep in the spare bedroom, okay?"

"I don't like to put you out by sleeping in a bed where you'll have to change the sheets and remake the bed."

"Cat," Gilley said, as if he found the notion ridiculous. "Come on. Sleep in a bed tonight. Washing sheets is no big deal."

"I'll wash them tomorrow," I said. "I have to wash the linens in the room Darius and Finley slept in tomorrow too."

Gilley sighed. "Whatever makes you feel more comfortable," he said.

I went to Chez Cat and changed into the same silk pajamas I'd worn the night before and headed back over to Chez Kitty.

Gilley was already in his robe and pajamas too. He yawned and said, "Did you want to stay up a bit?"

"No," I said. "I'm exhausted."

"Me too. See you in the morning?"

"Yes."

"You'll come get me if Shepherd calls with any news about Marcus?"

"I will. I promise."

"Good night, Cat."

"'Night, Gilley," I said before shuffling into the guest bedroom. I was asleep almost as soon as my head hit the pillow.

The next morning, I woke up to the smell of coffee. I grabbed my phone to make sure I hadn't missed any calls from Shepherd—I hadn't—and made my way to the kitchen.

"It's so early," I whispered when I found Gilley at the table, staring into space and sipping on a steaming cup of coffee.

"I woke up and couldn't get back to sleep," he said.

It was 4:00 a.m., and while I didn't feel fully rested, at least the hours of sleep I'd gotten were restful.

"Any news from Shepherd?" Gilley asked.

"Not a peep," I said, moving over to the French press to pour my own mug of brew.

"No news is good news, right?"

"It is."

"Who could've done that to him, Cat?"

I sat down and sighed. "I don't know, Gil. He's a defense attorney, and from what I understand of that profession, it's not an especially safe one. A client loses in court, gets some jail time, and comes back for revenge when freed. I mean, you saw his office, right? It was all top-notch security, and I'm thinking there was a reason for that."

"You're right," Gil said. "I just feel so helpless. I wish there was something we could do."

I knew what he meant. I felt helpless too. But then I had an idea about how we could fill our morning with purpose. "Hey," I said, tapping his arm. "What do you think about making not just one lasagna for Darius and Finley, but three? One for the D'Angelos, one for Tiffany and her parents, which will give us a chance to check up on her, and one for Aaron. I've wanted to call him since yesterday, when he was released."

"I think that's a great plan," Gilley said, with an eager eye.

I stood. "Then let's hop to it!"

We spent the next several hours making the lasagnas. Gilley even insisted on making the noodles from scratch. "What's the point of having a pasta roller and a noodle drying rack if you're just gonna go store bought?" he'd said when I'd questioned his laborious methods.

While Gilley tended to the pasta, I got started on his recipe for meat sauce, which was a complex series of steps, but when it was finally simmering, it filled Chez Kitty with an aroma that was heavenly.

Gilley placed two small fans in front of and behind the perfectly made pasta noodles and sniffed the air. "You did great," he said, squeezing my shoulders in a one-armed hug.

"How long will the noodles have to dry?"

"The fan cuts the time in half, so about six hours."

I looked at the time on the stove. "We can start assembling at eleven thirty, then?"

"Yep. It'll take about forty minutes to assemble all three, and another forty to forty-five minutes to bake, and then I'd give it at least a half hour to cool, which means we'll be good to go around two o'clock."

"What should we do while we wait for the pasta noodles to dry?"

"Make breakfast and take a nap."

"I love that idea," I said, grinning.

Gilley put together a quick quiche while I sent a text to Shepherd in the hopes that he might be up. His reply was quick.

"Is Shepherd up?" Gilley asked me. He'd obviously seen me sending a text.

"He is. He's heading out to the car lot to inspect Marcus's car, and he'll call me later."

"Did you ask him about Marcus?"

"I did. He says there's no news."

Gilley paused to wipe his hands on a dish towel and looked at me earnestly. "Do we still think no news is good news?"

"We do," I said, willing myself to believe it.

"Okay, then I won't worry more than I already am."

We ate breakfast together and talked over some ideas for Willem and Chanel's reception. We'd given our first impressions to Julia, but now that we had a chance to discuss the event between us, we were coming up with new ideas and jotting them down to send to her later this afternoon, after we got done spreading some lasagna cheer along the way.

Around nine o'clock I yawned. So did Gilley.

"Nap time," he said.

I grinned and asked, "Can I cuddle with Spooks?" Gilley had, of course, claimed the pup the night before, but Spooks gave me such comfort that I couldn't resist asking.

"Of course," Gilley said.

We headed back to our bedrooms, Spooks following me, and once again I fell asleep quickly.

By eleven thirty we were back in the kitchen, both feeling much more rested, and we got to work assembling the pasta.

"These noodles are perfect," Gilley said.

"They feel amazing," I told him. Soft and velvety, they covered the layers of meat sauce and cheese perfectly.

"Do you think we'll have enough for a small lasagna for us?"

"We should," Gilley said. "You made plenty of meat sauce."

"But is there enough pasta?"

"There is," he said. "If we cut the noodles in half and use a small casserole dish."

"I've got the perfect size at Chez Cat."

"Fantastic," Gilley said. "You can take all the ingredients over there and assemble our dinner, and put this third one in your oven while you're at it."

"Sebastian," I said.

"Yes, Lady Catherine?"

"Please preheat the oven at Chez Cat to three hundred seventy-five."

"Preheating initiated," Sebastian said.

"I love Sebastian," Gilley said.

"I love you as well, Sir Gilley."

That made us both giggle.

Gilley helped me across the driveway with all the ingredients for our small pan pasta and announced that he had to take Spooks for a walk.

"Careful he doesn't pull the leash out of your hand this time," I said.

"Trust me, from now on I'm holding on to that leash with a death grip."

He left, and I put the third lasagna into the oven, then assembled ours and was so pleased that the leftover ingredients were the exact amount I needed. After setting that completed casserole dish in the refrigerator, I peered through the oven glass and smiled at the bubbling concoction. Then I glanced at the time and hurried upstairs to take a shower and change before I had to pull the lasagna out.

When I stepped out of the shower, I got a text from Gilley, asking me to pull out the lasagnas at his place because he wouldn't be back in time.

I growled. He was cutting into my schedule now, but I donned a robe and dashed across to Chez Kitty just in time to hear the timer go off on the stove.

After carefully removing both casserole dishes, I set them on cooling racks, then hurried back across the drive to Chez Cat, looked at the timer on the stove, and said, "Sebastian, will you please let me know when the stove timer goes off?"

"I will, Lady Catherine."

After dashing up the stairs, I shimmied into a pair of leggings, a long-sleeved olive dress that fell just below my knees, and some low-heeled black boots.

I was almost finished drying my hair when Sebastian told me that the timer had gone off on the lasagna, so I abandoned the hair dryer and raced downstairs to pull the lasagna out of the oven. After setting the casserole dish on a cooling rack, I went back upstairs and finished making myself presentable.

By 1:15 p.m. I was ready for the day, but I didn't have a lot to do until the pasta cooled enough to be transported.

Making my way to the family room, I noticed how dirty the floor was, and so I hauled out the vacuum cleaner and got up most of the debris, which had been brought in by the birthday party guests. I then took the cordless vacuum upstairs, started in on the carpet in the hallway, and made my way to the boys' rooms.

Opening the door to Matt's room first and then to Mike's, I sighed. "I've raised slobs," I said. The boys' rooms were a mess!

I started cleaning their rooms by pulling off the sheets and tossing them into the washing machine and starting the load. I then moved to the guest room and found it neat as a pin. Darius had kindly made up the bed. After pulling those sheets off, I dumped them in the basket in the laundry room, making a mental note to wash them with the sheets at Chez Kitty when the first load was done.

Peeking at the time on my watch, I saw that I had twenty minutes left before meeting up with Gilley, so I headed to the worst disaster—Matt's room—and started sorting clothes scattered about the room into piles of darks and lights. It was as I was checking to see if anything had been shoved under the bed that I saw his duffel bag. After pulling it to me, I unzipped it and spread the flaps, only to be assaulted by the most god-awful stench.

His running shoes and sweaty clothes had been percolating ever since he left for school three weeks before.

"Oh, my God, child of mine," I said, pinching my nose and gingerly taking out the shoes and the clothes.

And that was when it hit me.

And everything clicked.

All of it.

I could see it laid out perfectly, each such a tiny clue, but leading to the final conclusion.

"Oh, my God," I whispered, rushing to my bedroom, where I'd left my phone. Snatching it off the bed, I realized that there were half a dozen texts from Gilley, sent only fifteen minutes before.

Ohmigod! I—shower—gone for ten minutes! He ate the whole thing!

Why aren't you answering your phone????

Headed to emergency vet!

Immediately I called Gilley.

"*Where have you been?*" he yelled.

"Honey, I'm so sorry! I was vacuuming and didn't hear my phone! What's happened?"

Gilley was sobbing. "I've killed him, Cat! *I've killed him!*"

I gasped. "Oh, no! Gilley, you mean Spooks . . . he's . . ." I couldn't form the words.

"In the back, with the vet," he said, still crying. "They're doing an ultrasound. He ate the whole damn lasagna, Cat! He figured out how to push a chair to the counter climbed up and *ate the entire thing*!"

I bit my lip. "Do you need me to come there?"

"No," he said. "No. I'll call you if I get news. But it might be a while. They're busy here today."

"Okay, sweetie. I'll wait to hear from you."

Clicking off the call, I stared at my phone. I hadn't

wanted to add anything to Gilley's brain, because he was so undone.

So I called Shepherd. I got his voice mail. Then a text, with the words **Can't talk right now.**

I got up and began pacing the room. An idea was forming to confirm my suspicions, and I wondered if I could pull it off safely.

"I'll just slip in and take a few pictures," I said. "I've already got a distraction. I'll be fine."

Still, I paced just a little bit more before reaching for my laptop and conducting several searches just to satisfy any lingering doubt. "The theater is only two miles from the park," I mumbled. "That's an easy run for someone so in shape."

I then looked up the safety features in Range Rovers and found what I was looking for easily. Next, I searched for a name that flashed through my memory, found it and, scrolling the associated web page, landed on the very item that tied every single thing together.

Standing up from my place on the bed, I settled on the endeavor before I lost my nerve. After dashing down the steps, I carefully placed my phone in my purse with the camera facing outward, put the lasagna in a warming bag, and rushed out the door.

Chapter 19

When I pulled into the drive, the garage door was up, but no car was in the bay, and there wasn't one to the side, either.

I had sat there for a beat, wondering what to do, when I saw a car pull into the drive right behind me. My pulse quickened, but I didn't let the fear get the best of me. I reached for the lasagna and my purse, got out of the car, and smiled all friendly-like.

"Catherine!" he said, smiling at me, as if he was genuinely happy to see me.

"Hello, Darius." I lifted the lasagna and said, "We promised to bake you one, remember?"

Darius opened the back door of his car and unbuckled his son, who was barely awake and fell limply against his father's shoulder.

"Aww!" I said, happy that things had also fallen in my favor. "He's so sleepy!"

Darius rubbed his son's back. "It's his nap time," he said, walking toward me.

I held out my free hand. "Can I?" I asked.

"Sure," he said and placed Finley against my shoulder while he took up the lasagna. "This smells amazing."

I grinned and shifted Finley to a more comfortable position for him. "Gilley insisted on homemade noodles."

"Wow!" he said, getting out his keys to open the front door. "I get the VIP treatment, huh?"

I laughed softly. "Well, mostly Finley, but also you."

Darius laughed. "Yeah, I get it."

He unlocked the door and held it open for me, but I pointed toward the garage. "Your door sticking again?"

He shook his head and sighed. "That stupid garage door never did work right. I gotta get a guy out here to get a whole new system put in."

I walked into the home and swiveled on my feet as Darius was closing the door. Whispering, I said, "Can I put him down? I miss my sons so much, and it would give me great comfort to lay him down for his nap."

Darius seemed to hesitate for just a moment. "Sure," he said. "Don't mind the mess in the nursery, though. I'm reorganizing a few things."

I smiled at him. "You're a wonderful father, Darius."

"Thank you," he said, and I could see the set to his shoulders relax a fraction. "This thing is still really warm. Should I put it in the fridge until we're ready to eat it?"

"I'd put it on a cooling rack for another thirty to forty minutes. Let it cool to nearly room temperature before you put it in the fridge and risk any other food spoiling."

He pointed a finger gun at me. "Gotcha," he said, then

made a clicking sound. When he turned to move into the kitchen, I took Finley up the stairs and into the nursery.

The place was a mess. Much of Finley's clothing had been pulled out and strewn on the floor. Almost all of it for cold weather. After moving to the crib, I laid Finley down quickly but carefully.

I then snapped a photo of the room, then hurried out into the hall on tiptoe, and eased open the door directly opposite the nursery.

Two large suitcases were standing upright against the wall, and various guitars in different states of repair were also set about the room. The guitars were the link between the two murders. Purdy hadn't been killed with a piano wire. He'd been killed with a guitar wire. Most definitely from the guitar that Darius had pulled from his car when we'd approached him in the drive the night of the murders.

I snapped two more pictures, one of the suitcases and one of the guitars. And then something else caught my eye. On the wall where the suitcases were set were a series of framed photographs of Darius, grinning next to a woman who, in each photo, was wearing a different wedding dress but atop her head in each photo was the same elaborately sized tiara. Every image showed the same pose for the two subjects, but clearly, they had been taken at different stages in both of their lives. I realized belatedly that the woman must be Darius's mother at some of her many weddings.

"Married to a queen," I whispered. I snapped a picture of the series of photos on the wall too and then tiptoed back into the nursery and up to another photo, this time of Sunny standing on the porch of her old home overlooking L.A.

The view was the same one shown in the listing that I'd found by looking up Andrew Yamanski, Darius's "real estate guy."

There was no condo. There never had been. This was the house on the hill that Yelena had been referring to. Lover Number Two wasn't Darius's uncle. He was Darius.

And Darius was also Lover Number Twelve. He was the lover that Yelena had pretty much begun and ended her show on. His mother had dressed like a queen at her wedding. She was wealthy and powerful, and willing to leave a giant portion of her money to her grandson.

And, no doubt, with her financial support, Darius had been able to keep the house in L.A. as a love nest for himself and Yelena. "Phoning for donations wasn't a political campaign reference. It was a reference to Darius calling his mother for money," I said to myself.

I snapped a quick photo of the image on the wall. And then I noticed a small photo in a frame nestled on a table with a lamp. I hadn't seen it before when I was here with Sunny, or I might've put things together sooner.

The photo was of the two of them, Darius and Sunny, taken in the early days of their relationship. Sunny was stunning, and she looked about twenty, as did Darius, but his hair was longer, his face thinner than it was now, and he resembled his daughter so much that there was no mistaking that he was Tiffany's birth father.

And Tiffany had been the fly in the ointment. I was certain that Yelena not only would've told Tiffany that she was her real mother but also would've given her the identity of her father.

And that was why, in her drug-induced subconscious state, Sunny had left her home after getting a call from her "dear" friend. Yelena had called to tell her that she and Darius had a daughter. The very woman babysitting her child.

Of course, Sunny would've translated that as a threat to her son. Finley stood to inherit a sizeable portion of his grandmother's money, but if the queen living in Singapore knew she also had a far older granddaughter, she could revise the terms of her will and switch the financial assets to Tiffany, which would no doubt be somewhat controlled by Yelena.

Darius must've known that his mother would make him her executor, giving him full control over her finances until Finley turned of age. He'd have a lot less money to be in control of if his mother recognized her granddaughter as family, since Tiffany was already of age.

That was why he'd killed Purdy. He'd been trying to pay off Yelena with the estate lawyer he'd hired through his shell corp and assigning him the task of delivering two hundred thousand dollars to her.

But Yelena had called him and told him of her plans. She'd called him on a phone registered to Sunny, because Sunny had opened up a family plan for the two of them. I'd checked the number on my one text from Darius when the three of us split up to go find Sunny. His subscriber number was 3838, the same subscriber number that Marcus had told me was in Sunny's plan.

And recalling the night Darius had sent me the text, it wasn't lost on me that he'd purposely pointed us toward the park, knowing we would likely find Sunny dead.

And the park was only two and a half miles from the theater. An easy run for a man in Darius's physical condition.

The clue had come from my son's duffel bag. The night of the murders, when Darius had gotten out of his car, he'd smelled terrible. Just as terrible as Matt's clothing when I'd opened up the duffel. I knew now that Darius's other clothes had been covered in blood, but he had had his duffel in the car and had changed into his dirty workout gear to hide his bloody clothing.

As I stood in Finley's nursery, I saw the murders unfold in my mind's eye like a movie: Yelena calls Darius and tells him of her plans to reveal his name during her performance that evening and alerts him to the fact that his wife's dear friends will be sitting front row center.

Panicked, Darius tries to buy her off with the two hundred grand. She accepts the terms, and he catches the first flight home from L.A. He then makes a withdrawal from his trust fund—which wouldn't have Sunny's name on it—for the two hundred Gs. He then goes shopping and buys the raincoat and personally packs it with the money before dropping it off to Purdy so that the elderly man can take it to Yelena. He then calls Sunny, and in that conversation, Sunny admits to taking some Ambien, but she also lets him know that Tiffany is there with Finley.

Darius goes about his day, hiding from anyone who might recognize him, and just before he's set to go home, he gets a call from Yelena. She tells him the deal is off, and she's already told Sunny everything. She demands that he introduce his daughter to his mother, or she'll do it herself.

Furious, Darius hangs up on Yelena and frantically tries to reach Sunny. She has already gone to the theater and has left her phone behind. When she doesn't answer, Darius assumes she believes Yelena, so he goes to the theater to get his revenge.

He plans on sneaking in and waiting for her in her dressing room, but when he gets there, he finds Sunny is already waiting. Maybe she's still loopy, or maybe she's out of it, and Darius thinks he has a good chance of getting her out of the theater and convincing her, should she remember anything, that it was all an Ambien dream.

As he's pulling Sunny along out of the dressing room, Yelena appears backstage and is enraged to see both of them there. She and Darius get into a physical fight. He grabs the nearest weapon he can find, which is Aaron's letter opener, and he stabs Yelena.

Sunny becomes lucid enough to try to get between the pair, but she manages only to smear blood on herself as Yelena collapses.

As he throws away the letter opener, Darius grabs Sunny's hand—they've got to get out of there—but as they're leaving through the exit door, covered in blood, they literally bump into Purdy, smearing his hand with Yelena's blood.

Putting two and two together, Purdy realizes that Darius has killed Yelena, and he makes a run for it.

Darius quickly moves Sunny to his car, grabs the guitar wire, and chases after Purdy, but he can't catch up before Purdy ducks into the coffee shop.

Darius sees him through the window, lit up from the lights inside, and he watches him move to the back of the shop. That's when Darius rushes to the alley to wait and see which way Purdy will go.

After washing off the blood in the restroom, Purdy goes out the back way, and Darius, hiding in the shadows, jumps out and wraps the guitar wire around Purdy's neck and kills him. He then shoves Purdy's body into the crevice between the wall and the stack of pallets. But he doesn't have time to grab the cash, because he has to get back to his wife, and so he rushes back to his car.

She's in the car and a little out of it, but she's also now a probable witness to murder, so Darius drives her to her car. Maybe it's parked down the street, or maybe in the parking garage, but he finds it and places Sunny in the car, grabs his gym duffel from his own car, and heads toward home, but not before he coaxes Sunny to take a few more Ambien.

When he gets home, he probably didn't park in the driveway, but at the curb down the street from the house. Darius then sneaks over to the house and uses the outdoor shower to rinse off and change into the workout clothes he has in his duffel bag. He shoves his bloody clothes into the duffel and heads back to the car to remove Sunny's bloody clothes and shoes. Taking these with him he returns to the house, this time sneaking around to the back and looking in the well-lit windows to see where Tiffany is. He spots her on the treadmill, so he sneaks inside through the garage, hurries down the hallway and into the laundry room. There he rummages through the laundry basket for some clothes for him and Sunny, but he can't find any clothes that don't stink for himself because he's been gone for a month and Sunny would've done his laundry weeks earlier, so he's stuck wearing what he's already changed into.

He can't stay long inside the house, lest Tiffany discover him, so he shoves Sunny's bloody clothes and her shoes to the bottom of the laundry basket and takes whatever's on top for her to change into.

Once he's back at the car, he coaxes Sunny to the outdoor shower and rinses her off, getting his clothing wet in the process. What I had mistaken for sweat was actually the water from the shower. And it's also the reason Sunny's hair was damp and she was barefoot when Gilley and I found her in her Range Rover at the park.

Once Darius has got Sunny rinsed off and changed, he takes her back to the car and drives her to the park. After he's got them parked in a spot at the end of the lot, he forces Sunny to take all the rest of the Ambien with the bottle of water that he takes with him from the supplies in the garage. Then he places the empty pill bottle in Sunny's hand, removes the water bottle with his fingerprints on it and leaves the key fob in the car, but he can't lock it that way, because the car won't let you lock the doors if the engine is off and the key is inside the car. So he takes the key fob with him, shuts the door, locks the car from the outside, and jogs back to his own car, parked somewhere near the theater.

On the drive home he plans on sending Tiffany away, before waiting until perhaps the next day for the call that tells him that his wife has committed suicide in her car parked downtown.

But Gilley and I are already in his driveway when he shows up, spoiling his plans.

Seeing another angle that will push any suspicion away from him, he sends us to the park, knowing that's exactly where he's left Sunny's car. He knows we're the ones that will find her dead body, and he can then play the role of grieving husband.

Complicating things is the fact that Sunny is not dead when we find her, so Darius holds his breath until he can privately question her about any memories she might remember of that evening. Maybe she confesses to a terrible dream, or maybe she doesn't, but Darius is prepared for any memory that might bubble up by playing up her depression to her doctors. Which is what keeps her so long inside that mental health facility.

Darius thinks he's totally in the clear when Sunny arrives home, as another man has already been charged in Yelena's murder, but then Sunny discovers the bloody clothes at the bottom of the laundry basket which he has forgotten all about until she presents them to him.

Darius tries to talk Sunny out of confessing, if only to keep the suspicion as far away from him as possible, but Sunny cannot let an innocent man go to jail when she believes she murdered Yelena. So she sneaks away from Darius long enough to drive to my house with the bloody clothes, where she confesses to her brother in front of a large crowd.

Darius must be relieved when he learns the case against Sunny is so solid. He's happy to let her take the blame, all the while playing the role of distraught husband and devoted father perfectly.

While he's thinking about what to do next, Marcus keeps him informed of all the details in the case, which is why, after Marcus calls him yesterday to ask him to come along for the interview with Sunny so that she can explain the two phone numbers associated with her name, Darius knows he has to take care of Marcus first, to slow down the case, and he has to make a run for it—with Finley and probably to Singapore—because the walls are closing in.

I snapped a picture of the framed photo. "And so they are," I whispered.

Downstairs I found Darius in the kitchen, already eating a piece of lasagna.

"Sorry," he said through a big bite of warm pasta. Chewing quickly, he added, "It's so good!"

I laughed, waving my hand nonchalantly. "No, please, eat away!"

Darius took another huge bite and pointed to the casserole dish and looked at me, as if asking me if I wanted a bite.

"I'm fine. I just ate lunch," I lied. Switching topics, I said, "I folded up all the clothes on the floor of the nursery and set them in piles."

I hadn't, but it was a good excuse to explain why I'd taken so long upstairs.

"Thanks," he said. "Taking care of a toddler is hard work."

"Don't I know it," I said. "I raised twin boys, although I had help. I can only imagine how much more difficult it must be for you now that Tiffany can't babysit."

Darius eyed me carefully but said nothing. I had no doubt that he hadn't heard about Tiffany's fall and broken foot.

"I really hope her foot and ankle heal up quickly," I said into the awkward silence. "That was quite a spill she took, and her ankle and foot swelled up so fast."

Darius's expression relaxed. "Yeah, tough break for that kid."

I pretended to look around the kitchen for another topic and then said, "Say, what happened to Sunny's car?"

Again, that quizzical, careful expression returned to his features. "Her car?"

"Yeah. You know, her Range Rover. It's not in the garage."

Darius was sweating a little, and his face was a little flushed. "The rumors are true," he said, pushing a playful smile to his lips. "Those cars spend more time in the shop than they do on the road."

Victoria Laurie

I knew there was absolutely no chance Sunny's car was in "the shop." It was someplace hidden. Like a junk-yard. The police were, after all, looking for the car that'd hit Marcus's and might still have some of the car paint from Sunnys's car on the fender.

"Ahh," I said. "Yeah, I told Sunny that model had a terrible maintenance record, but there was no talking her out of it."

"She wanted one bad," he said. "I wanted her to get a Mercedes."

"You love yours, huh?"

"I do."

"Good," I said. "Oh, and did you sell your condo yet?"

Belatedly, I realized that I'd probably asked one question too many, because Darius's look turned from playful to suspicious. It was subtle, but it was definitely there.

"Not yet," he said, setting down his plate. His eyes flickered to the knife block across the kitchen. It was a very quick movement, but I saw it.

I was about to announce that I had to dash when my phone rang. Relieved beyond measure, I snatched the phone out of my purse and opened up the screen. After placing it to my ear, I said, "Shepherd! What a coincidence that you'd call right when I was chatting with your brother-in-law!"

"What?" Gilley said. "Cat, it's *me*!"

I laughed loudly and winked at Darius. "No, he's tak-ing wonderful care of Finley, not to worry. The tyke is up-stairs in his crib, and we're down here in the kitchen, chatting while Darius has some of Gilley's lasagna." I wanted to let someone know where we were should I need the cops to break in and rescue me.

"What the heck are you talking about?!" Gilley shouted.

"Of course I'll save you a piece, lovey. What time will you be home from all that detecting you're doing?"

There was a pregnant pause on the other end of the call, and then Gilley said, "Are you in trouble?"

"Yes, yes, I am. I'm looking forward to it too."

Gilley sucked in a breath.

Across from me, Darius stared at me with narrowed eyes. I might've been trying too hard to appear casual. "Let me talk to him," Darius said softly, holding his hand out for the phone.

I couldn't help my immediate reaction, which was to widen my eyes in fear. Recovering quickly, however, I said, "Hold on, Shep. Darius wants to talk to you."

Before I handed over the phone, I pressed my thumb on the END button. The phone made a small beeping sound, and I pulled my hand back in surprise. "Oh, no," I said. "He must've hung up."

Darius crossed his arms. "Show me your list of recent calls, Catherine."

I could feel the blood draining from my face. I knew he knew that I hadn't been talking to his brother-in-law.

"Why?" I asked.

"To prove that it was him on the line."

"You think it wasn't him, Darius?"

"I do."

"Well, that's not very nice. In fact, it's downright rude! And here we made you such a delicious feast." I settled my purse on my arm and took two steps toward the front door. Darius took three. He was bigger, stronger, and faster than me, and I knew he could get to the door before I even made it out of the kitchen.

Feeling a panic settling in, I couldn't think of what to do! And then my phone rang, and I gasped both in surprise and relief. "Oh, look!" I said, swiveling the face of the phone toward him. "See? It's him calling back."

I had punched the green TALK button, ready to clue Shepherd in, when Darius snatched the gadget from my hands.

Before I could even recover from the shockingly fast move, Darius took my phone and slammed it facedown into a corner of the kitchen island.

It broke apart into at least a dozen pieces. Then I watched in abject terror as Darius reached for me. I ducked and spun and managed to twist my way toward the hallway leading to the front door, trying to move as fast as my feet could possibly go as I made a break for it.

I had gotten only a few feet when Darius's hand clamped down on my shoulder and pulled me back right off my feet.

My head hit the wood floor with a loud whack, and my vision darkened to gray, with lots of sparkles. Putting my hands up in front of my face protectively, I did my absolute best to remain conscious, but that was about all I could manage.

I then felt cruel hands grip my shoulders, lift me off the floor, and place me on my feet. I wobbled and felt my knees weakening, but Darius kept me upright while he pulled me forward.

My vision was still blurred, though some of the darkness had lessened.

I tried to form words, but all I could get out was a low moan.

Still, Darius pulled me forward. Suddenly the light

was too bright, and I brought my arms up to shield my eyes. Darius responded by shoving me hard. I would've fallen flat on my face if he wasn't holding tight to my arm.

I heard a car door open, and I was shoved inside, smacking the middle console before crumpling onto the front passenger seat in the fetal position.

The car door opposite me opened, and Darius got in. "You got your key fob with you?" he asked.

My head throbbed with pain while I twisted around to sit sideways in the seat with my back against the door and my knees pulled up to my chest protectively. As I looked dully at him, I could see that Darius's expression was filled with deadly intent, and it was startling to see in someone who played the Dr. Jekyll part of his character so well.

"Whah . . . ," I said, still unable to form coherent words.

Darius pressed the START button, and my car hummed to life.

In the distance I heard the wail of sirens, and I thought, *Oh, God! I'm saved!*

Darius put the car in reverse and stomped on the gas while pulling hard on the wheel, spinning the car around, and I bounced against the passenger side door, nearly blacking out again.

"I bet you think you're safe, huh?" he said.

I could only blink my lids slowly at him.

"You'd be wrong," he said. "You're about to have the same accident my wife's car had."

I tried to make sense of what he was saying. Was he about to hit someone else with my car?

But then, as we sped down the road before taking a

sharp left, all the while those sirens drawing closer, I realized where he was taking me. I could feel the immediate incline as the car sped up the hill.

The same hill his uncle had lived on.

"So that's what you did with her car," I said. Realizing I'd actually spoken coherently, I wanted to smile, but my mind's ability to move my body wasn't exactly cooperating.

"Yeah. It was beautiful. I didn't think the Rover would make it. It got smashed up pretty good, but it did. All the way off the cliff."

My chin drooped while I looked up at him with half-lidded eyes.

He looked at me and scowled. "I was gonna take the flight to Singapore tomorrow, but I guess taking it tonight doesn't make much of a difference."

Again, I blinked at him, all the while my head drooping on my neck.

I knew we had to be near the top of the hill by now, so I turned my head ever so slightly to stare out the windshield. The sirens were no longer approaching. They'd stopped. No doubt the police had arrived at Darius's house.

But I wasn't there.

And in a moment, I wasn't going to be anywhere.

Suddenly there was a whoosh of air, and I turned my head again to see Darius had opened the car door and was beginning to lean out while gripping the steering wheel with one hand. My feet were resting on the seat while I was lying back against the door.

Using all my willpower and strength, I lifted my legs and slammed my feet into Darius's arm. He let go of the wheel immediately and went tumbling away from the car.

And then I barely managed to lift my hand, clamp down on the wheel, and turn the car to the left. I had no idea if this would save me or kill me, but I had to try something to save my life.

The open door swung wide, then came whooshing back and slammed shut. My car bobbled along, shaking the interior—and me—and then slowed down, until it bumped into something and stopped.

Panting hard, I picked my head up and looked around, blinking furiously all the while. My car had hit something that was out of sight. Probably a rock. Thank God the airbags hadn't deployed.

After pulling myself up into a sitting position, I crawled into the driver's seat and was just about to turn the engine off when, out of nowhere, Darius's bloody and dirt-stained face appeared in the windshield to the left of the car.

"*You stupid bitch!*" he screamed.

The rush of adrenaline helped to clear my thoughts. Darius was already scrambling forward to reach for my door handle, so I threw the car in reverse, punched the gas and turned the steering wheel left again, hard. Darius was thrown away from the car once again, and I raced away.

Somehow, I managed to get back down the cliffside road, and I thought it was probably a good thing I didn't actually know how close I'd come to going off the top of the cliff.

When I got to the bottom and the main road, I hit the brakes and just sat there, panting heavily again. I felt nauseous and dizzy and unable to drive even an inch farther. So I laid my head down on the steering column, reaching up to push weakly on the horn with my left hand.

The horn bleeped, and I let up on the pressure and then pressed down again to give another short beep, then three long beeps and three short beeps. I kept that pattern up through sheer force of will until there was a knock on my door.

I stopped hitting the horn and gasped, thinking it was Darius again, come to finish me off.

"Cat?" Shepherd said.

Lifting my head ever so slightly and opening one eye, I saw him wearing a frantic look and trying the door handle, but the automatic locks had kicked in.

"Cat! Let me in!" he said.

I turned my face away, closed my eyes, and fumbled around for the door handle. After pulling on it, I felt the door open and a rush of fresh air hit my cheek.

"Cat?" Shepherd said, laying very gentle hands on my shoulders. "Cat?"

"I need help," I squeaked. Tears leaked out of my closed lids.

"I'm here," he said. "I'm here."

Chapter 20

I was on a solid week of bed rest and bored out of my mind. Gilley propped me up with a dozen pillows, and every four hours he fed me a little something to help with the lingering nausea. I'd sustained a terrible concussion, and the doctors had told me I'd need at least a week of bed rest until my dizziness subsided, and then I'd have to take it easy for the next few months, while my brain healed.

The CT scan hadn't shown any bleeding, thank God. That would've been a fine kettle of fish.

Shepherd came to stay with me every single night, after he got off from work. He and Santana had been able to put all the pieces together once I told them how I thought both Yelena and Purdy's murders had gone down.

Even better, when they found video of Darius purchasing the size ten raincoat from a local department store, *and* discovered that he'd withdrawn two hundred thousand dollars from his private savings account on the day of Yelena and Purdy's murders, they knew they had Darius dead to rights with the circumstantial evidence.

When presented with all the evidence, and the fact that only the worst attorney in the Hamptons would take his case after what he'd done to Marcus, Darius had confessed, simply to save himself from ending up at Rikers. The deal he made with the DA meant he'd be sent to another maximum-security prison in Kentucky.

Sunny had been cleared of all charges, and at least Darius had insisted that she'd had nothing to do with any of the murders. She was back home, still recovering from the shock of discovering that her cheating husband had fathered a child out of wedlock, murdered one of her closest friends, had attempted to kill her, Marcus, *and* me, and had allowed her to take the blame for at least one of those murders.

Let's just say it was a *lot* to process.

Gilley had floated between Chez Cat and Sunny's house, playing nursemaid and helping her with Finley. He would sweetly bring Spooks up the stairs to me every time he was about to leave me go to Sunny's for a few hours.

"How're we doing today, sugar?" he asked when he brought in my breakfast tray, Spooks padding along faithfully behind him.

I patted the bed, and Spooks jumped up and took up his usual spot, on the pillows next to me, his head resting on my shoulder.

"I'm feeling better each day, Gil."

"That's good!" Gilley said, setting the tray table down across my legs.

"How's Sunny?" I asked.

"She's getting better every day too. I think she's over the shock and finally moving on to angry."

"Let's hope she doesn't stay angry for too long."

Gilley crossed his fingers with one hand and removed the silver covering to the plate on the tray, revealing the most delicious set of blintzes I'd ever seen.

"Blueberry's your favorite, right?"

"Oh, my God," I said, clapping my hands in delight. I am a huge fan of blintzes.

Gilley flipped out a cloth napkin and placed it over my lap. "Pain pill today?"

"No," I said. "I'm starting to crave them, so . . . no."

"Good idea," he said, pocketing the vial. "I'll take these back to the pharmacy to be properly disposed of tomorrow, after I know that you don't still need one before bed."

I took a bite of a blintz and moaned. "That is insanely good, my friend."

"The trick is to have two pans going. You don't want your first crepe to dry out before you've cooked your second."

I wrapped my hands around one of his. "Thank you."

"You're welcome," he replied, swishing his hips happily. "Oh, and Marcus would like to come over for a visit."

I stared in shock at him. "Marcus? Marcus Brown?"

Gilley smirked. "The one and only."

"He's already out of the hospital?"

"Oh, yeah. He got out two days ago. He's allowed to move around for short periods of time. He's hired a driver and a nurse, and he wants to check in on you and Sunny, of course."

"Please tell him I said absolutely yes."

"I will," Gilley said. "Now, if you'll excuse—"

Gilley's phone rang, and he and I both jumped at the sound. After taking his cell out of his pocket, he stared at the screen.

"It's Michel, isn't it?" I said.

Gilley nodded.

"Gil, please, please talk to him. Please put the two of you out of your misery."

Gilley looked up at me, took a deep inhale, then pressed the TALK button. "Hey," he said.

Then he walked out of the room, taking my best wishes for him and Michel with him.